WHAT THE HEART WANTS
(May or May Not Happen)

A Novel

LINDA ELLEN LYNCH

Crippled Beagle Publishing
Knoxville, Tennessee
dyer.cbpublishing@gmail.com

ISBN 978-1-970037-36-4

Library of Congress Control Number: 2020916156

Cover design by Jody Dyer

For Brenda, Randy, and Sean.

Thank you. Without your help this book would not have been written.

WHAT THE HEART WANTS

PART 1

CHAPTER 1

Raw bewilderment followed by a feeling of utter betrayal raced through the mind of beautiful, tall, blonde, blue-eyed Janice Crenshaw. At first she blamed herself for what took place. As time went on she came to the realization that what happened was not entirely her fault, but that would not happen until she experienced the grief of a broken heart, self-doubt, and the uprooting of her life. That uprooting involved a cross-country move to California—a location almost 3,000 miles from where she was betrayed. Amid tears of unbearable emotional pain and insecurity, she was forced to question her decision to make such a drastic move and wondered if she would ever be capable of trusting or loving anyone again.

It didn't take long before Janice became aware she mistakenly trusted two people who thought nothing of using a generous, loving person like her to get what they wanted. These were two people she thought she knew well. It would become painfully clear she did not know them at all. Her experience could be likened to believing she found gold and later learning it was nothing but pyrite. It glitters like gold but is of no value when compared to the real thing. Will she be able to accept a difficult journey? Will she be able to resolve intense feelings of hurt, betrayal, and disappointment? Will she be able to forgive? Will she be able believe anyone? She cannot help but entertain the thought of seeking retaliation for the cold, cruel manner in which she found herself betrayed by what she believed to be a committed relationship after more than five years of widowhood. Friends and family kept encouraging her to put the ordeal behind her and move forward with her life rather than live alone. In spite of such encouragement, she informed all of them that her sense of trust, especially in men, was shattered possibly beyond repair.

CHAPTER 2

Janice reminded herself she was not looking for love when an acquaintance of twelve years, Jack Fairchild, called from an adjoining state to invite her out to dinner.

"Hi Janice," said the deep male voice that could have belonged to a radio announcer, a voice she didn't recognize at first. Her first impulse was to hang up, but the person calling used her given name. This sparked a sense of curiosity she felt could not be left unchallenged.

"May I ask who is calling?" she asked with unmistakable coolness.

"It's your friend from Tennessee, Jack Fairchild," he responded, with an intonation that conveyed he felt she should have recognized his voice.

"Jack!" she exclaimed. "I'm sorry. I didn't recognize your voice. It has been a while since I last spoke with you, and you were under a great deal of stress at the time." She couldn't help wondering what prompted him to make a phone call when they had been in long-term contact via e-mail during the debilitating illness, subsequent death, and celebration of life ceremony for his wife Sabrina. It had been six months since Sabrina died after a six-year battle with metastatic breast cancer.

Before Sabrina's death, Jack initiated e-mail conversation with Janice, who lived in Georgia. He began the dialogue by asking questions about how Janice had handled the illness and death of her husband Clayton. Jack and Janice had met at a writers group meeting when Janice lived in Tennessee. She was referred to the group by a friend who thought that being around people with similar interests, namely writing, would be helpful for Janice as she dealt with profound grief after Clayton's demise. Janice lost her husband only four months prior to joining the group.

"I thought I would give you a call to see if you were free for dinner next Friday evening instead of sending you an e-mail invitation," Jack offered, sensing her wonder at why he would call instead of using the typical e-mail.

"It would be nice to see you but isn't that a long drive just to have dinner?" questioned Janice. "Last time I checked it's close to a three-hour drive in light traffic from where I now live in Georgia to your home near Knoxville, Tennessee."

"I will be visiting my niece who lives in your area, so I thought it would be a good time to visit you, too," he responded. Janice continued to think it strange he would want personal contact with her, taking into consideration there is a substantial distance between them and because it was so soon after Sabrina's passing. At the time of Sabrina's death, Jack expressed in an e-mail that he felt he was too emotionally distraught to immediately schedule and plan Sabrina's celebration of life. This admission was in addition to asking questions about how Janice handled the legal and emotional aspects of Clayton's death.

Understanding and having compassion for Jack's grief, Janice accepted his explanation of already visiting a niece in a town close to Janice's home.

It was approaching five years since Janice lost Clayton to a rare, incurable, blood disease. She found Jack's phone call somewhat troubling. She wondered why he would be seeking female companionship in the form of a dinner date, especially with her now living so far away.

As she and Jack continued to talk she convinced herself accepting his dinner invitation would not be a real date but a meeting of two friends over a simple meal. It had taken her more than three years to go on a first date following Clayton's death, but family and friends were pressuring her to "get back out there in the dating world."

If asked, Janice would explain she wasn't prepared to handle casually dating men introduced to her by her friends. Those encounters had been un-nerving. She was shocked to learn the men expected more than a handshake and a thank you following coffee, an evening of dinner, and/or a movie. Out of the dating scene for many years as a married woman, she was not prepared for such expectations; even with the time span and changing attitudes regarding casual sex.

She gave Jack's invitation more thought as they continued trading memories of their past collaborations on various projects with the writers group. This gave her time to convince herself having dinner with Jack would be safe due to theirs being a platonic relationship based on emotional support via e-mails.

She had not been involved in any direct person-to-person contact with Jack or his son, Steve, since Sabrina's celebration of life ceremony. If Jack had not mentioned that Sabrina's celebration would probably not be held for at least two months following her passing, Janice would not have mentioned or attended it. Out of respect for Sabrina, and in spite of the fact Janice suffered a stroke a month earlier, she ended up agreeing she would try to attend the celebration if possible. Jack said he understood, but he would really appreciate it if she could see her way clear to be there. "I am aware you suffered a stroke, and I'll understand if you can't be here. I want you to know Sabrina thought a lot of you. Plus, you did a lot to help both of us through those last few months of her life by cooking and bringing meals to our home and spending time with Sabrina, even traveling to see her after you moved to Georgia." He grew silent for several seconds before proceeding. "I can't begin to tell you how much your e-mails have helped me through the bad times before and after her passing."

Jack agreed he would be in contact with the details soon. Then he added, "You don't think it is inappropriate of me or disrespectful toward Sabrina's memory if I wait to pull myself together before having the celebration of life, do you? I don't want people to think I'm being, I don't know . . . not grieving properly."

"No, I don't think you are being inappropriate. You need to do what feels right no matter what anyone else may think," she replied. "Everyone needs to grieve in their own way." After ending their conversation, Janice liked to think Jack spoke with a sigh of relief as he thanked her for being an understanding friend.

Janice's friendship with Jack and Sabrina included dinners out with groups of friends, events at various writers' group members' homes, preparing meals for Jack's family during Sabrina's illness, and sitting with Sabrina when Jack needed to be elsewhere. There were times the two women were able to talk about the reality that Sabrina was terminally ill, a topic she revealed others were reluctant to discuss with her. During these encounters Janice always thought of Jack as nothing more than a big brother and Sabrina as the sister she had always wanted and never had in her life.

After the tragic ordeal of her husband's death, Janice had given little thought to ever becoming romantically involved with a man again. The memories of her long marriage were good ones until Clayton's final days. When his brain began to become increasingly deprived of oxygen due to his illness, their relationship became difficult for her. She realized he didn't mean some of the things he said, but that didn't totally erase their sting. This played a major role in her reluctance to go out on dates arranged by well-meaning married friends for several years following Clayton's death.

That reluctance became a firm, "No, thank you," after two unsatisfactory dates. In her estimation those men turned out to be the proverbial frogs—the types of men women share a laugh about over lunch. These were men she had quickly shown the door when their intentions became clear; they expected the evening to end in her bedroom. It didn't take much brain power to figure out they were looking for a sugar momma to take care of their financial needs and someone to cook and clean for them, in addition to those tasks of a sexual nature. Janice was not the least bit interested in fulfilling any of these men's needs or fantasies, especially when expressed on a first date. She had the feeling such men viewed her as an easy target now that she was a widow.

She had worked much too hard to attain her independence after being forced to face the future alone. At that time, her two adult children lived hundreds of miles away. She had always envisioned Clayton and her enjoying a healthy and fulfilling life well into old age while walking hand in hand into the sunset. Clayton had been her rock. In spite of a lot of time passing since his death, she still remembered sitting alone on the edge of the bed they shared after the hearse had taken his body away to be cremated. The impact of knowing that, in one breath, she was no longer a wife was overwhelming. The impact was so strong she could not even cry for days; the new widow understood she was now relegated to the life as a fifth wheel in social situations. Clayton was gone, and he wasn't coming back. It was a strange feeling to be forced to realize and accept the fact that her life would never be the same.

Janice and Jack's present conversation continued. "Since you are going to be in the area visiting your niece, why don't you come to my apartment for dinner?" suggested Janice. "I will be happy to cook. In fact, why don't you bring your niece? I would love to meet her. That will make it easier for you to spend some time with her and for us to talk and catch up on mutual friends without shouting over cell phone calls, disruptive or crying children, and the usual din found in area restaurants, even the upscale ones."

Jack was silent for a moment before he responded that his niece and her husband had already made plans for the evening that did not involve him. Janice thought it odd they would make plans that did not include a visiting uncle, but she resisted the urge to mention it. She assumed they could have made those plans before Jack let them know he was coming for a visit. Thus, it was mutually agreeable he entertain himself for a few hours on the Friday evening in question.

"If you insist on cooking dinner, how can I refuse?" replied Jack. "I remember those tasty dishes you used to bring over to the house when Sabrina was too sick to do any cooking. I have to confess, my cooking skills have not improved beyond those of making coffee, frying a couple of eggs and some bacon, dropping bread in the toaster, and slapping on some margarine. If it hadn't been for friends like you, we would have had to rely on microwavable frozen meals that weren't all that healthy."

"Then it's settled. I'll see you here on Friday around 4:30 for a little wine and cheese while we get reacquainted. How about eating dinner at 5:30? I hate to admit it, but I don't remember if you have any food allergies or if there are foods you don't particularly like. I know that's a little early for dinner, but 4:30 will get you here before rush hour traffic gets heavy in earnest and back to your niece's home at a decent hour so that you have some time to spend with her and her husband."

"I don't have any allergies, and I've never met a food I didn't like," Jack responded. "Give me the address to your apartment. I can log it into my GPS." he replied. "I like to hear the lady with the British accent give directions. If I still manage to get lost, as sometimes does happen, I can always phone you." Janice gave him the address and some general landmarks to look for on the approach to her apartment, along with her location within the large complex, before they said their goodbyes. Janice was relieved to think Jack sounded like he was in better spirits after she suggested they dine at her apartment.

"That was an unexpected call," she mused aloud before she resumed working on the manuscript she was developing. Busy writing, she gave little thought to his call beyond momentarily wondering what to serve for their meal.

At age 51, willowy, honey blonde, sky blue-eyed Janice, was an attractive former model, registered nurse, business owner, and now writer. She had become relatively content to live alone in a lovely, roomy, first-floor apartment across the street from her son in a suburb northeast of Atlanta, Georgia. She made the move two years before, following the sale of her large home and acreage tucked on a mountainside in in rural Roane County, Tennessee. She learned to accept living alone on the eight acres of wooded mountainside surrounding the home she designed. She even served as the general contractor while it was being built. She would have preferred to continue living there if her two adult children, Jason and Belinda, had not talked her into selling the property. They kept insisting it was not safe for her to continue living alone twelve miles from the nearest small town reachable by car only by a narrow, curvy, mountain road.

In a matter of months after listing the property with a realtor, the lovely home with three bedrooms, a den, two bathrooms, and an attached, two-car garage situated on wooded acreage was sold, along with most of the well-appointed contents. Janice reluctantly moved into an apartment across the street from her son Jason in a suburb of Atlanta, Georgia. Alpharetta is an upscale community twenty miles northeast of downtown Atlanta. While it was a lovely and spacious apartment with all of the amenities, including two Olympic-size swimming pools (one indoors and heated, one outside not heated), tennis courts, a clubhouse, and picnic facilities, she knew immediately after the move she could never truly consider it home. She loved the outdoors and walking the rustic hills with her faithful rescue dog, Goldie. Such was not found in this complex that housed approximately 3,000 people in high rise buildings. Oh, there were lots of pine trees. The heavy droppings of pine needles and the light green pus-colored spring discharge covered everything. The intrusive pines were no comparison to the variety of oak, cedar, maple, and other flowering trees, not to mention the fresh mountain air of East Tennessee.

Many of the occupants living in the large complex were yuppie types in their late twenties to mid-thirties. They worked in the many technology and financial institutions centered in the Atlanta area. Their idea of a lifestyle, along with that of entertainment after working hours and on weekends, consisted of hanging out in bars and clubs. The lifestyle was definitely not Janice's cup of tea.

Still, she tried to make the best of it. She had her writing, shopping, and occasional in-house events provided by the condo association, such as the chili cook-off, which she won. This helped keep her occupied a majority of the time. Plus, she had a good relationship with her son, her son's live-in girlfriend Suzanne, and Suzanne's mother Monica. Seventy-year-old Monica lived alone only two streets away in the same apartment complex. It was a good thing romance was not on Janice's bucket list of things she wanted to include in her life. The pickings of desirable men were slim to none.

Janice had no idea what awaited her on that fateful late hot August afternoon when she would open the apartment door to find an old acquaintance and now recent widower, Jack Fairchild, standing there. It's a good bet as an intelligent, self-sufficient independent woman, that, had she known her life was about to change in ways she could never imagine, she may not have opened that door.

"Why, hello there stranger!" exclaimed Janice. "I wasn't expecting you for another hour. Dinner isn't quite ready but come on inside out of this miserable heat and humidity," said Janice as a sweet smile played across her lips.

Jack didn't know it, but when she said she preferred to cook dinner for them rather than go out to a restaurant, her motive was to make sure he was the honorable man she thought him to be. This was in light of the fact that she was fooled before when she reluctantly accepted two blind dates that turned out badly.

Janice arranged for Jason and Suzanne to come calling during the evening to make sure things were going well. She explained to Jason that Jack had founded her Tennessee writers group and that his behavior toward her had always been appropriate. She enjoyed reading and editing Jack's redneck humor novels and found his editing of her work to be helpful even though their styles were markedly different. She considered Jack a friend, but if it turned out he didn't measure up, her son would be close at hand to insist that he leave.

When she lived in Tennessee, Janice frequently prepared various foods like soups, stews, and fruit cobblers for Sabrina and Jack during the final years of Sabrina's illness. She also made time even after the move to Georgia to make the drive to Tennessee to sit with Sabrina when her metastatic breast cancer spread to her lungs and brain. As a retired registered nurse, Janice offered knowledgeable comfort that helped Sabrina come to grips with terminal illness. The last time they were together was in late April when Janice made a short visit. Privately, Sabrina told her she would not be alive when Janice planned to visit in September. Sabrina was right. She quietly passed away less than a month later at home under hospice care. Jack's e-mails left no doubt in Janice's mind that he was lost and inconsolable for at least two months before he could even think of planning and hosting for family and friends a celebration of life in his wife's memory.

As she mentioned to Jack in their ongoing e-mail correspondence and referenced on the phone call, Janice was still in the process of recovering from a stroke when he e-mailed her with the date, location, and time for the celebration of Sabrina's life. She warned him that her speech was still slow and she sometimes slurred her words. It was also difficult for her to walk without the aid of a cane due to a balance issue. But she was determined to attend the celebration and honor her friend's memory. Her son accompanied her and reserved rooms in a local hotel. Janice did not have the stamina for such an emotionally charged round trip in one day.

Upon the arrival of Janice and her son at the community park where the celebration was to be held, which is located near Jack's home on the banks of the Tennessee River, Jack appeared happy to see her. So did the other people she had known and considered friends during her years in Tennessee. Jack had told her the event was a covered dish affair. Janice baked a ham and made a blueberry cobbler for her contribution, knowing those items would be easy to make and transport in a cooler.

While still a little unsteady on her feet and aggravated by a halting speech pattern, Janice managed to spend time visiting with many of the guests and Jack's family members, all of whom seemed amazed she was progressing so well. While pleasant, Jack was not overly attentive toward her throughout the afternoon until it was time to leave. She presented him with the book *When Bad Things Happen to Good People*. Then he became tearful and gave her a hug, asking if it would be all right if he continued to stay in e-mail contact. He need advice on coping with the loss of a spouse and how to take care of legal matters. Of course, without the slightest hesitation, Janice agreed to his request.

"I will do my best to help you during this sad and stressful time by sharing the things I encountered and what I did to manage them," she told him. "But please keep in mind as I mentioned before, no matter what anyone tells you, there is no right or wrong way to grieve. I cannot stress enough that everyone must grieve in their own way."

Janice's work as a registered nurse, especially her time in a supervisory capacity at a large teaching hospital gave her substantial experience that could help her friend. She continued to e-mail Jack with encouragement on a regular basis. His request to remain in contact didn't seem unusual or raise any red flags when he continued to make contact even after she moved to Georgia. To her, it seemed natural for him to ask questions throughout the last months of his wife's final illness and even more so after her passing.

"I'm continuing to contact you for help since you went through a similar situation when your husband died," he wrote in an e-mail less than a week after the celebration of life for Sabrina. Janice did her best to share her experiences, hoping to make life easier for him (if that is possible when someone is forced to face the loss of a loved one). At the time, she continued to think of Jack as a big brother in need of emotional support. Considering them big brothers is how Janice socialized with all men she had contact with following her husband's death. This demeanor helped keep the men interested in unsavory dating experiences at bay. She did this to draw a line and reassure wives or girlfriends that she wasn't looking to form personal relationships with their partners beyond that of friendship. In the cases of single men, it was to let them know she wasn't ready for a relationship. So far, this approach had worked well most of the time, but the circumstances with Jack had changed. He was now a widower who not only continued e-mails, but he also went out of his way to make phone contact with her to ask for a dinner date. It was apparent to Janice from their back and forth e-mails that Jack needed someone to tell him he had done everything possible to ease his wife's suffering, and when she passed, it was okay to give away her belongings and think about starting a new life—just as Janice had done. It wasn't entirely clear to Janice why he chose her for solace. From time to time he mentioned contacts with other local women who made it clear, even before Sabrina's passing, they would jump at the chance to offer him comfort on a more personal level than just e-mails or tuna fish casseroles. Throughout the time Janice had known Jack, she could honestly say that she had never given him any indication she was interested in him beyond friendship. She kept telling herself his interest in her was purely platonic. Her conclusion was based on the content of his e-mails, but the dinner invitation tossed a monkey wrench into that line of thinking.

"Your advice will help me get through this painful time. I need to know what to expect and if I could have done more to help Sabrina," he had written not once but multiple times in his e-mails to her while Sabrina was still alive. And when she died, Jack kept sending even more frequent e-mails wanting to know if he was crazy for wanting to dispose of Sabrina's belongings and redecorate the home they had shared for 22 of their 27 years of marriage as one method by which to move on with his life.

Janice let him know he wasn't crazy to feel that way, and she would do her best to help him by sharing the steps she took to handle things such as collecting life insurance, removing Clayton's name with the auto license bureau, bank accounts, credit cards, voter registration rolls, etc. At the same time, she made an issue of pointing out he would experience emotions for which she could not offer solutions. "Only you can experience this part of the painful grief process; everyone reacts to grief differently. And, no, you are not crazy for wanting to make changes to your house and give away Sabrina's belongings." Janice told him patiently, not once but several times, "I won't lie and tell you it will be easy. It was very difficult for me when I had to clear out Clayton's clothing and personal effects and even harder to see his empty cupboard shelves and closet space afterward. When I considered asking family members and friends for their help in disposing of his belongings, I realized this was something I would have to handle on my own as part of the healing process. I cried a lot during this time. I ended up hanging some of my clothing in what had been Clayton's side of the walk-in closet so it didn't look so empty and break my heart every time I opened the door. I kept one of his white dress shirts and wore it around the house for a long time before I could give it up. Just do what feels right and don't look back or allow others to tell you what you should or should not do. I know this is going to sound harsh, but first and foremost, you have to face the fact that Sabrina is gone. She isn't coming back, but life will go on. Keep in mind she doesn't need the things of this world anymore. I had to come to grips with that following Clayton's passing." Jack wrote back to tell her this advice, while painful, was helpful. A companionable e-mail correspondence between two friends continued.

Instinctively, Janice was hesitant to accept his dinner invitation. She was concerned so little time had elapsed between the invitation and Sabrina's death only six months earlier. She thought their meeting might be awkward and inappropriate. Jack kept assuring her he had come to terms with his wife's death and was ready to move on when

Janice questioned the short interval. This should have been a red flag, but he sounded so convincing she believed him (against her better judgment). She was well aware that studies show men often need to find a new partner more quickly than women, and that contributed to the little voice in her head that said, "It's too soon."

Janice mentioned the phone call and her reservations about having dinner with Jack to her son several days after Jack's call. She felt this was something she should do face to face so that Jason did not get the impression she was forgetting about his dad. "Are you okay with me having dinner with my old friend from Tennessee, Jack Fairchild?" she asked.

"I don't have a problem with it," Jason replied with no hesitation. "I remember Jack, and he seemed like a nice person. Mom, the two of you should go for whatever makes you both happy," he told her. "I know losing Dad has been awfully hard for you, but it's coming up on six years since he died. I was there when he told you he wanted you to have a good life, even when he knew he wasn't going to make it. If renewing the connection with Jack makes you happy, go for it with my blessing."

"This is happening only because he has a niece living nearby and he is planning to visit her. There are no strings attached. We are just friends," insisted Janice. Jason just smiled.

Her daughter, Belinda, reacted in much the same manner when Janice called her in California. "Go for it, Mom. Dad wanted you to move on with your life. The few times I've interacted with Jack he seemed like a real nice guy."

The responses of her children and several close friends helped lessen feelings of betrayal to Clayton—but not totally. In her heart she continued to feel married; and as a married woman, she had never cheated on her husband. For that matter, she had never been dishonest with anyone she ever dated.

The Friday afternoon Jack was due to arrive, Janice was finishing the main course for the oven when several firm raps sounded on the apartment door. "I wonder who that can be?" she questioned aloud. "Jack isn't due to arrive for another hour, and I'm not expecting anyone else." Looking through the door's peep hole, there was no question in her mind about who was standing there. It was Jack Fairchild. He was neatly dressed in khaki colored Bermuda shorts, a red knit shirt with a collar, and tan leather sandals with white cotton athletic socks reaching half way up his calf. While she found it necessary to suppress a chuckle at the sight of the calf-high white socks, she smoothed her hair and removed her apron, giving it a quick toss through the pass-through window between the nearby entrance area and the kitchen. It landed on the sink counter.

A momentary feeling of trepidation flooded her before she opened the door to greet him with a smile. "Why hello there stranger!" exclaimed Janice. "I wasn't expecting you for another hour. Dinner isn't quite ready but come on inside out of this miserable heat and humidity," said Janice as a sweet smile played across her lips.

"Hello yourself, Janice," said Jack as he stood there, a disarming smile spreading between the well-groomed beard and moustache on his tanned face. "Sorry I'm early, but I didn't know how long it would take for me to get here. I know freeway traffic can be a bear, especially on late Friday afternoons. I didn't want to be late. My, you are looking good these days," he added with an unmistakable expression of admiration. "I like your red outfit. Red is your color."

No, red isn't my best color, thought Janice. He's just being nice—that and he must like red since he's wearing a red shirt. Blondes don't look that good in red, but I'll take the compliment. Blushing, Janice responded, "Thank you for the compliment, but please don't continue to stand out there in the hallway. Come inside," she offered graciously while stepping aside to give him room to enter. The feeling of butterflies in flight developed in her stomach at the sight of his smile, the carefully trimmed facial hair, and broad shoulders. Suddenly, she wasn't sure she should have invited Jack to her apartment or prepared their meal. Even with the knowledge her son would be stopping by in about an hour, it was hard to quell her thoughts.

Jack wasted little time after stepping inside the apartment to ask if he could give her a hug as he opened his arms wide. She hesitated before allowing him to embrace her. While doing so, she was unaware his eyes swept the well-appointed combination living/dining room. By the looks of things she appeared to be doing well, financially. The hug lasted a little longer than Janice was would have liked, but she brushed aside any thoughts of impropriety on his part as she stepped back to offer him a drink. *After all*, she reasoned, *hadn't they shared information through e-mails most people don't often get the opportunity to share? Didn't he deserve the benefit of the doubt?* These were the thoughts passing through her mind as she led him to the bar area adjacent to the kitchen. "I did remember you like wine, but I must confess, I couldn't remember if you prefer red or white. Excuse me while I get some Chablis from the fridge . . . if you like white wine. "

"I prefer red," Jack replied. He approached the bar and proceeded to select an expensive imported bottle of merlot rather than one of the more popular and modestly priced wines produced in the Napa Valley of California. Janice noticed, but she thought, *What the heck? We haven't seen each other for a while, so his selection isn't that big of a deal.*

"Red it is, but you will have to open it. I'm all thumbs when it comes to opening wine bottles," Janice told him. "Glasses are on the shelf under the bar. Please pour me just a little. I shouldn't be drinking at all due to the medications I'm currently taking for a heart problem. While you pour, please excuse me while I go into the kitchen to pop our entrees into the oven."

Jack continued to smile as he, with a well-practiced flourish, deftly inserted the silver colored metal corkscrew into the bottle's cork. There was a slight muffled sound when the cork released. He sniffed the cork and handed it to Janice for her approval as she passed by to make her exit into the kitchen. "This wine smells delicious," commented Jack. "And here I thought red wine was supposed to be good for what ails you," he commented as he reached under the bar for two glasses. "That should tell you I don't know a whole lot about medicine and drug interactions with alcohol." Janice smiled and continued on her way into the open concept kitchen to put finishing touches on their entrees. Jack quickly followed with two glasses of wine and allowed his gaze to fix on her attractive, well-rounded bottom as she bent over in front of the open oven door to place the individual baking dishes inside.

"In most cases it is true that wine in moderate amounts can be of value," said Janice over her shoulder. "It's a curse that I happen to be taking one of those medications that doesn't mix well with alcohol. But I have every reason to believe this will change with my visit to the cardiologist on Monday. I've heard there is a new medication available that doesn't restrict alcohol intake." When she stood and turned to face Jack she blushed again. "That doesn't sound right. What I said sounds like I will be able to drink more than I need to."

"You see a cardiologist?" he questioned. "I didn't realize you had a heart problem. You never mentioned it. I hope it's nothing serious."

Janice laughed. "I like to say I'm not wired right. My heart's electrical system is a little on the crazy side, but I'm doing all right following cardiac ablation along with daily medication to keep things more or less under control."

Jack handed her one of the delicate, crystal, stemmed wine glasses filled with deep ruby liquid. Hers held just a swallow or two. "You made the comment about excessive drinking. I didn't," he said with a mischievous grin. "You look like a lady who knows when she's had enough to drink before it gets out of hand." He raised his glass to hers. "Here's to our friendship." Their glasses touched, giving off the clear ringing sound only good quality crystal can make, and they both took sips. His nostrils flared as he began to sniff the air before taking another generous sip of his wine with relish. He swallowed and said, "Mmm. Something sure smells downright good enough to eat!" he declared.

"Please stay here in the kitchen. That's if you don't mind," offered Janice. "I need to do some last minute

preparations. Or you can take a seat in the living room."
Jack let her know he preferred being in her company. "In
that case, I will let you know you smell the sauce I made for
the chicken parmesan. I hope it's a dish you enjoy."

"It's one of my favorite dishes, but there aren't many
foods I don't like, as you can probably tell." Jack patted the
slightly rounded stomach he tried to hide under his loose-
fitting, untucked shirt. "If I won't be in your way, I prefer
staying here in the kitchen. My guess is you haven't lost
your touch when it comes to cooking," he added through a
mouthful of bread dipped in the leftover sauce Janice
offered him from the tongs of a fork. "God, that's good! I
could make a meal out of nothing but bread and this
sauce," he said. She resisted the strong urge to wipe the
smidgen of sauce from his carefully trimmed moustache
with her finger like she would have done for her husband,
Clayton. Instead, she offered Jack a wet paper towel. *Now
is not the time to get personal*, she thought.

A few minutes later during a tour of the apartment,
Jack didn't miss the signed artwork hanging on the walls of
the living room, guest bedrooms, and hallway, or *objets
d'art* carefully arranged on occasional tables. He didn't
even try to dismiss the thought he comfortably could live
here but was wise enough to keep that to himself. "You
must have hired an interior decorator. Everything is just
perfect," he commented as they went from room to room.
"I especially like the way you've decorated the master

bedroom." His gaze lingered on the king bed with its floral, needlepoint-embellished bedspread featuring the color turquoise. "Turquoise is one of my favorite colors, and you have used it to an advantage with just a touch of that color in the drapes, pillows, print chairs, and bedside ceramic lamps. It's amazing how those touches really set everything off." *So does the idea of waking up every morning lying beside you on silk sheets*, he silently mused. Again, he was smart enough not to voice those thoughts, at least not yet.

"No, as a matter of fact I didn't hire a decorator. I did the decorating myself," she responded. "Perhaps I should have been an interior decorator instead of a nurse, business owner, and writer," Janice replied with a charming, yet nervous smile. It was proving to be more than a little awkward to have a man, even if he was just a friend, in her bedroom.

Jack gave her another one of his best smiles. "You appear to be talented in all of those areas. Not only are you a promising author, successful entrepreneur, and from what I've seen so far, a fantastic interior decorator, you were a notable nurse with an impressive career. You are quite an accomplished lady." His praise of her talents made her feel uncomfortable rather than flattered. To lessen the uneasy feeling, she started making her way toward the bedroom door. She hoped he didn't pick up on her sense of discomfort associated with him being present in what she considered her private space.

"The first time my husband and I sold a home the buyers wanted to purchase the furnishings as well," she lamely offered. "The lady told me to give her the key and leave everything just as it was. I told her to get out her checkbook, and to my surprise, she did. Would you believe she bought everything in the house with the exception of our personal items and some signed artwork I didn't want to sell? We became friends after the transaction. My husband and I moved into a nearby oceanfront condo located on Hutchinson Island. It's an Atlantic Ocean barrier island located near Stuart, Florida. It was just like coming home every time we were invited to the house for cocktails and dinner." Jack saw a wistful look appear on her face as she continued to speak. "The lady passed away two years after the purchase, and I haven't heard anything more from her husband. He wasn't in good health, so I assume he passed away, too. There was a FOR SALE sign in the front yard of the house the last time I was in the area to visit friends. I was almost tempted to contact the realtor and make an offer to buy the house back. I say *almost* because when I really thought about doing it, I realized this was one of those times when you can't go back. The neighborhood residents would have changed. Clayton was gone, and the children are now grown. By then, Belinda was married and living elsewhere. When I stopped by six months later on my way for another visit, the same sign was still in the front yard and the living room drapes were shut. I knocked on the door several times, but nobody answered, so I left."

Jack made it a point to sound empathetic about the loss of her friends. The two continued into the den Janice had made into her office. He was impressed with the custom-built, ceiling-high, wooden cabinet that housed her computer, printer, landline phone, and office supplies. He stopped to admire the matching, free-standing shelves housing a variety of books, including several he had authored.

"The same thing happened when I sold my last home in Tennessee," continued Janice. "I found it almost impossible to believe someone would want to buy the furnishings twice in a row. I didn't believe it until the checks cleared the bank."

"I can see how buyers would want to buy everything in your houses if this apartment is any indication of how you decorate a home. You have excellent taste. Say, you wouldn't be interested in helping me redecorate my place on the river in Tennessee would you?" asked Jack. "It is really in need of help."

"Oh, I think you should find someone specializing in interior design closer to where you live," blurted Janice. "I'm sure there are a number of qualified people available in your area. Talk to some of your friends and ask who they recommend. If my memory serves me correctly, it would be more than a three-hour drive each way for me to drive from here to your house." Janice found herself quickly replying in an effort to establish what she viewed as valid reasons not to redecorate his home. She knew she was rambling, but she couldn't seem to stop talking. "I would have to rent a hotel room for a place to stay, and my son and his girlfriend would miss me if I were gone for who knows how long. Plus, they would have to pick up and forward my mail if things took more than a week." She didn't know why, but his question concerning the redecoration of his home made her feel very uncomfortable, as did his next comment. She wasn't ready to spend any appreciable time in close proximity to this man, even though she considered him a friend. The short time since Jack's wife died played a big part in her not wanting to help with the redecoration of what was their home. But it became clear Jack wasn't quite ready to give up trying to convince her to help him.

"I'm sure you haven't forgotten, from the times you visited our home, that I have a nice waterfront guest bedroom with an adjoining bath," Jack countered. Without waiting for her response he continued. "I think it's way past time to make some major changes so I don't continue to feel like I'm living with Sabrina's ghost. I happen to think with your talent you could make that happen. We had a cleaning service come in every two weeks while Sabrina was sick. I still do, but all they do is sweep the floors, dust, and clean the bathrooms and kitchen. I hate to admit it, but

I'm afraid I'm not much of a housekeeper, nor do I have an eye for what it would take to make a comfortable and stylish waterfront home. Most of our furnishing could be best described as 'early marriage.' He took a deep breath followed by another sip of wine while he waited expectantly for her to respond in what he hoped would be in a positive manner.

While Janice felt sorry for Jack's plight, she put him off without making a commitment to help him redecorate. "I think the chicken should be about ready. Shall we get started with the salads?" Her response, while disappointing, helped Jack realize he should not keep trying to persuade her to help him, at least not now. Besides, he liked the idea of a challenge. He told himself he would be content to bide his time until he had her eating out of his hand just like his clients used to do when he was still working sales promotions for a large communications company.

They were eating their salads when Janice remembered comments she had overheard him make at a party in Tennessee. He had bragged to a friend that he always got what he wanted in one way or another. At the time such a comment didn't mean much to her, but now that she thought about it, she was not impressed with that statement. *Not this time, my friend*, she thought as she excused herself and exited the dining room table to retrieve their entrees from the oven. *You can find locals to do your redecorating. This is one lady who will not be manipulated by you or anyone else!*

Dinner progressed well in spite of her thoughts amid Jack's repetitive compliments regarding the food. He interspersed those with light conversation about the happenings in the lives of people they both knew and what they had been doing during the two years since she'd left Tennessee. His primary goal was to keep her mind occupied so she did not ask questions about the niece, who did not exist, whom he was in Georgia to visit.

Right on time an hour later, just as she had planned, Janice's son Jason and his soon-to-be wife Suzanne knocked on her apartment door. Janice was about to serve coffee and fresh fruit topped with whipped cream for dessert. As planned, they accepted her offer to join them after acting as though they didn't know Jack was there. Jason had met Jack several times when he and Belinda helped with writers group fundraising projects.

Jack pushed his chair back from the table and stood to shake hands with Jason. "It's nice to see you again. In case I didn't remember to tell you at the time, I appreciate you bringing your mom to my wife's celebration of life," he offered. "And I remember all the times you and your sister helped us put those fundraisers together, especially when you helped set up those large unwieldly tents to shelter our paying guests. Without tents in those storms, it wouldn't have been possible to hold the event and earn the funds necessary to give awards to students in our annual writing competition. That and your mom calling in favors for free music from her groups of musician friends," he added.

"It's good to see you, too," Jason cordially replied . "Yes, I remember those times. Not to change the subject, but I would like for you to meet my future wife, Suzanne Rutherford." Instead of offering her hand, Suzanne stepped forward to give Jack a hug. Janice noticed he reciprocated in an appropriately chaste manner. *You just earned some Brownie points*, thought Janice.

"When is the big day?" asked Jack as he turned to again take his seat at the head of the table. Jason and Suzanne took this opportunity to take seats side by side to Jack's left and opposite Janice.

"June first next year," replied the beaming pair in unison as they settled at the slate-topped, wrought iron table.

"Congratulations in advance. I wish you both much happiness. My wife and I would have celebrated our 28th anniversary if she had beaten cancer." Jack squared his shoulders, took a deep breath, and smiled wanly in Janice's direction. "I have your mother to thank for helping me though some tough times." He paused before continuing when Jason, with a mouth full of fruit, was not able respond immediately. "She sure helped me through my loss by writing all of those e-mails about how she dealt with your dad's illness and her own loss. Otherwise, I don't think

39

I would have been able to handle Sabrina's death as well as I've managed to do."

"That's my Mom," Jason finally agreed after swallowing the fruit. "She always looks for that glimmer of hope in situations, but losing my Dad has thrown her for a loop for way too long. I'm really sorry about your loss."

As soon as Jason finished speaking Suzanne voiced her regrets for Jack's loss as well. "I lost my dad a year ago," she offered. "I know how hard it can be when you lose a loved one. I can't even begin to imagine losing a life partner. How did you and Janice meet?" she quickly added in an effort to guide the conversation toward more pleasant circumstances.

"We met through a mutual friend four months after her husband passed away," offered Jack. "I didn't have the opportunity to meet Clayton since Janice and I didn't know each other then. People I've met who knew him tell me what a great guy he was. The members of my writing group are grateful Janice has given scholarships in his memory for the past five years. We host a school writing competition. I'm ashamed to admit it, but I didn't know how much your father's passing affected your mom until my wife got sick and died. Before then I didn't really fully understand what she was going through during the months she attended our weekly meetings. She said little during that first year of widowhood. Fortunately, she gradually came out of her shell with some good ideas for fundraising and began displaying excellent writing abilities. That's why I made contact with her again after she moved here to Georgia. When it became clear Sabrina wasn't going to make it, I hoped your mom could help me by sharing her own experience," he said, looking for their reactions. *The fact that your mom is still a lovely woman with money and writing talent doesn't hurt either*, he thought as he maintained a sad smile on his face. His goal was to portray understanding. With satisfaction, he noted the sympathetic looks he sought were achieved from not only Jason and Suzanne but also from Janice.

As always, Suzanne was able to change the subject and fill conversations with comments sure to evoke laughter. Her lack of a filter when it came to her often colorful views on any given subject allowed her to make comments most people usually reserve for close friends or family members. This lapse in judgment on Suzanne's part embarrassed Janice, but Jack's facial expressions and hearty laughter gave her the impression he enjoyed the off-color remarks.

When dessert and coffee were finished, and he was satisfied everything was under control, Jason announced he and Suzanne needed to return home to feed their dog. "We'll see you tomorrow, Mom. Nice to see you, Jack," said Jason, extending his hand after he and Suzanne pushed back their chairs to stand. Jack stood to bid them goodbye and said it was time for him to be leaving, too, but added the comment he would like another cup of coffee first.

The door was hardly closed behind them when Suzanne started to giggle. As they walked through the short exterior hallway to make their exit from the apartment building into the parking lot, she asked, "Did you pick up that your mom's friend is putting the moves on her?" she announced. "Are you okay with him doing that, Jason?"

"I am," he replied with a grin. "Mom deserves to have someone special in her life. From what I have observed by the choices made by of some of her friends, she could do a whole lot worse than Jack Fairchild. He seems like the decent sort. It does bother me a little that it hasn't been that long since his wife died. I know that bothers Mom, too."

"It's a known fact that men move on from the death of a spouse faster than women do. I read that in a self-help book," replied Suzanne, solemnly. "Anyway, I think they make a cute couple." Jason gently patted her bottom and did not respond to her comments.

"My niece is expecting me to stay at her house tonight," Jack lied as soon as Jason and Suzanne had gone. "It's an hour's drive away, so if it's not any trouble, I need a little more caffeine before I head out." He mentioned this when, in fact, he was staying at a nice chain motel not two miles from Janice's apartment. "I'm not looking forward to that part of the drive," he remarked again with an exaggerated sigh. He hoped by making this comment Janice might take the hint and make an offer for him to spend the night in her guest room, thinking it could be an inroad into the master bedroom at some point in the near future, if not tonight.

OH, NO! was Janice's immediate mental reaction when Jack asked for more coffee. *Here it comes. He is looking for an excuse to stay since Jason and Suzanne have gone home.* Twenty minutes of only small talk passed before Jack reached the conclusion Janice would issue no invitation for him to stay longer. He finished his coffee, got up from the dining room table, and said it was time for him to be going. Janice got up as well. She did not make further comments beyond the small talk in which they were engaged while seated. At the door, he paused to take her offered hand in both of his, thanked her for a lovely evening, and left without a hug or kiss—to her immense relief.

After he had gone and she was cleaning up the kitchen, Janice thought perhaps she may have momentarily misjudged him. She came to the conclusion Jack had ended up behaving like the person she believed him to be, and she was correct in her assumption that he could be considered a gentleman, at least for the time being.

Late the following Sunday afternoon, Janice received an e-mail from Jack letting her know he made it home to Tennessee without any problems, other than the long wait in traffic due to road construction, and what a nice time he had during their visit, especially seeing Jason and meeting Suzanne. "I hope there will be other occasions for us to get together," he added.

Janice felt guilty for setting him up with her offer to cook dinner and confessed to what she had done by letting him know he passed the gentleman test with flying colors. "I hope you weren't offended by my actions." Jack responded he wasn't the least bit offended by what she had done. His e-mail included a smiley face icon added to the message, in which he was not only flattered but also thought what she had done was truly imaginative.

Janice was caught off guard when the offer to set up a book signing for her at a library near where he lived was included in the next paragraph of the e-mail. "I know you've just published your first novel. I've read it, and it's a good one," Jack continued. "The first weekend in September after Labor Day, there is another book signing in a larger town northeast of here. I'm planning to attend. That one involves multiple authors. I'm sure you would be welcome to participate. I can schedule the signings back to back so you would only have to make one trip up here to Tennessee. All I have to do is make a couple of phone calls to the ladies in charge." He wrote this part of the message with his figurative fingers crossed, hoping she would accept his offer including and the subsequent offer to stay at his house. He was on pins and needles when Janice was slow to respond. She reminded him that she had suffered a stroke two months earlier, and while well on the road to a full recovery, she wasn't sure she wanted or needed to make the long, roundtrip attempt from Georgia to Tennessee and back.

"Let me think about it and get back to you," she responded.

"Oh, come on. You can do it!" challenged Jack in his next e-mail less than an hour later. "You are doing great. I wouldn't have known you had a stroke if you hadn't told me. You can stay at my place. I told you I can make both events happen back to back. The library book signing would involve only you on Friday evening. The multiple author event is scheduled for two hours Saturday. Janice, you know you can't rely on digital downloads and paperback sales on websites for that many book sales," he argued. "You are only one of thousands of people with books on those platforms. You have to get out in the public and meet your readers in order to get your name out there if you expect any long-term success as a writer."

Janice knew Jack's argument made sense, but she wasn't ready to spend the night in his home. It just wouldn't feel right to be there alone with him. She didn't hesitate to let him know she had her reputation and his to consider. When she e-mailed her feelings to Jack, he pooh-poohed her, "I'm now a single man. It's nobody's business who spends time at my house."

He felt a heightened sense of anticipation while he waited for her response. After 24 hours passed with no word from Janice, he was tempted to give her a call. He brought her number up on his cell phone but thought better of it and snapped the phone shut. He didn't want to appear too anxious and scare her off. Another long twelve hours would pass before she got around to sending a response.

"Okay, you've convinced me to make the trip to Tennessee, but I will be staying at the small motel out near Interstate 75. You will need to arrange a ride for me to that town you mentioned for the second book signing. I'm directionally impaired and would more than likely end up in Canada if left to my own devices. I'm sorry it took me so long to respond, but I was checking availability of motels in the area to make sure I had a room before making a commitment."

Although disappointed Janice wouldn't stay at his house, Jack muttered, "At least she will be in the immediate area." In his next e-mail he promised to personally provide transportation for her to the second book signing on the designated Saturday morning. "But you will have to call me that Saturday morning at 5:30 a.m. to make sure I'm up and awake," he cautioned. "The signing and sale start promptly at 9:00 a.m., and it's a minimum two-hour drive. It will take me at least a half an hour to have my coffee, shower, dress, and drive twenty minutes or so from my house to your motel. Then there's breakfast to consider." Janice thanked him for his offer of transportation and agreed she would give him the early morning call. She ended the message by thanking him for making the necessary arrangements for her to be included in the second book signing and the event at the local library.

Only minutes passed before he responded. "I can hardly wait until I can give you a hug again. I can't believe I waited so long to see you." Janice found his response a little more intense than she was ready to accept.

It was only a get reacquainted dinner, and the main reason he came here to Georgia was to visit his niece. It isn't like it was a real date with me. He simply needed something to fill the time before his niece returned home, she mused as she stared at the computer. *Maybe I should back out of attending those book signings . . . Aw, what the heck! We will be in contact only a couple of hours each day and like he mentioned, I do need the exposure to get the attention of more readers. What can it hurt if I accept his offer, especially if I stay overnight at the motel? He is only being nice as a response to my cooking dinner when he came to visit his niece.*

The Friday evening, two-hour book signing at the small local Tennessee library proved to be successful in a modest way for Janice. She sold two dozen of the four dozen copies of her novel she brought along, in addition to five of the fifteen copies of her latest cookbook. They were not huge numbers by any means, but she had to take into consideration she was still a relatively unknown author who had not lived in the area for the past two years. *Out of sight, out of mind*, she thought.

She felt a sense of accomplishment when former friends and several acquaintances attended the signing and reception. This was in addition to three people who came just to meet her and buy signed copies of the books.

After the event wrapped up she, Jack, and several of her old friends decided to go out for dinner at a local Mexican restaurant to celebrate her success. Jack ended up taking a seat at an angle across from Janice at the wood-grained, rectangular table after the others claimed their places. Anyone there may have thought Jack paid no more attention to her than he did the other people at the table, but every time Janice glanced his way she sensed Jack was watching her while trying his best not to appear obvious.

At the library Jack offered to drive both of them to the restaurant. She declined the offer. She thought he was a little too eager to spend time alone with her. As the evening progressed she was glad she had insisted on driving her car. "It doesn't make sense for you to drive all the way out to the motel after we eat, drop me off, and then have to turn around and backtrack to your house when you are coming back that way to pick me up in the morning," she argued when he mentioned her refusal in a joking way. She explained, "Think about it. If you take me to the restaurant in your car you would have to drop me off back at my car at the library. Then I would have to make the drive back to the motel." Jack continued to show disappointment that she didn't take him up on his offer but found there was no way to argue with her without admitting he hoped for an invite into her motel room for at least a cup of coffee and perhaps something a little more intimate. *Thank goodness our friends are making a joke out of this conversation*, thought Janice.

"Looks like I struck out again," Jack muttered as he watched her drive away after dinner and a brief hug in the restaurant parking lot. This small gesture only added to the fact he would have to figure out another way to gently gain her confidence. He was aware from her e-mails that she had dated little. He assumed this meant she had not formed an attachment to any particular man following her husband's death. That knowledge encouraged him and made him more determined than ever to move their relationship beyond that of a platonic friendship.

The next morning Janice called Jack promptly at 5:30 a.m. just as she said she would. She peeked between the drapes to find the sun had not yet risen above the mountains. "Good morning, Jack. Are you up and awake?" she asked while trying to stifle a yawn, surprised he did not sound sleepy when he responded to her question.

"I'm sitting out here in the motel lobby drinking coffee and reading the newspaper," he replied. "I woke up at 3:00 a.m. and was afraid to go back to sleep for fear I wouldn't hear the phone ring. I don't own an alarm clock. So, I got up, showered, dressed, and drove here about an hour ago."

"Oh my goodness, you're here at the motel!" exclaimed Janice. She was a little piqued at the thought he didn't think she would call him as they had agreed. "I didn't expect you here at the motel until 6:30!" She wasn't about to invite him to her room while she took care of such matters as showering, dressing, and applying her minimal make-up. "Sit tight and I'll get ready as fast as I can. Then we can have breakfast in the dining room if that's all right with you. It's located to the right just off the lobby. They serve waffles, oatmeal, scrambled eggs, bacon, bagels, toast, coffee, several juices, and fruit. That way we won't have to find a restaurant open this early. I don't know about you, but I really don't want to eat at one of those fast food places . . . too much fat and salt. It would be free for you to eat here since breakfast is included in the price of the room. I don't think anyone would mind if you joined me. If they do, I can have it put on my bill." She still couldn't help wondering why Jack didn't go back to sleep when she had agreed to call him but dismissed the thought in her haste to shower and dress without making him wait any longer than necessary.

"I can see the breakfast room from where I'm sitting," replied Jack. "In fact I can already smell food warming in the steam tables. When I wandered in there earlier the lady setting up the breakfast buffet graciously offered for me to help myself to some coffee while she was preparing the sausage gravy. Having breakfast here is okay with me. Take your time. I'll be right outside," he answered.

"Damn it!" he cursed under his breath after hanging up. "I thought she would invite me to her room."

Jack didn't have a clue Janice was resolute in her moral code to never allow a man near her beyond a handshake or brief hug, especially after her husband passed away. Clayton was the one and only man she had ever been intimate with in her entire life, and that wasn't about to change anytime soon; especially in this day and age of promiscuity and sexually transmitted diseases, some of which last a lifetime or can result in a painful, prolonged death. She had no idea about Jack's sexual history. She assumed he had been faithful to Sabrina, but she had no way of knowing. The thoughts made her blush, so she quickly put them out of her mind.

Half an hour passed before she joined Jack in the motel lobby. "My, but you sure are an early bird," she teased. "It's a good thing I'm drip dry and don't wear much makeup or you could have found yourself sitting out here for an additional hour or more. Come on. Let's go grab some breakfast. I don't know about you, but I'm hungry. They should have opened the buffet a few minutes ago according to what the desk clerk told me at check in yesterday."

Not only did Jack partake liberally of the suggested items, he added a generous helping of biscuits and sausage gravy; something he obviously did not need standing five feet ten inches tall and weighing in at a solid 235 pounds. While he wasn't jiggly fat, Janice could easily see he needed to shed a few pounds under his colorful, loose-fitting, blue, Hawaiian shirt. Obviously, he dressed to hide those extra pounds around the middle. Coupled with the fact he had already been through two major heart surgeries, she, a former nurse, knew those extra salt and fat-laden calories were not something he needed. At the same time, she didn't feel she knew him well enough to mention it. *I'll clue him into healthier eating habits using an e-mail after and IF I get to know him a little better*, she thought to herself. *I don't want to hurt his feelings so soon after reconnecting.*

After breakfast, the two started out in Jack's car to make the drive north on Interstate 75 in the pre-dawn hour. They were headed for a destination neither one of them was sure of as they tried to follow incomplete directions provided by a writers group member. They laughed and joked about the possibility of becoming lost. They oohed and aahed over the spectacular sunrise above the mountainous hillsides like two old friends are prone to do. This type of conversation allowed Janice to feel comfortable in Jack's presence.

Janice found herself a little dismayed when she learned Jack had arranged for them to sit at different tables at the book signing. They arrived at the destination, the town's large historical library, which was a gothic, dull red brick structure built in the 1800s. Jack sat down and arranged his books next to Elaina Albright, a female member of the writers group. Janice knew Elaina was married but always sensed the woman had designs on Jack. She once joked with Janice, as they exited a meeting several years before while Janice was still living in Tennessee, about becoming a friend with benefits with Jack long before the death of his wife. Janice had not forgotten the tasteless remark. Her opinion had not changed. She wanted to believe Elaina was joking, but her sixth sense told her otherwise as she observed how Elaina looked at and interacted with Jack. Janice convinced herself it was not of any concern to her that Jack and Elaina were seated next to each other today. After all, she and Jack had no ties that would invoke jealousy on her part.

During a lull before the doors opened to the public, she had no reason to disbelieve Jack when he wandered over to her table to offer an explanation as to why he had not joined her at her sales table. "I thought you would have a better shot at selling books at a location closer to the door where people enter the room," he offered. "I didn't know they would lock that door." Out of the blue he added that Elaina was nothing more than a friend. Janice had not requested or expected an explanation regarding his relationship with this woman. In fact, she thought it strange he made a point of mentioning she was just a friend, so Janice smiled and said, "It looks like they are about to usher in the first wave of customers, so you probably need to get back to your table."

Janice dismissed any thoughts concerning Jack or Elaina as people started to circulate among the tables piled high with books for sale. At least 30 authors were present. Janice became occupied with selling her books and chatting with potential buyers. This helped the day quickly pass. Before she realized it, it was 1:00 p.m. and the sale was over. The authors began packing up unsold books. It was time for all of the writers to enjoy a potluck lunch.

Jack had made a crockpot of white bean and sausage soup. She also brought several different kinds of canned mixed nuts and a store-bought cake since she was not able to prepare anything more substantial in a motel room. In spite of the vast array of foods, there were no leftovers of her items. She noticed little had been eaten of Jack's soup. She felt badly for him when he tried to laugh it off.

Janice remarked that she did sell the remaining ten copies of her cookbook but only one copy of her new novel. While this was disappointing, several more people had asked how they could obtain the novel online, explaining they spent their money before reaching her display near the side door. Jack's assumed favorable spot had actually routed people away from her. At lunch Jack and Elaina reported they did not sell any books, but from her viewpoint across the room during the sale, Janice observed they seemed to have a good time laughing and talking, which didn't bother her. After all, Jack was just a good friend providing transportation and looking out for her best professional interests, or so she chose to believe.

The two-hour drive back to the motel was as amicable between them as the drive to the book signing had been, perhaps even more so. She and Jack laughed and talked about a lot of different things; other drivers' stupid moves, places they wanted to visit, including Mexico, and memories of when they worked together on the writing group scholarship fundraising. Janice found herself becoming more and more comfortable with this man.

While accompanying her husband to various events at his instance, Janice had found it necessary to discourage unwelcome advances by several of Clayton's superiors. She tried to do so in a manner that would not damage her husband's close relationships with colleagues. She let Clayton know what was happening. He laughed when she mentioned her discomfort to him. "It doesn't bother me. I trust you completely," Clayton assured her. In fact, he admitted he enjoyed knowing he was the one she would be going home with, leaving other men with "their tongues hanging out like dogs on the heels of a bitch in heat." Janice cringed at the analogy but knew Clayton was just being Clayton. She also knew he was correct in that she would be going home with him and that, as a married woman, would never accept a clandestine date with any man. She never dressed or acted in provocative ways and had always taken her wedding vows seriously.

"Is it okay if I come in for a cup of coffee before I make the drive back to my house?" asked Jack as he pulled into the motel parking lot. "It's been a long day, and I'm tired." Knowing Jack's history of heart surgeries, Janice did not hesitate to invite him in for coffee. She addressed the afternoon desk clerk as soon as they entered the lobby to let him know she was having a male guest in her room and there would be no hanky panky. "He's an old friend who needs a cup of coffee before he heads home," she assured him. "We're just catching up. I've been gone from the area for two years, and we have a lot to discuss." Knowing her from other times she had been a guest at the motel while visiting friends after her move, the desk clerk expressed his approval for Jack to accompany her to her room. The two of them headed for her room, which was located just around the corner from the reception desk. Janice proceeded to make coffee using the coffee maker, ground coffee packet, and small four-cup glass pot provided by the motel. With the task completed, she then turned on the TV to an old western movie while Jack used the bathroom facilities.

When Jack came out of the bathroom they took seats opposite each other near the window overlooking a scruffy tree-lined hillside. A dark-stained, wooden, card-size table was between them. He drank his coffee while they watched the movie starring John Wayne. They continued their conversation focusing on the day's activities. She sipped on cold bottled spring water she had taken from the mini-refrigerator. She thought he was ready to leave when Jack asked if he could take a short nap. This request took her completely by surprise.

"You can lie down and take a nap, too, if you want to," said Jack as he sat down on the side of the bed and provocatively patted the king bedspread and sheet-covered mattress beside him. This comment and gesture immediately put Janice on guard.

"I'm comfortable here in the chair," she replied. *This is not a good idea*, she thought when Jack unbuttoned his shirt, took it off, and tossed it across the back of the chair where he had been sitting. She could not help silently wondering, *What do I do now?* She felt slightly less apprehensive when, quickly, his loud snores began to permeate the room. She let him sleep for the better part of an hour before getting up from her chair to walk hesitantly toward the side of the bed and lightly tap him on the right shoulder. He awakened with a start.

"Time for you to go home now," she said softly. "The desk clerk might want to charge me for having another person in the room if you stay here much longer." Jack appeared to be fully awake and up on his feet in an instant.

57

"Is it all right if I use the bathroom to splash some cold water on my face?" he asked without reaching for his shirt. Janice tried to keep her eyes focused on the television program, rather than the hairy nakedness of his upper torso. She quickly returned to sit in the chair rather than stand beside the bed. Still, there was no discounting the fact she had seen his bare muscular shoulders and chest, and the sight sent goosebumps up both arms and at the base of her neck. It had been almost six years since she had seen a man in any state of undress, let alone in a motel room.

"Sure. Help yourself. Towels on the rack are clean," she managed to reply while struggling to maintain a casual tone. A few seconds after the bathroom door closed, she couldn't help hearing the muted sound of him urinating then flushing the toilet. She then heard the sink turn on and off. A minute later Jack emerged, put on and buttoned his shirt, then headed toward the door and prepared to leave. He extended his hand. Once again Janice experienced the same immense relief she experienced when he left her apartment in Georgia without any unwanted advances. After she thanked him and gave Jack a brief hug, she closed and locked the door. She couldn't help but think this had been a strange and unsettling day. She could not explain her next move. She prepared for bed, got in, and pulled the pillow on which he had slept under her head. The faint odor of his aftershave still lingered on it. She found it comforting as she drifted off to sleep. Upon awakening the following morning, she chided herself when she fully realized what she had done. "What kind of silly school girl thing is this?" she muttered, tossing the pillow and sheet aside before heading to the bathroom for her morning shower.

"I won't see him again for a long time, if ever. I'm being utterly crazy to even think about Jack being anything more than a friend," she said out loud during the long drive back to Georgia.

It didn't take long before Janice's son and girlfriend arrived at her apartment door. They wanted to hear about her book sales and how everything went with Jack on Sunday afternoon. "I want to hear everything, so don't keep me waiting," said a beaming Suzanne the minute she entered the living room.

"The first library book sale went reasonably well. I can't say the same for the second signing on Saturday. Only one novel sold, but several people took my business card for future reference. I did manage to sell the rest of the cookbooks."

"I'm not talking about the book sales. I want to know how it went with Jack," insisted Suzanne. Janice smiled.

"Leave it to you to be a nosey little miss. But if you must know, we had some good conversations." She did not mention what had gone down at the motel after the second book sale, that Jack had already sent an e-mail asking her to come back to Tennessee so they could spend more time together, or her mixed feelings about becoming romantically involved with him so soon after Sabrina's passing.

"Just conversations?" Suzanne questioned as she raised one eyebrow. "Come on! And here I visualized the two of you dancing in the moonlight, sipping champagne, and sharing a bed."

"Suzanne! Stop it! Jack and I have just recently reconnected. Have you forgotten his wife died only a few months ago? Anyway, I'm not about to become seriously involved in a romantic way with Jack or any other man until I feel it's the right thing to do. I hasten to point out that I have not reached that point in my life, nor do I plan to in the immediate future!"

"I think it's time for me to take a walk and leave you two to sort out this conversation," interjected Jason.

"Coward!" replied Suzanne. "I'm sure you want to know the details just as much as I do." Jason did not respond before he left, so Suzanne continued, "You don't need to get all huffy, Janice! It has been almost six years since Clayton . . ."

Janice held up her hand in a motion meant to message Suzanne to stop talking. For once, Suzanne had the good sense to back off and keep her mouth shut, but her knowing look said more than Janice was willing to acknowledge. Not being someone easily silenced, Suzanne's demeanor strongly suggested she was not done speaking her mind and Janice knew it. "I think it is time to change the subject," Janice announced with a forced smile. Thankfully, Suzanne got the less than subtle message this time. "How about we go get some lunch and do some shopping?"

"If you insist," replied Suzanne.

"I insist," answered Janice as she picked up her purse from the antique, maple rocking chair sitting nearest the door. She turned to her future daughter-in-law with a bow and wave of her hand toward the door. "After you, my dear, and just to let you know who's the boss, I get to choose the restaurant." This left Suzanne little choice but to proceed ahead of her future mother-in-law out the now open door. It was that or risk what could turn out to be an unwanted confrontation she knew she could not hope to win.

CHAPTER 3

Upon returning from lunch and shopping with Suzanne, Janice found another e-mail from Jack waiting on her computer. "I wonder what he wants from me now! I don't have time for this. We relived our past and said our goodbyes," she whispered. Tempted to ignore the message, at least for the rest of the day or even until tomorrow, an hour passed before she gave in to curiosity and read it.

"I had a great time the past two days and hope you did, too," it read. "When can we get together again? I know the old gang and I would be delighted if you happened to show up for the Thursday evening writers group meeting the third week of September, or even a day or two earlier so we could spend some time together. It's still warm enough to take my boat out for a ride on the river, or we could drive up into the mountains for one of those picnics you told me you and Clayton often enjoyed. I am handy at barbequing burgers or hot dogs, and I could pick up some potato salad and drinks at the local grocery store. The leaves will just be starting to change colors, and we'll be planning the final touches for the October fall writers group fundraiser. I'm sure you can offer Elaina some ideas you used that were successful. As vice president, she's in charge of the event. She has never done anything like this before and, frankly, that has me worried. We need a good turnout to earn enough money to reward our annual competition winners. If I sound like I'm begging for your help, I am. I know it's a long drive back here on the heels of the book signings, but I would love to see you. Please get back to me so I have time to get the boat cleaned and gassed up. I haven't had her away from the dock for quite some time, so she will definitely need a good scrubbing."

"Why don't you drive down my way to Georgia and we can do some sightseeing around the Atlanta area since I just made the trip to Tennessee? That would save you the time and effort of cleaning the boat," countered Janice in her e-mail later that same evening. "There are some pretty lakes down here, and the marinas offer boat rentals. Plus, our mountains aren't far away. I'm sure Elaina will do just fine with help from you and other club members."

"Sorry, but I can't make the drive down your way right now. I have too many commitments. You are welcome to stay at my place as long as you want if you make the trip this way. That will save you the expense of renting a room at the motel. Once again, I'm begging you to help Elaina with the fundraiser. Let me know what you decide to do." The e-mail was signed simply, "Jack."

Janice couldn't help wondering why he would want her staying at his home if he had so many commitments that he couldn't see his way clear to make the trip to Georgia. It didn't make any sense until she gave his message some more thought and read it again. This clinched her decision to not respond to his invitation to Tennessee. "I need to give this e-mail a little more thought after I have my dinner," she softly said aloud.

"Oh dear me," she murmured when she read the message for the third time several hours later. "I just got home from Tennessee, and it's only two weeks from now when he wants me to come back . . . wait a minute . . . he has a birthday coming up about that time. I'll bet he doesn't want to be alone. It will be his first birthday without Sabrina." Janice immediately e-mailed Elaina. Although she wasn't especially fond of Elaina, Janice felt she was the right person to contact and could be of assistance in carrying out the plans she had in mind.

After several attempts to come up with a satisfactory e-mail, she finally sent the following: "We need to set up a surprise birthday party for Jack at the writers group meeting on September 29. It will be his first birthday since Sabrina died. What do you think? His birthday is actually on Wednesday, September 28, so he won't be suspecting anything at the Thursday evening meeting. I'll drive up on Wednesday afternoon and invite him out for dinner that night to act as a decoy. He invited me to come to the Thursday meeting to help you plan the fall fundraiser. Would you be so kind as to take care of contacting club members, members of the library staff, and the board to let them know what's up? Could you also make sure tables and chairs are set up in the library meeting room? I'll provide the cake and some substantial snacks if you provide the coffee and iced tea."

Elaina promptly e-mailed back to let Janice know she thought this was a great idea, with the exception of the dinner invitation with Jack on Wednesday. "I'm sure he will have already made plans," she wrote.

Janice replied, "I didn't get the impression from his last e-mail that he was planning to do anything special, which doesn't surprise me since it will be his first birthday without Sabrina."

"Oh, I suppose you could be right, but just keep in mind he may have already made plans and you would end up making the trip for nothing," Elaina wrote in response. "Besides, I think I have everything under control for the fundraiser and won't need your help for that or the Thursday evening birthday party. You don't need to make the long drive."

Elaina made it obvious she didn't want any help from Janice and that Janice wasn't needed to pull off the Thursday party. Janice decided she would not tell Elaina how Jack pleaded for her assistance with the fundraiser since her efforts had proven so successful in past years, or that he was unsure about Elaina's first attempt at managing the major fundraising event. That was likely a bad call on Janice's part, but she wouldn't know it for quite some time. In addition, there was that little voice in the back of her head. She could not help wondering why Elaina did not want her having dinner with Jack or visiting with any friends in Tennessee. These questions helped confirm that she would indeed make the trip and hopefully get some answers.

"Since I do plan to make an appearance and supply food for the party, it would not be a wasted trip. I have friends to visit if Jack has plans Wednesday night. Jack and I have been friends for too many years for me not to make the effort," Janice replied in a carefully worded response.

Janice wasn't surprised when Elaina curtly responded in her next e-mail, "Suit yourself. I was only trying to save you a long drive."

Sure you were, thought Janice. *It's clear to me that you don't want me to come to Tennessee for whatever reason. Sorry sweetheart, but I'll be there with bells on, and if you don't happen to like it, that is just too bad!*

Janice felt excitement building as she carried about routine shopping and housekeeping tasks during the two-week interval before returning to Tennessee. Providing a family dinner for her Jason, Suzanne, and her mother helped the time fly. She decided not to mention the trip to Tennessee for Jack's birthday to any of them until the day before she planned to leave. When she did reveal her intentions, just as she suspected, she once again got knowing looks from Suzanne, but Jason gave his intended bride a glare that told her to zip it, for which Janice was thankful. She proceeded to pack her weekender suitcase in time to hit the road back to Tennessee and surprise her widowed friend on his actual birthday without contacting him. The drive to Tennessee proved to be long and, thankfully, uneventful. Her heart began to beat faster when Janice saw the touch of color visible in the early fall, tree-lined foothills of the Great Smoky Mountains off in the distance. She felt a brief sense of melancholy knowing she had left the place where she had been so happy prior to Clayton's death. Try as she might to avoid it, a tear rolled down her cheek. *Stop it!* She mentally chided herself. *You know it was past time for you to move on before you sold your mountain home, so stop with the waterworks already!*

Before she called to let Jack know she was in the area, she stopped to check into the same motel where he had napped in her bed after the book signings. She maintained it wouldn't look right to stay overnight at his home, even though he had ultimately ended up behaving like a gentleman when he spent time in her room at the motel.

She asked for and was given the same king-size room located close to the front desk. She checked her watch to note she was running later than anticipated, so she didn't feel the need to remove her suitcase from the trunk of the car and take it directly to the room following check-in. "I can take my luggage to the room later," she said to the desk clerk as she tucked her credit card and room key into her purse. As she placed the card in a secure place, her cell phone caught her attention. "I need to call Jack," she mumbled. She hit the send button to Jack's number during the walk across the lobby and through the automatic doors to her car still parked under the portico. Janice knew she was taking the chance he might have other plans, but this didn't matter since she would be attending his surprise birthday party the following evening at the library anyway. If he said he was busy, she simply wouldn't let him know she was in Tennessee and would spend the evening visiting friends. She felt relieved when Jack finally answered after the fifth ring, just as she began to think he wasn't home. He sounded surprised, but at the same time delighted to hear her voice.

"Hey there Big Brother!" exclaimed Janice.

"Hey there yourself, Sis," he replied. He immediately regretted using the term *Sis*, but it came out automatically since that was how he had often addressed her in the past. "What's up?"

"How about meeting me at the restaurant where all of us used to go so we can celebrate your birthday tonight? That is, if you don't have any other plans," she blurted out, in spite of her earlier plan not to mention dinner until she knew he was free. Jack didn't hesitate before saying he had no plans and he began to chuckle. His first thought was, *YES! She came back already. Maybe I do stand a chance for a relationship with her.*

"Don't tell me you are back in town already? You just left a little over two weeks ago, and when you didn't respond to my invitation to join me at the meeting this coming Thursday evening, I figured you wouldn't be coming," he continued smoothly. "To what do I owe this honor?"

"I was hoping to help you celebrate your birthday, silly," said Janice. "I know this is short notice, but I thought I would take a chance. I was driving up here to attend the writers group meeting tomorrow night and figured I would give you a call." She felt a sense of delight when Jack said he had no plans. She was grateful when he didn't ask what she would have done if he were obligated. Janice had no way of knowing that Jack actually did have other plans. He knew he could cancel them, so he accepted her offer.

"I wasn't about to let you celebrate your birthday all alone." continued Janice. "I ask you. What kind of friend does that? Will the restaurant out by the freeway, just this side of Kingston, at six sound good? I'll be the lady wearing red."

Jack sounded even more delighted as he immediately accepted her offer for dinner. "That sounds great to me! I thought I would be celebrating my birthday alone. I was beginning to feel sorry for myself, but then you called," he responded.

At the same time, Janice began to wonder if she had acted a little too quickly in making the drive to Tennessee or planning his birthday celebrations but realized it was too late to back out now.

"How did you know it is my birthday?" he questioned. "I don't remember mentioning it during our phone and e-mail conversations."

"I remembered the party Sabrina had for you two years ago. Members of the writers group were invited." Janice immediately felt terrible that she mentioned the party. "I'm sorry. I didn't mean to stir up old memories."

"There is nothing for you to feel sorry about," interrupted Jack, even though her comment felt like a sucker punch to his gut—something he would never admit to Janice or anyone else. "I'm glad you are here, and I look forward to having dinner with you tonight." He literally danced around the room as soon as their conversation ended. "She's here, and she is taking me out to dinner," he said with glee to a fluffy, multicolored cat. The animal belonged to the neighbors and often wandered inside Jack's house through the open sliding door to his back deck. "What more can I ask for? Except, I *might* be able to convince her to stay here at my place for the night instead of that damned motel!"

Jack didn't waste any time cancelling his previous plans at such a late hour. He did so without second thoughts, even in the face of chastisement by the person he was committed to see in just two hours. It was already four o'clock, so he set about selecting a classier set of clothes than what he had planned to wear. He gave his beard and moustache a quick trim while mentally cursing himself for not visiting his barber for several weeks. After taking a shower and dressing, he stood back to take a look a look at himself in the full length mirror fastened to the inside of the closet door. Satisfied he had done the best he could on such short notice, he hit the road for the twenty-minute drive to the restaurant. He was a happy man. Any thoughts involving the angry words hurled his way by his intended date were erased from his mind the moment he snapped his cell phone shut ending that conversation.

Janice noted her arrival at the appointed restaurant was barely five minutes before Jack was due to join her. She had made a stop at a grocery store on the way to purchase a Mylar, helium-filled, birthday balloon. After being seated by a hostess, Janice tied the balloon to the table's condiment holder. The stop had cut short the time she had to prepare. She quickly caught the eye of a waiter and ordered an appetizer to be ready when Jack arrived. She did have the foresight to take one of her famous homemade banana walnut breads from the freezer. She knew he liked them because she used to take them to the writers group meetings, and he always complimented her baking skills. She tied a colorful red bow around the loaf. An appropriately funny birthday card lay beside Jack's bread plate. Warm cheese artichoke dip and corn chips arrived. She congratulated herself for remembering he liked that particular dip. When Jack walked into the restaurant a couple of minutes later, she slid out of the red leather booth to give him a big smile and a quick hug as soon as he approached her. "Happy Birthday you sweet old man," she said in a light-hearted way. "How does it feel to be another year older? Dinner is on me, but don't expect me to pick up the tab when we meet again . . . well, maybe next year on your birthday," she teased. "From now on it is 50/50."

Jack didn't miss the fact she had said "WHEN we meet again" instead of IF we meet again. He returned her smile, thinking she was at least beginning to think about him in her future. He readily agreed they should go Dutch on future meals. He offered no comment about how he felt about becoming another year older. He simply scrunched up his nose, adding a wrinkle to his forehead, as he slid into the seat opposite her. He smiled broadly at the sight of the balloon, card, gift, and appetizer. "You didn't miss a thing, did you?" he commented as he dipped a corn chip into the warm artichoke and cheese dip and lifted it toward his open mouth.

"I tried," said Janice. "But you need something to drink besides ice water. What will it be? Wine? Or how about a cocktail? After all, this is a special occasion, so name your poison my good man!"

Jack couldn't help laughing. "You are correct, my dear lady. I think the occasion does call for a gin martini with two large, pimento-stuffed green olives," he responded before aggressively chomping down on the generously dip-covered chip.

"Then a martini with two pimento stuffed olives is what you shall have," she replied.

Janice had little doubt Jack was pleased with all the attention given to him by her and the restaurant staff as they enjoyed their salad and steak dinners, he with a gin martini with the specified olives. His bright blue eyes glowed with delight when the servers presented him with a huge slice of chocolate cake topped with a glowing striped candle accompanied by a generous scoop of vanilla ice cream on the side. While the servers began to sing Happy Birthday, other diners joined in.

"Blow out the candle and make a wish, but don't tell anyone what you wish for or it won't come true," Janice said sternly when he picked up a fork before even blowing out the candle—he wanted to dive into the delicious-looking cake without delay. Janice couldn't help but notice the look on his face was not unlike that a child opening a brightly wrapped present on Christmas morning. She found his look endearing. In response to her admonition Jack hesitated, the fork in mid-air, before he blew out the candle and asked for another fork, which was quickly delivered. This allowed him time to make a wish and for Janice to share the cake and ice cream. She had no idea when he blew out the candle and closed his eyes that he wished that she would spend the night and share a bed with him. When the dessert and his coffee were finished, the conversation began to lag. This is when they both reluctantly agreed it was time to give up the booth.

"This has been an unexpected pleasure to find myself spending time here with you this evening, and I don't want it to end," declared Jack.

"Thank you," was all Janice could muster in a reply.

On the way out the door to the parking lot, Jack asked Janice if she'd come to his house not far from the restaurant for a glass of wine out on the deck overlooking the river. "That, and you could change your mind and make use of my guest room. You did say you would join me at the writers group meeting tomorrow evening." He knew she had not agreed to attend the meeting but thought she might not remember. He implied she had confirmed she would be there.

"Thanks for the invite, but I will have to take a raincheck on the wine tasting and invitation to stay at your house. I'm tired after the long drive here, and I've already checked in at the motel for the night. How about we meet for breakfast tomorrow morning before I head back to Georgia? I've heard Alice's Restaurant has a fantastic pecan cinnamon roll," she replied. Jack did his best to look confused.

"You are headed back to Georgia tomorrow? I thought you were going to stick around in order to attend the meeting tomorrow evening."

Janice hated not being totally honest, but she could not recall accepting the invitation, and at the same time, she didn't want to spoil the birthday surprise party scheduled for the following night. She didn't miss the look of obvious disappointment flashing across Jack's face but knew she would not be comfortable spending the night at his home, nor did she want to accidentally let it slip about the party. She reasoned that she was being truthful when she said she was tired, but couldn't shake the feeling that she was lying: she needed to spend the night at the motel in order to pick up the cake she had ordered the following morning and deliver the other goodies to the library, where the party was to be held; plus, she had promised to meet old friends for lunch the following day, all of which significantly shortened her free time before the party.

She crossed her fingers believing this nullified the fib she was about to hastily tell. "I need to get back to Georgia tomorrow, so I can't stay for the writers club meeting like I must have said in an e-mail. I promised Jason and Suzanne I would help them get ready for four out-of-town visitors, two of whom will be staying in my guest room tomorrow night. Jason has only one guest bedroom."

Jack had the feeling she wasn't being truthful, but neither was he in making her think she had agreed to stay for the meeting. He didn't voice his suspicion for fear it would nix any possible future contact with her.

"That doesn't mean you can't stop at the house. Won't you even consider following me out to the house to at least taste the elderberry wine? I've promised some of it to a local charity, and if you don't think it's quite up to par, I can donate another variety from my stock," he replied. There was no mistaking the pleading look he gave her.

Janice was aware he had donated gallons of the barely drinkable, homemade, fruit-based concoctions to various charities for use at many of the fundraising events she had attended in the past while living in Tennessee; thus she wasn't as excited as he seemed to be about tasting his latest wine. She suspected he donated the homemade beverages to ensure not only his acceptance by members of the various organizations, but also to give him something to do following an early retirement buyout from his mid-management job four years earlier. The hobby must also help him face the fact he was living alone in a somewhat remote riverside home. He had told Janice about his employer's early buyout of his contract six years ago in their conversation during the drive from the out-of-town book signing. This knowledge allowed her to put two and two together and speculate this is where the money came from to buy the riverside property, build, minimally furnish the house, and purchase the sleek, yet modest yacht berthed at his redwood dock. But where the money came from didn't matter to Janice since there was not a connection between them beyond that of friendship, as far as she was concerned, of course.

Rather than disappoint him on his birthday she thought she should relent, go to his home, taste the wine, and then leave shortly thereafter.

"Thank you for the invitation. You have managed to convince me to go back to your house and spend a little more time tasting your latest liquid contribution to the human race, as long as you understand I can't stay long," she said with a grin. "Then I must be on my way to the motel in order to get my beauty sleep. If we meet for an early breakfast that means I'll have to get up even earlier and be there when they open the restaurant door in order to get a reasonable start for the three hour-drive back to Georgia. I don't relish the thought of hitting afternoon, rush hour traffic to deal with all of those crazy Atlanta drivers, many of whom seem to have a death wish." She kept her fingers crossed on both hands tucked in her lap out of sight. This was a habit learned from her grandmother when she fibbed in order to keep a secret. Jack's smile spread even wider across his face in its usual charming, boyish way.

"I take that to mean you will follow me back to my house?"

When she nodded in agreement, he thought his birthday wish was about to come true. He was glad he had straightened up the house that morning and changed the sheets on the queen size bed in the guest room following a brief visit by his son two days ago. Another bedroom where he normally slept, now as a matter of habit, held two twin beds to accommodate what had been his wife's illness. This had become their nightly routine for more than a year after Sabrina informed Jack that his restless tossing and turning during the night kept her awake when they shared the same bed.

Janice's "taste the wine and leave" theory went by the wayside as they spent time talking about experiences concerning emotional pain, medical decisions, and legal ramifications associated with illness and loss of a spouse. Jack fought a losing battle with tears as he related the eight years of heartbreaking struggles with his wife's repeated hospitalizations and the final bout of cancer that spread to her lungs and brain. He briefly mentioned his own bout with prostate cancer, elaborating more on the two major heart surgeries and resulting phlebitis in his left leg after veins taken from there were used to improve blood flow in his heart. This surgery was followed shortly by the need for a new heart valve. Janice was aware of the heart surgeries, but not that he'd had to deal with prostate cancer. As a former nurse, she knew the resulting effects of radioactive seed implants involved significant negative side effects, none of which he had disclosed in his e-mails. She was aware a major side effect of this treatment was of a personal nature, so she decided not to offer any comments on the subject, and neither did he.

Janice felt encouraged to share some of the details of her own life. She talked about her long-term struggle with a collagen disease, heart problems, and the illness and loss of her husband, coupled with her efforts to overcome uterine cancer and the recent stroke. She had not felt closer to any man, with the exception of her now deceased husband, than she did to Jack during this conversation. She wanted to reach out, take him in her arms and offer comfort, but she felt this could give him the wrong impression, not something she should do. She was afraid this would lead to him asking her to stay overnight, as he had done in previous e-mails and verbal conversations. If the truth were known, she was afraid she would not be able to tell him no out of a sense of wanting to alleviate the obvious pain he was exhibiting due to the death of his wife. *Now is not the time in the friendship to become physical, even in a platonic way*, she mentally reminded herself.

She breathed a quiet sigh of relief when what turned out to be a mutual friend and his current girlfriend pulled a car into the parking area in front of Jack's house. Jack hastily wiped his eyes and took a large gulp of wine when he heard their footsteps approaching the front porch. Janice said she would answer their knock on the door. It was a really fortuitous timing.

"Would you look who's here!" declared the gentleman visitor. "Gosh it's good to see you again, Janice. Life in Georgia must be agreeing with you. You look great. This is my friend Mary Ann. We just decided to drive over to wish this old man a happy birthday."

"It's nice to meet you Mary Ann," said Janice, extending her hand. "And good to see you again as well," she said, turning back to the gentleman. "Come on inside. Jack and I were sitting at the kitchen counter talking."

By this time Jack managed to pull himself together and joined her in welcoming the guests.

"Come in and join us," he said, although the strain in his voice and extra rosy color of his cheeks belied the smile on his face.

They all sat on high-backed wicker bar chairs placed around the kitchen island and chatted as they sipped on Jack's latest batch of elderberry wine. Janice did not comment on its rough taste, nor did he ask for her opinion, which he had claimed to care about, as per their conversation at dinner. It didn't help matters when the gentleman visitor made a comment about how beautiful it was to wake up to the sunrise on the river flowing behind Jack's house, while giving Janice a knowing look. There was little doubt he made the assumption Janice was planning to spend the night. Janice was cool in her response. "I will have to take your word for it in regard to the morning river view, since I will not be waking up to it. I came here tonight to taste Jack's latest offering of wine after treating him to his birthday dinner. Then I'm going back to a Comfort Inn, the one near the interstate, where I've already checked in. Tomorrow morning we'll meet at Alice's Restaurant for breakfast, and after that I will head home to Georgia."

She crossed her fingers, hoping the male visitor wouldn't let the cat out of the bag concerning the surprise birthday party the following evening. He was a member of the writers group, so she felt reasonably sure Elaina had invited him and his girlfriend to attend the surprise birthday party for Jack. She breathed a subtle sigh of relief when he held his tongue. She did leave a few minutes after the visitors left, but not before experiencing an intimate hug from Jack that left her heart racing and a feeling of weakness in her knees. She reluctantly turned her lips away, allowing his kiss to land on her right cheek instead of his intended target.

"See you at Alice's tomorrow morning at 7:00 a.m. sharp," she said before disengaging herself from his embrace to make the short walk down the curving concrete sidewalk extending to the gravel-covered parking area where her car waited. She pretended not to notice the look of dejection on Jack's face in the glow of the yellow porch light when she passed by him. She knew she was not prepared to face what could happen if she gave into that look. She had a distinct feeling that if she did, there was a good possibility that would mean changing plans to include awakening to the river view to find Jack lying next to her; and she believed neither one of them were truly prepared for that to happen.

The next morning Janice put on a happy face and toyed with her breakfast at Alice's Restaurant. Jack seemed glum, almost morose. "Don't tell me you have the birthday blues?" she voiced with genuine concern between taking tiny bites of scrambled eggs. He hesitated and took a deep breath before answering.

"It just dawned on me that a lot of people will now consider me an old man," he offered. He didn't mention the main reason for feeling down was the fact he ended up sleeping alone last night. The sleeping alone comment was something he very much wanted to say out loud if only to get Janice's reaction. Once again, he held his tongue for fear she would get up and walk out, thus killing any chance he might still have of her becoming interested in pursuing a more intimate relationship.

"Nonsense! You are still one handsome man who is aging well. You can take it from me that you have a lot of good years left ahead of you. Besides, you are only as old as you feel," replied Janice in an attempt to raise his spirits. She smiled before taking a fork full of the huge pecan cinnamon roll the waitress had placed in front of her a few minutes earlier. She moaned in delight at the taste of the delectable pastry before breaking off another generous bite and offering it across the table to Jack.

He shook his head. "No thanks. Leave it to you to be the eternal optimist," he replied before draining his second cup of coffee and raising his hand to signal the waitress for a refill. "How about coming back to the house for the rest of the morning? That would get you home before rush hour traffic if you left at say, noon. That would give you plenty of time before your son's expected guests arrive. Or you could wait to leave until around three o'clock. That would get you home after the evening rush hour... or you could change your mind and spend the night here. I'm sure your son has a house key and could let his friends into your apartment should you happen to be late or decide to stay in Tennessee. Nobody is occupying the guest room. Also, I have begun work on another book, and I would really appreciate it if you could help me with some editing."

"You don't give up easily, do you?" replied Janice with a half-hearted, unmistakable, lopsided grin. Swallowing the mouthful of roll followed by a sip of water she continued. "You know I would love to help you with the editing, but I really must get back to Georgia to host Jason's friends. You can e-mail me a couple of chapters of the book. I will take a look at them and get back to you with an opinion as soon as I can."

Once again, she felt guilty about lying but couldn't tell him about the party tasks she had to accomplish before her late luncheon with friends. For some unexplained reason Janice felt like Elaina would not go out of her way to make sure the room at the library was ready for a party, which left her with the feeling she needed to arrive at the library a little early.

"Enjoy the meeting with the writers group this evening and fill me in. I'm really sorry I can't stay to attend, but Jason and Suzanne are counting on me," she told him as she got up and stepped away from their table. She felt it was time to leave, or things could get complicated since she was not a good liar. She started walking toward the front of the restaurant with Jack close on her heels. She stopped at the glass display counter featuring a variety of pastries, fumbled in her purse for her wallet in order to pay the cashier for her meal, in accordance with the agreement to go 50/50 on any future meals they would share.

Please God, don't let him ask me to spend the night at his house again. I don't think I can say no. It was a prayer she continued to silently pray as they stood facing each other in the parking lot while standing beside her car to say their goodbyes. Following a hug and a peck on the cheek, she ignored another unmistakable look of longing on Jack's face. He held the car door open for her a little longer than necessary, then reluctantly shut it after she was seated before stepping back to watch her drive away with a wave of her hand. "I must be losing my touch," Jack dejectedly mumbled while walking to his car.

"It's too soon for me to become involved with him on a more personal level," Janice whispered on the drive back the motel in order to freshen up then head on to the bakery. At the same time she did admit to herself she was beginning to have an attraction to Jack she couldn't quite understand, and it was unsettling. "It is much too soon for us to become involved on a more personal level," she kept muttering. "He needs more time to grieve. Even though he tells me he has moved on, I'm not so sure that's the case."

On his drive down the familiar country roads back to his home, Jack groused aloud. "Damn! Looks like I've struck out with her again! So much for making a wish on that confounded birthday candle last night."

He was totally unaware Janice had spent a long and sleepless night in the motel room, tossing and turning alone in her bed, just as he had in one of the twin beds at his home.

The Thursday evening surprise birthday party was not as heavily attended as Janice had anticipated. Elaina had not gone out of her way to alert that many club members, including the visitors who'd come to Jack's house the previous day, nor any of the library board members about the party. As a result, Janice ended up purchasing too much cake. To her dismay the on-line order for one large sheet cake had been overlooked. She ended up purchasing three small cakes, insisting these words be placed on each cake: The first one, a chocolate cake read, "Happy", the second, a carrot cake, "Birthday" and the third one, vanilla with butter cream icing, "Jack." She dismissed the sour look on the face of the woman carrying out her wishes.

While driving to the library after the purchase, she made a mental note to arrange the cakes to form a centerpiece down the middle of the oblong table before he and the other guests arrived. To her chagrin, she found the table and chairs needed attention first. She had been correct in her assumption that Elaina would not go out of her way to make an effort to arrange them. The chairs were still sitting haphazardly around the room just as they had been left by a group of young children making craft items earlier in the day. She quickly cleaned the bits of leftover colored construction paper and scraped globs of glue from the table top, arranged the chairs, and spread out a white lace tablecloth (she remembered it was kept in one of the library's kitchen drawers) over the oval table. That taken care of, she placed the chips, dips, and a sliced cheese, green grapes, and salami platter on each end of the table.

She was about to make the coffee when Elaina made her grand entrance huffing and puffing with two plastic jugs of tea in hand inside plastic bags. Blaming heavy traffic for her late arrival, she hurriedly waived Janice off while making her way to the kitchen to make a pot of coffee using library stock. She let Janice know in a condescending way she had purchased two, half-gallon bottles of tea, one sweet the other unsweet, and the ice cubes would come from the library kitchen refrigerator freezer. The nondescript paper cups, sugar packets, and creamers would also come from library stock. Elaina then curtly informed Janice she made the decision not to buy ice cream since she thought nobody would eat it. "Everyone is watching their weight," she said, primly. *Everyone but you Elaina*, thought Janice as she appraised Elaina's ample figure clad in a tight-fitting, cream-colored sweater and tan pants that would have looked more flattering on her plump body in a size or two larger than what Elaina was wearing.

Elaina was all smiles at the party and spent the majority of it making it seem to the guests, and especially Jack, that she had planned this party and purchased the food. Janice found this irritating, but she couldn't see any reason to say anything to correct that impression in front of the guests. To her it wasn't a big deal, but apparently it was a big deal for Jack; Janice would later have reason to regret that she failed to speak up and set the record straight as to who planned the party and paid for a majority of the refreshments. Jack kept telling everyone he couldn't believe nobody had ever made such a fuss over his birthday like Elaina had done. He made no mention of the long drive, dinner, balloon, card, and banana walnut bread Janice provided for him the previous evening. In fact, Elaina did not give him a birthday gift, only a sentimental inexpensive birthday card, the gushy kind Janice knew came from the local dollar store. Janice was left to assume Jack didn't realize or care that his insensitivity hurt her feelings. Being a caring person, Janice gave him the benefit of the doubt and chose to think he didn't know she was hurt by his reaction. What bothered her the most was how Elaina made a concerted effort to place herself between Janice and Jack at every possible opportunity, even going so far as to prevent a hug when it was time for her to leave when the party broke up; and Jack did nothing to alter the situation.

CHAPTER 4

Janice returned home late Friday afternoon to find a new e-mail waiting for her from Jack. "That was a great surprise birthday party Elaina planned for me at the library, wasn't it?" the message began. It seemed like an afterthought when he added, "It was nice of you make the drive here to take me out for dinner on Wednesday and stay over at motel to attend the party she planned for me." To Janice's chagrin, he didn't miss a beat as he continued. "Will you come back to help Elaina pull off the big writers group yard sale and fundraiser to be held at the VFW the end of October? Like I mentioned before, she has never done anything like this. You have organized several successful fundraisers. I'm planning to donate a lot of Sabrina's things for the yard sale to be held Friday and Saturday mornings that same weekend, along with other stuff like Christmas decorations and a variety of items that I know I will never use again. I'm grooming Elaina to take over the day-to-day operations as president of the writers group and want her to be successful. I'm ready to step down, and I don't want her to feel overwhelmed. Maybe you didn't know. She is getting ready to file for divorce from her husband and will need all the help she can get." Jack kept writing without allowing a chance for her response to the information concerning Elaina's impending divorce. "As you know from attending the party, I'm sure you heard the theme for the fundraiser this year is a Halloween costume party. My brother and his wife are coming from South Carolina to furnish entertainment free of charge. He has a band, and they are pretty good. I know it's a lot to ask, but I would really like to have you here to help out. Let me know ASAP." Then he dropped a bombshell by adding that he was scheduled for a nuclear stress test of his heart the following Monday morning. Janice read between the lines and sensed he was apprehensive about the test, but as an ex-Marine, he would never admit it. Her hurt feelings gave way to a feeling of sympathy for him once again. She knew raising a lot of money for the student writing competition was important to ensure the ongoing success of the program and chose to think about that rather than dwell on her hurt feelings; and the heart test had to be causing him a great deal of stress.

Janice e-mailed him back without mentioning her negative feelings about the fact he was still under the distinct impression Elaina had planned his birthday party at the library or that Elaina had made it clear she didn't want or need Janice's help regarding the fundraiser. "Be glad to assist at the yard sale and fundraiser if you think it would be helpful, but Elaina tells me she has everything under control. You know this writing competition project for the school kids has always been near and dear to my heart ever since it began," she responded. Then she added, "Do you have someone to go with you for the stress test?"

He quickly e-mailed back to answer her question concerning the test. "No, I plan to go for the test alone. I've asked several friends to go with me, but everyone has plans or is going to be out of town. That's my fault for not asking anyone sooner. As for needing your help at the yard sale fundraiser, that is a definite yes!'

"What the heck were you thinking on Wednesday or last night? Obviously, you weren't thinking! You should have told me about the test and I would have made arrangements to stay longer to take you," scolded Janice. She immediately chided herself for her harsh response but was not sorry she had written it.

"I was under the impression you needed to get back to Georgia and help your son and his girlfriend, so I didn't say anything," Jack wrote back, defensively.

Janice wanted to respond by telling him any idiot would have figured out she told him that to keep the party a secret, but she didn't write it. Instead she responded by writing, "You shouldn't go through this test alone." Without taking time to think it through she added, "Would you like for me to come back and go with you? I've had this same test done, and I needed someone to drive me home afterward." Having made her point, she didn't dwell on the fact he waited for almost an hour to respond to her chastisement and consequent offer to return. As a retired nurse and caring friend, her only thoughts were for his safety and comfort and not her inconvenience of having to turn around and make another long drive alone to Tennessee during the wee hours Sunday.

Jack finally responded. "Sorry. I wasn't thinking with all the excitement of you being here and Elaina's great birthday party. I would really like it if you came back . . . if it isn't too much trouble." This message was sent at 7:00 in the evening, and the stress test was scheduled for the following morning at 7:30 a.m. It wouldn't be until much later that Janice would wonder why Jack didn't seem to be concerned about her driving alone for hours on a major interstate highway or back roads during the night to reach his home. Her only thought at the time was that Jack needed her, and as a friend and former nurse, she wasn't going to let him go through this test alone. Knowing he had undergone triple bypass heart surgery followed by a mitral valve replacement, there was the very real possibility his test results may not contain good news.

"I'll be there by 6:30 in the morning," Janice replied without hesitation. She did a quick load of laundry, took a shower, repacked her small suitcase, and tried to catch an hour of sleep on the recliner. She planned to be on the road no later than 2:00 a.m. Monday morning. She decided to not let her son know what she was about to do. She knew he would object to her driving alone at night on the interstate, let alone on the poorly-lit hilly backroads that led to Jack's home. She promised herself she would call Jason and explain her actions once Jack's test was finished.

In spite of her best efforts, she didn't make it on the road promptly, and she scolded herself for sleeping half an hour longer than anticipated. She knew this allowed little time for any type of delay. She arrived at Jack's home at 6:15 a.m. without incident with only a brief stop to gas up at an all-night truck stop. She was grateful it had been smooth sailing time-wise due to the lack of heavy car or truck traffic she would have encountered during the daytime. In fact, it had been almost too uneventful traveling alone, with few headlights to break up the night time monotony or the caravans of eighteen wheelers that usually filled the highway in daylight hours. Several times she found it necessary to turn up the radio and roll down the driver's side window to allow the sound of rushing wind and cool night air to hit her face in an effort to prevent her from falling asleep at the wheel. The thought that she should not make the trip did not enter her mind.

To his credit, Jack was barely awake and did not hear her pull into his gravel driveway. He stumbled out of bed a few minutes after her arrival and turned on the porch light but didn't see her silver car. Janice would later assume it was a combination of the fog off the river and a red, four-foot-high Chinese maple shrub growing between the parking area and front porch obstructing his view, although he turned off the porch light almost as fast as he had turned it on. Janice continued to sit in her car and attempt to doze rather than knock on the door, thinking she could be interrupting him taking a shower and dressing.

Jack walked off the porch and down the recently poured concrete sidewalk at 6:40 a.m. to take a closer look. Unseen or heard by a napping Janice, he tapped firmly on the passenger side window. Awakening with a start at the sound of the tapping noise, Janice unlocked the car doors as soon as she realized it was Jack standing there. He opened the passenger side door and slid into the front bucket seat without speaking. Janice found it necessary to remind him to fasten his seat belt before she began to back out of the driveway onto the narrow paved roadway.

"Sorry about that," he muttered as he grappled over his right shoulder and pulled the seatbelt aggressively across his chest, then struggled with the buckle. "I'm not awake, yet. I hope you haven't been waiting out here long," he offered instead of saying hello or good morning. "I checked outside a little while ago, but I didn't see your car. I got dressed since I can't have anything to eat or drink."

"I've been here about fifteen minutes," she replied before adding, "Hello and good morning to you, too."

The way she said it made Jack realize she was a little miffed he had not greeted her the way he should have done or acknowledged her long drive throughout the wee hours of the night to get there.

When it dawned on him he replied, "Sorry. I should have told you good morning and said thank you for making the drive."

Janice gave him a tight-lipped smile in response before speaking. "Not a problem," she replied rather than make a big issue out of it. "We need to get started if we're going to make it to the testing center by 7:30. I asked you to get buckled up out of concern for your safety." Jack grunted in response before mumbling something barely audible under his breath, which she chose to ignore.

During the drive to the test site Jack wasn't all that talkative. He did speak up to complain bitterly about the fact he couldn't have his morning coffee or eat any breakfast before the test would be administered. Janice wrote off his irritated muttering to him being nervous at what the test results could possibly reveal. The fear factor was more evident after he fastened the seatbelt by the way he fiddled with it with one hand and tapped his fingers on his right knee with the other. Janice decided it would be best not to engage in small talk, instead concentrating on the increasing morning traffic as people began driving their cars to work on the four-lane highway heading to the Oak Ridge medical test site.

Janice sat in the waiting area of the clinic, which was adjacent to the main hospital, and chatted with people waiting to be tested or seen by their doctors. Jack stood at the front desk filling out the paperwork required before the first portion of the test, which involved a treadmill to check his heart. This and unexpected wait time due to overbooking took the better part of three anxious hours.

The initial phase of the test would not begin until around 10:30 a.m. They were both tired of waiting. Janice could not help but notice Jack was becoming more and more agitated by the way he kept flipping through the pages of an old magazine he picked out of one of the waiting room stacks. She reached for Jack's hand, gave it a squeeze and murmured, "I know it is hard having to wait, but don't borrow trouble. I have a feeling everything will turn out all right, and if there is a problem, we can deal with it. You have an excellent doctor." Her words of encouragement fell on deaf ears—Jack didn't even try to smile or respond.

"I sure hope you're right," he replied later, a worried expression evident on his face. He did manage a return squeeze to her hand before he got up and started to pace the length of the glass-enclosed room until he was finally called into testing. Janice resisted the urge to join his pacing and continued to thumb through the magazine she had selected, in order to give him a chance to work off his energy.

"Think positively," Janice called after him when he walked behind the technician to disappear behind a set of double metal doors. Except for admissions office personnel dressed in street clothes, everyone else wore blue cotton scrub suits with no visible nametags to distinguish professionally licensed personnel from technicians. Janice found this disturbing. When she worked as a nurse she was required to wear a white uniform, including white shoes, white stockings, a white cap with a black velvet band, and the pin representing the college she attended for her training, along with an easily read name tag pinned to her uniform. Not to have been dressed in this manner would have involved chastisement and possible firing.

It turned out Janice's instinct was right on target about the initial treadmill results. Jack made it through this portion of the test without any apparent problems. "They told me I have an hour and a half before the second phase of the test can be done," he told her. Janice gave a sigh of relief although she was concerned about the delay between the two portions of the test.

"I say we take this time to find somewhere to grab a bite to eat. I'm hungry!" continued an unsmiling, somewhat pale Jack. Janice agreed, aware the next phase of the test is when nuclear-infused fluid would be injected into a vein after another IV is started. It would travel through his heart's circulatory system after being administered by a certified tech with a doctor in attendance nearby. Janice knew the reason for this procedure was to show the heart's function of how well the replaced mitral valve and grafted veins were functioning at the same time the MRI is taking place. When she tried to let Jack know what to expect he literally growled at her. "The cardiologist already explained the procedure to me! It's not like I haven't had this test done before. I don't want to go over everything again!"

"I'm sorry," apologized Janice. "It's just that I hate to see you look so worried, or I would never have said anything."

Jack immediately regretted his gruff manner and backed off. This time he was the one to reach out and take her hand. "I'm the one who needs to apologize," he offered. She merely nodded, gave his hand a squeeze, and acted as though nothing negative had transpired between them before she let go. He knew he would have felt a whole lot better if she had yelled at him. But she didn't, and it made him take a long hard look at this woman who had been and continued to be willing to help him through the loss of his wife and this stressful procedure. I've got to stop behaving like a total jerk, he told himself, or I'll never get to first base with her!

"I think getting some lunch is a good idea," remarked Janice in order to change the subject. "I haven't eaten anything since a light dinner last night while I waited for my laundry to finish washing and drying. I'm sure you are hungry. I say we head for that nearby popular soup, salad, and baked dessert restaurant." Jack readily agreed, and they walked to their car parked outside.

A few moments later, while stopped at a red light, Janice turned toward Jack and asked, "Please be honest. How are you feeling?"

Jack reluctantly admitted to feeling light-headed as a result of the treadmill portion of the test. Janice wasn't surprised he felt that way and was relieved when he said he was not experiencing any chest pain or shortness of breath. "Since you didn't have breakfast or coffee before the test, I'm sure you will feel better after we eat," she reassured him. Once again, she had the same feeling there would not be a serious problem, just like the feeling she had before the treadmill test. She said a silent prayer that the lack of food and coffee would be the reason for his paleness and lightheadedness. After eating a large bowl of chicken noodle soup, some cornbread, and drinking two cups of coffee, Jack became his usual charming and chatty self during the short drive back to the outpatient area, where phase two of the test was scheduled to take place.

Janice spent the better part of an hour in the waiting area during the final phase of Jack's test. He came out smiling to announce with a grin, "That part of the test was a piece of cake! Remember when we talked about getting passports during your last visit? Let's go get them," he strongly urged.

Janice questioned the prudence of this idea. "Are you sure you want to do this so soon after the test?" she asked.

"I don't see any sense of us hanging around here or going back to my place. I feel fine," argued Jack. "I won't get the test results for a couple of days. I've already told the guys working on the lawn back at the house about the changes I want done. There's a post office in downtown Knoxville where we can get our passports done today."

Janice was still skeptical amid a feeling of anxiety about driving in heavy city traffic, along with him wanting to make the trip so soon following the stress test, but she agreed to go. She did not remind him it had only been nine weeks since her stroke and only two weeks since she felt comfortable enough to start driving again. The two trips back and forth between Georgia and Tennessee were the longest trips she had made behind the wheel of a car since being cleared by her doctors to start driving again. Even though she probably should have reminded him of all this, she dismissed her thoughts.

The post office turned out to be located on a narrow side street. Had it not been for the American flag fluttering in the breeze on a pole in front of the small brick building, they would not have found it. By the time they waited their turn for service, filled out the lengthy forms, and paid the necessary fees, it was approaching bumper to bumper five o'clock, rush hour traffic. Jack chided her for slowing down to make sure the approaching lane onto the ramp of I-75 was clear enough to safely enter the steady stream of rapidly moving cars. She knew from the experience of living in the area for almost fifteen years that she needed to be cautious. Once again, she didn't say anything even though Jack's comments upset her. After what he had gone through that morning, she didn't want to speak her mind and upset him by voicing her displeasure at his back seat driving, to which he seemed oblivious. She understood he was anxious to learn if the heart valve and harvested leg veins transferred into his heart were functioning as they should. She remembered something he had asked her when they had coffee back in her motel room after the book signings: "What happens if the heart valve or veins malfunction? Does that mean I'm a goner?"

She remembered saying, "I guess we kill another pig, implant a new valve, and then have a pig roast. If a new vein is needed it can be harvested from your other leg so you will have a sexy matched pair of scars ," Janice had said to lighten the mood. While the flippant comment made Jack laugh, she knew those remarks did not lessen his anxiety.

Jack's mitral valve had been replaced with that of a pig instead of a mechanical device. He said he chose that option because he didn't want to hear the clicking sound emitted from a mechanical device to remind him of the valve replacement every waking moment for the remainder of his life.

With the passport applications behind them, Janice made the drive back to Jack's house expecting to drop him off and return to the motel in time to have dinner alone at a nearby restaurant, get some much needed rest, and head for her Georgia home early the following morning. Jack did not exhibit any overt signs of distress. She didn't ask him to join her for dinner after he told her he had food prepared ahead for his own dinner. She didn't realize Jack had other ideas on his mind.

"You should stay here in my guest room at least tonight, Janice," he insisted. "I know you are tired. It doesn't make any sense for you to drive all the way back out toward the interstate when you can stay here and get a good night's sleep." Janice knew what he said was true. She was exhausted. Plus, she should be close by if any problems were to develop during the night as a result of Jack's tests. He did have a triple by-pass followed by a pig valve replacement, she reminded herself. What if he passes out, falls, or throws a blood clot? He's out here in the boondocks all by himself, twenty miles from the nearest hospital, which would only be of help if he could call 911. He could die and nobody would know it for possibly several days. *If that happened*, Janice thought, *I couldn't live with myself.*

It took less than a minute before she made the decision to spend the night in the guest room. "Okay. Once again you win. I'll stay," said Janice. "I'll call the motel and cancel my reservation. I left my suitcase in the car trunk and can return the room key tomorrow on my way out of town."

While she made the call Jack didn't waste any time asking for her car keys so he could bring her small suitcase into the house from the car. He had an unmistakable feeling of anticipation while placing the suitcase in the guest room on top of a trunk sitting against the far, wood-paneled wall. They ate cold meatloaf sandwiches and salads Janice prepared for their dinner. Jack told her he made the meatloaf yesterday morning using the recipe from one of her cookbooks, which she had given him almost a year before during one of her brief visits to Tennessee.

After eating, Jack settled into his brown leather recliner placed at an angle in front of the fieldstone fireplace. He rested with a glass of wine in his hand. Janice sat on the nearby, quilt-covered sofa facing the fireplace trying her best not to yawn. Unable to keep her eyes open any longer, at 8:30, she got up, excused herself, and headed toward the guest bedroom. "I'll see you in the morning, but please don't hesitate to wake me if you have any problems like chest pain, shortness of breath, or leg pain where the graft was taken. I know you had a problem with phlebitis before, and we don't want to wait for medical treatment if it shows up again," she advised.

Jack got up from the recliner to intercept her near the guest bedroom door, thanked her for coming to his rescue, and asked for a goodnight hug. "You sure smell good," he commented as he began to nuzzle her neck before he kissed her. To shorten a long story, they both ended up in the guest room bed for the night. Nothing of a sexual nature took place. They spent the night holding each other while alternately talking and dozing. Janice felt a sense of closeness she had once felt with her husband as she lay there nestled beside him with her head on his shoulder, his arm draped across the waist of her pink floral night gown.

When she awakened, the first rays of sunlight were just beginning to stream between the inch-wide openings between the red, Roman shades covering the two large bedroom windows. She felt a momentary sense of panic when she realized Jack was no longer beside her! The clock on the nightstand read 6:00 a.m. She crept out of bed to don her bathrobe and slippers before opening the bedroom door to walk across the wooden floor of the dining room, not knowing what she would find. There was no sign of Jack anywhere in the open dining/living room, the kitchen, at his computer desk on the far wall, or outside on the wooden deck overlooking the river. She took a closer look when she noticed another door across from the dining room. It was ajar just far enough for her to see Jack asleep on his right side in one of the twin beds. She tip-toed closer until she could see the rhythmic rise and fall of his chest before she returned to the guest room where she tried to decide what to do next. She didn't wash her face, put on lipstick, or comb her hair. Janice could not explain why she wanted him to see how she looked upon awakening. By the time she returned to the living room half an hour later, still wearing her nightgown, slippers, and robe, Jack was up and dressed in a red, long-sleeved sweater, khaki pants, white cotton socks, and no shoes. He was sitting in front of his computer engrossed in reading and responding to e-mails. He wasn't aware she had silently walked up behind him until she spoke and lightly touched his shoulders. The sound of her voice and touch made him jump and turn sideways in his chair. He smiled and said good morning as she leaned into him and lightly kissed his cheek and the top of his head. "Good morning," he said with a smile. "You look bright-eyed and bushy-tailed."

"Good morning," she whispered back while standing behind his chair. "This is what I look like first thing in the morning. Kind of scary isn't it?" she announced as she began to gently massage his shoulders and kiss the back of his neck.

"If I were a cat I would be purring," he joked before turning more sideways in his chair in order to be able to look directly into her eyes. "You don't look all that bad," he replied. "I sort of like the mussed up hair look, especially when I had something to do with mussing it up."

"You scared me when I woke up and you weren't there beside me," she murmured. Her concern brought a slight smile to Jack's face. He made no move to get up from his chair, continuing to shrug his shoulders under her firm, yet gentle fingers while she continued to massage them.

He groaned contentedly before offering an explanation as to what sent him off to a different bed. "I was awake early and wanted to let you sleep. It was only 4:00 a.m.

when I woke up. I didn't want to disturb you since you looked so peaceful. I got up and made some coffee, then decided to try and catch 40 more winks in one of the twin beds since someone in the guest room bed kept me wide awake most of last night, not that I'm complaining. Sorry if I scared you." At this point he leaned his head back to rest between her ample, braless breasts with a contented sigh. She continued to stand behind him and leaned her cheek to rest on the top of his head while encircling his shoulders with both arms.

"I'm usually an early riser and apparently you are, too. I can go back to the guest room or go out on the deck and let you continue with what you were doing," offered Janice. Jack leaned forward enough to disengage her arms from around his shoulders so he could get to his feet to face her.

"No, please stay here with me. It's chilly out there on the deck. I want you to see how the morning mists rise off the river. Let me open the bamboo slider curtains so they don't block the view. Then you can take a closer look at how the sun and currents form ribbons on the river." He walked over to the oversized, triple glass slider and pulled back the bamboo curtains mounted on the wall above the doors. Then he turned his attention back to her, slid his arm around her waist and pulled her slim body against his side, kissing the top of her head. They stood there side by side, for several minutes, to look at the changing water patterns along with a covey of mallard ducks swimming close to shore before Jack said he needed another cup of coffee. He gave her a gentle squeeze before releasing her and headed for the small open kitchen to prepare his coffee. "Can I make a cup for you?" he asked.

"Thanks, but I don't do coffee. Can't tolerate the caffeine," she replied. "Your friend was right. The river is lovely," Janice breathed, continuing to stand there in front of the glass doors for several more minutes before returning to the guest room to prepare for the day, closing the door behind her.

She returned to the kitchen a short time later to make their breakfast of crisp bacon, scrambled eggs, and toast. Jack made another cup of coffee in one of those machines requiring small containers of grounds to make each cup. Though the kitchen was small, they were able to move about freely and didn't get in each other's way. Neither of them felt any sense of guilt, remorse, or embarrassment for what had taken place last night or this morning. In her mind they were simply two good friends who needed each other to make it through the night. She assumed Jack felt the same way. He acted as if nothing out of the ordinary had taken place between them; in fact, he said he had *appreciated* what had taken place.

He ate the breakfast she prepared while he talked about the need for some repairs on his boat before he began to elaborate on plans already underway to renovate his gardens and lawn. This would involve the removal of a heavy growth of pampas grass and the overgrowth of ivy on what had once been an active waterfall cascading down a steep, rock-covered incline in the side yard. It was the kind of comfortable conversation that would have taken place between a loving husband and wife.

"I've found a guy who wants the pampas grass for his landscaping business and will haul it away as part of the payment for his work," Jack proclaimed proudly. "The boat mechanic is supposed to call before he stops by, too," He paused to drink more of his coffee before continuing, "Do you have to leave today?" he questioned as she stood and started gathering up their dishes to take them to the dishwasher. When she didn't answer right away he added, "I like having you here. Why don't you call your son again and let him know you aren't coming home for a few more days?" He wasn't asking. He was pleading. They both knew their relationship had gone way beyond that of "Big Brother" and "Sis".

Janice closed her eyes and took a deep breath while trying to decide what she should do next. Her heart said stay, but her mind kept saying, *No, you need to leave. He is doing just fine. There is no need for you to stay here any longer and complicate our relationship any more.* She continued to stand in front of the dishwasher, wiping her hands on a red and white striped dish towel to buy more time. She knew her son would not be pleased if she were to stay. "Please God help me make the right decision. I've never done anything like this before," she prayed softly under her breath. "Should I listen to my head or my heart?" Her heart ended up winning the argument.

At Jack's insistence Janice wound up staying with him for another five nights. In fact, he asked her to stay indefinitely that night as they prepared for bed. This is when she learned what she already suspected. He was impotent due to radioactive seed implants to eradicate prostate cancer. The seed implant and resulting impotence was something he had failed to mention in their earlier conversations or e-mails. Until now it had only vaguely entered her mind this could be the reason Jack had not made love to her last night after the passionate kisses they had shared before and after going to bed; along with their close proximity throughout the night while holding each other. At the time Janice wanted to believe his lack of becoming aroused was because he was tired from the long day of testing he had undergone. *I should have known*, she lamented silently. *I was a nurse. I should have known something wasn't quite right.*

"I thought that if you knew, you'd think I wouldn't be man enough for you," he whispered, a note of hesitancy and sorrow in his voice, before walking up behind her to wrap his arms around her waist the second night. He kissed the back of her neck and rested his head against her left shoulder, letting go only when she slipped out of her clothing and into her nightgown. The nearness of him caused desire to flood through her body, even though she knew there was no possibility for them to have intercourse without a surgical penile implant. She knew Jack was not a good candidate for this type of surgery due to his heart problems, and it would present an ongoing situation. But at the time it didn't matter to her. The pale blue nightgown slipped to the floor.

Blame what happened next on the full moon shining on the river reflecting through the large glass windows when Jack neglected to lower the bedroom Roman shades; or the overwhelming sexual desire felt by two people who had been denied that basic human need for so long through no fault of their own.

"Lack of an erection is not a problem for me," Janice said tenderly as she turned in his arms to face him. "I have a little secret to tell you – on second thought, make that a big secret I've never told anyone before. My husband was impotent for the last ten years of our marriage following his heart attack, along with the MDS we didn't know he had then. It didn't change my love for him, and it won't change how I feel about you." She looked into his eyes with a mixture of desire and mischief. "I think you are a whole lot more than a penis. Haven't you heard the old saying there's more than one way to skin a cat?" At those two comments they both started to laugh to ease their tension.

"Would you care to elaborate on the cat comment?" asked Jack as he returned the unmistakable look of desire while continuing to hold her close to his now naked body. He placed his hand under her chin to lift her face up so that he could give her a passionate kiss, to which she responded without any reservation.

"It might be easier to demonstrate," replied Janice with a come hither look after she caught her breath when they came up for air. The look she gave him caused Jack to become more sexually aroused than he had ever experienced before, even though it was mentally. The ice was broken and passion took over. They both ending up naked in bed and satisfied by suggestive words and touch as they explored each other's bodies.

Janice felt this marked the time a barrier was crossed for both of them. In her heart she felt she was in love for the second time in her life. Jack said he found their encounter a blessing because he wasn't aware of what could happen with a loving partner without an erection or invasive surgery to facilitate an erection. The next morning he would ask her if it was all right with her if he didn't undergo any more surgery following the prostate treatments and two major heart surgeries. Janice agreed that surgery wasn't necessary. "After what happened between us last night, I don't have any concerns about our sex life," she replied.

Those five days were idyllic for both of them. They alternated between him supervising the renovations of his lawn, her cooking their meals, grocery shopping together, and sometimes going out to eat just like any newly married couple would have done. It was all they could do to keep their hands off of each other each time they came in close proximity. At the same time Janice realized she could not continue to stay with Jack, as much as she wanted to continue playing house with him. She had a life, home, and family back in Georgia; and she needed her family's approval for Jack to be a part of her life as more than just a good friend with benefits.

In her mind it was one thing to date Jack casually and quite another to play house with him. "Honey, I have to go back to Georgia," announced Janice. "I've been gone almost a week, and my son isn't thrilled about what I've done by coming here literally in the middle of the night and continuing to stay. I didn't bring that many clothes. I'll be back in a couple of weeks to help with the yard sale and fundraiser. I think with everything you have planned involving the yard renovations and boat repairs, you won't have time to miss me all that much."

"Only every night when I am forced to sleep alone and in the daytime when I have to cook and eat without you here," he replied sadly. "Before you go you have to see the costume I'm wearing for the Halloween fundraiser party," Jack insisted. He went to a cabinet in the corner of the room to return with a metal helmet and a suit made of cloth that looked like the type of armor worn by a Roman Soldier. When he put on the helmet and held the suit up against his body Janice couldn't help but burst out laughing. He looked absolutely adorable and she said as much. He beamed at her reaction. "Next you have to see my wine cellar before you go."

She knew Jack was stalling for time to delay her leaving, but his joy was like that of a little boy. She didn't know how she could tell him no. So they went out onto the deck and down the steps to a ramp leading to the basement. They had to lean forward through the entrance door to keep from hitting their heads on the ceiling rafters when they entered what turned out to be a four-foot-high crawl space. Jack switched on an overhead light. Janice could see there were three large glass containers he called carboys filled with various stages of fermenting fruits, a lot of cardboard boxes, and empty wine bottles.

Jack offered her a three-legged milk stool a friend had made for him to sit on while he worked to test the alcohol content of the fruit during the fermentation process. When she attempted to sit, she promptly fell flat on her back when she tried to sit on the unsteady stool. Stunned at first, she was able to get herself upright by clinging to the nearby concrete block wall for support and willing her body to get up to a semi-standing position without any help from Jack. Also stunned by her predicament, he continued to stare in disbelief at what happened before offering a hand to help to her fully onto her feet. Amid gales of laughter by both of them she quipped, "Boy, you sure know how to sweep a girl off her feet!" They would often laugh about what had taken place during the months to come after she assured him there was no damage done except to her ego. "Well at least I can laugh about it," Janice told him. "I hope the time never comes when I can't laugh at myself." Had she known such a time would come a whole lot sooner than expected, she may not have uttered those words.

It was a long three weeks, even with morning and nightly e-mails between them, before Janice planned to return to Tennessee. Something in the back of her mind kept telling her their relationship was moving along a little too fast, so she again decided to check in at the motel rather than stay with Jack on the return trip to help with the yard sale and fundraiser. Jack made it clear he was not thrilled with her decision, but he later had to admit the decision turned out to be a wise one on her part. Jack's brother and wife decided to stay in the guest room she and Jack would have shared. She nor Jack felt ready to share their newfound relationship with other people. It didn't seem appropriate to share this information since less than a year had passed since Sabrina's death. Local custom dictated at least a year needed to pass before the partner left behind should seek companionship. While difficult, they played it cool at the

Friday and Saturday yard sale and the Halloween party fundraiser later on Saturday night.

It didn't take long before Jack's brother sensed something was going on between them. He took Janice aside to tell her his brother was a good man who needed someone like her in his life. Janice responded by saying she felt that way, too, but thought Jack needed more time to grieve and accept Sabrina's death before they became involved in a public way. She reminded him it had only been a little over eight months since Sabrina had passed away.

Even though Jack told her on numerous occasions he was ready to move on, and she was aware that, statistically, men are usually ready for another relationship more quickly than women are, she hesitated in elaborating on their budding relationship to Jack's brother. She had to come to terms with how nice it was to be held and kissed by someone, to feel she was a good fit and be made love to again, if only in a limited way. "I know Jack insists he's ready to move forward, but I'm not totally sure about that," she kept repeating to his brother. She didn't add, *I need to be certain that I've completely accepted my loss of Clayton. I'm not totally sure I'm ready to enter into another committed relationship, even if Jack insists he is.*

Jack and Janice tried their best not to flirt and blow their cover throughout the yard sale or the evening of the Halloween costume party fundraiser, but it wasn't easy. The yard sale had been a rousing success while the fundraiser turned out to be a total bust. Elaina Albright, the person who demanded to be in charge of the event without Janice's help, decided not to send handwritten invitations to potential attendees, which meant intended guests could not RSVP. She failed to do this in spite of Janice's suggestion that she send invitations with RSVP requests at least four weeks in advance of the event so guests could co-ordinate their social calendars. Not only did Elaina poo-pooh this advice, she also kept no record of those who responded positively or let her know they could not attend. This was when Janice decided to cease offering any further advice. She found Elaina's smugness (in letting Janice know she was relying on a couple of newspaper ads to draw people to the event) irritating. Elaina didn't seem to understand not everyone would see those ads and that it was chancy to rely on people to learn about the event at the yard sales. Elaine did little to ensure a large turnout.

Janice's misgivings turned out to be accurate; only twenty paying guests attended the fundraiser. It irked Janice even more when Elaina responded to the lack of guests to say, "Oh well. We made enough money at the yard sale to cover our costs." It didn't seem to bother her she had ordered enough food to serve 90 people based on the response of past fundraisers overseen by Janice. The cost of renting the VFW hall was $300.00 plus a guaranteed tip for each of the two bartenders of $75.00 each. This was in addition to the cost of food and several door prizes which Elaina had not even tried to have donated. Had it not been for the overwhelming success of the yard sale, they would have lost money and not had enough to cover the underclass student awards or the senior student college scholarship for competition winners. Janice was taken aback even more when Jack kept telling Elaina it wasn't her fault that so few people showed up. Janice knew, beyond a reasonable doubt, it was Elaina's fault. It puzzled her that it didn't seem to upset Jack that Elaina didn't want to be bothered with sending the invitations, which had been custom under Janice's watch, or for that matter, taking her advice about keeping track of responses in order to know how much food and beverages would be needed, so as not to waste food or money.

Elaina's words about the newspaper ads kept running through Janice's mind, along with Elaina adding, "Besides, I've e-mailed a couple of people who kicked in big bucks in the past. I'm sure they will contribute again." It turned out a majority of those individually contributing large sums in the past did not come through, but Elaina failed to mention it and rambled on. "I don't see any reason to spend time or money on handwritten invitations or postage. My psychic powers tell me the fundraiser will be highly successful. Janice, you worry too much about such details and need to learn not to sweat them."

At that comment, after the poorly attended event, Janice justifiably reminded Elaina she had tried to give helpful advice to someone arrogant, who in reality knew little or nothing about raising money for a cause. Elaina merely laughed, giving Janice a brief feeling of satisfaction when she was able to make the comment after it was clear Elaina's approach had not worked. "See what it got you?" remarked Janice. That comment, too, fell on deaf ears when Elaina turned and walked away. "If she is the psychic she claims to be she should have known people who contribute large sums of money to a cause want to be wooed by a handwritten invitation," angrily muttered Janice under her breath within ear shot of one of the attending writers group members who overheard the exchange between Janice and Elaina.

"Elaina should have known personal contact or a written invitation usually pays off. That is just common sense," agreed the woman. "That's one of the many reasons why the writers group started falling apart when she took over the day to day operations. She's a foul-mouthed little witch who thinks she's a great writer. As far as I can see her only writing accomplishments are trashy anthologies she pays to have published. And as for her claiming to be a psychic, I refuse to even go there!"

"In my humble opinion she's no more psychic than my grandmother's dead cat!" declared Janice. "She's a fat, dumpy little scammer who capitalizes on weakness she senses in others by working for one of those phony psychic phone lines that prey on insecure people. But I have to admit she's particularly good at convincing others she has mystical powers by telling them what they want to hear. Forgive me. I think I've said more than enough. It seems she brings out the worst in me." The woman patted Janice's arm and told her she only said out loud what other people were already thinking.

At a time before this encounter, Janice tolerated Elaina as a member of the writers group in spite of what she considered her shady occupation, foul mouth, and refusal to accept advice proven to be effective. That feeling of minimal acceptance would dramatically erode over the next several months as the truth began to slowly emerge regarding the fundraiser fiasco, along with other bits of information regarding her behavior involving Jack.

Janice stayed behind to help with the cleanup when the poorly attended fundraiser ended early. She did this even though she was a paying guest who had provided some of the food and helped with the decorations and serving. Jack stayed close by her, telling Janice he would not have recognized her in her sorceress costume, complete with a black and silver veil and magic wand. Janice felt he did this in a poorly disguised attempt to redeem his earlier responses involving Elaina.

A little later that evening, Jack's brother approached Janice during a break to encourage her relationship with Jack. Janice told him, once again, she thought Jack was a good person but felt he needed more time to grieve

Sabrina's death before they considered becoming romantically involved, especially in a public way. "It's much too soon. People will talk," she protested.

He was finally able to understand her concern, but at the same time, he told her not to wait too long before letting people know that she and Jack were in a relationship before some other woman made a play for Jack. Janice kept her suspicions concerning Jack and Elaina to herself.

"Sabrina was a great woman and we all loved her, but she is gone, and the two of you have to face the fact life is too short not to have someone to love in it. If people want to talk let them," insisted Jack's brother. "He needs someone like you to take care of him." Janice didn't know what to say, so she said nothing and excused herself, saying she needed to check on the cleanup in the kitchen.

Janice made an effort to keep her focus on the people seated next to her as Jack kept staring at her from across the table during and after they had eaten. She continued avoiding eye contact with him when prizes were awarded for the funniest, prettiest, and most unusual costumes, even when Janice won for most unusual. This made it necessary for her to walk to the front of the room to accept the prize. She felt Jack's eyes on her but resolved not to acknowledge him then or on the return trip to her seat. She was still feeling disappointed at the way he had defended Elaina's poor performance.

"You look very mysterious," he had commented, having moved from across the table to take a seat beside her. "I would not have known it was you until you took off your mask in order to eat." Janice knew what he said was not true because she had described her costume to him in detail, but she saw no sense in challenging his statement with others within earshot.

She responded, "I am mysterious—very mysterious," while flashing him a hint of a smile, just enough to be sociable. Intrigued by this statement, Jack was right there at her side to help remove table coverings and place decorations back in their respective boxes as soon as the few paying guests left the hall. When the main hall cleanup was completed, he insisted that he walk her to her car parked in the dimly lit lot next to the VFW building.

She stiffly offered her cheek for a goodnight kiss before getting into her vehicle. Instead of the quick peck she expected, Jack took her firmly in his arms and planted a passion-filled kiss squarely on her lips. Janice pushed him away and chalked it up to the moonlit night and the large amount of wine he had consumed. She expressed hope that nobody had seen what had just taken place. Thankfully, a quick scan of the parking lot revealed all of the guests had gone. The only people remaining were Jack's brother and wife and three band members, all of whom were busy packing instruments and sound equipment into their vans at the other end of the lot. There was no possible way the two bartenders and Elaina, still finishing up in the kitchen, saw anything. This assured Janice none of them had witnessed the passionate embrace and kiss.

Jack's voice was husky when he responded. "I don't think my brother or his wife would care if you spent the night with me. I can shove the twin beds together."

"Maybe they wouldn't mind, but I don't think that's a good idea," replied Janice. "Your brother and I had a little chat while you were in the restroom. He knows something is going on between us. I told him I thought you needed more time to accept Sabrina's death. If I were to show up for the night and end up in your bed that would make me a hypocrite, especially since he finally agreed with me that you do need more time to grieve. You need to keep in mind it has only been a little over eight months since Sabrina passed away."

Jack frowned and started to protest, but finally admitted Janice was right. Rather than sound like a jealous fishwife, Janice didn't mention his repeated attempts to downplay his defense of Elaina and her responsibility for the poor turnout at the fundraiser.

Janice drove to the motel alone. She wasn't happy about it, but she didn't want to intrude on Jack's family time or give them the impression she was putting the moves on Jack. She also knew she wasn't ready to admit she was more than a little angry with Jack for his defense of Elaina's poor judgment. Instead she told herself Jack and his brother didn't get together often due to the distance between where they lived, and they needed some private time. She expanded those thoughts to include that the memories of shared moments with Jack, while nice, were a thing of the past when she made light of his kiss in the parking lot and told him she thought they should not become more involved. And there was that small, almost imperceptible but persistent, voice in the back of her head telling her something was going on between Jack and Elaina.

That night she awakened with a song in her head at 3:00 a.m.—a song declaring the unexpected, strong feeling of love she was feeling toward Jack. She would include those lyrics along with other songs she promised to send to Jack's brother for possible recording; this is something she would later regret, even though at the time it seemed like the right thing to do. After she wrote the song, she was ready to let go of what they shared. She convinced herself the distance between them was too great for a meaningful relationship to flourish. She decided to dismiss any thought of Jack and Elaina as anything other than them being friends.

Somehow, Janice didn't realize Jack wasn't finished trying to win her over. His e-mails kept coming her way. Not wanting to appear rude or totally insensitive in light of what had transpired between them after the stress test, she answered each one as generically as possible without allowing any undue emotion to cloud the issue. As of now, advancing their relationship wasn't on her bucket list, yet she still felt herself caught up in the process of falling in love with this man, despite the fact her sixth sense was telling her it would only end in heartache if she didn't listen to her gut. *I could be wrong about this whole Elaina thing,* she kept telling herself. *Maybe it's only my overactive imagination. I don't want to spend the rest of my life alone and neither does Jack. He once told me to reach for the brass ring, so what's keeping me from doing it?*

CHAPTER 5

Several days later, Janice instinctively knew it was the wrong move on her part the minute she called Jack and invited him to spend Thanksgiving Day with her family in Georgia. The words were barely out of her mouth before her brain became fully engaged in what such an invitation would mean to him. She had just contradicted her speech in the parking lot after that fateful night of the fundraiser.

He didn't hesitate for an instant to accept the invitation. He was well aware she was headed for California to spend the winter at her daughter and son-in-law's vacation home in Palm Springs after the holiday, something she had done for five winters since Clayton's death. Janice didn't know Jack had been hoping for an invitation to spend time there with her and felt giving her a call would provide the opportunity for that to happen if he played his cards right.

Additionally, Jack wasted little time hinting about coming for a visit in California when he arrived at her home on the Tuesday before Thanksgiving. He arrived early with the explanation he wanted to avoid the heavy interstate traffic expected as the holiday approached. This made sense, but Janice decided not to extend an invitation to California until after she saw how things went with her family in Georgia. Her daughter Belinda and husband, Tom, had flown in from California to join the festivities for the extended weekend. This would be the first time Tom had the chance to meet Jack. She would value their opinions regarding Jack.

At Jason's insistence, Belinda and Tom planned to stay in Jason's only guest room. This meant Jack would have to stay in Janice's apartment guest room. But as it turned out, he had no intention of staying in her guest room. Without any words passing between them, Jack took his suitcase directly to her bedroom and placed it on the off-white damask bench at the foot of the bed as soon as he walked into the apartment. Janice was aware none of her family would have a problem with him sharing a bed with her, even though nothing had been said openly between them to indicate that was going to happen. It didn't take a rocket scientist to determine what was taking place in their relationship after her stay with him in Tennessee, but Janice still had reservations about his alliance with Elaina.

All anyone had to do was look at them, and it was obvious from the glow on their faces that Janice had forgiven him after the fundraiser fiasco. Her son made it clear again when he told her privately that at their ages and circumstances, she and Jack should take whatever joy they could find in each other without feeling any guilt. Belinda and Tom expressed the same opinion after the second day in Jack's company.

She and Jack visited back and forth between the apartments of her family members. They went exploring the historic downtown area of nearby Roswell and held hands as they wandered the sidewalks, stopping at a small café for something to drink. Suzanne prepared a typical Italian dinner the first night and the evening went well. They all went to a local upscale restaurant the following evening as guests of Belinda and Tom. Janice had to admit to herself she had not been this happy for a long time, and Jack appeared to be enjoying himself as well. At the dinner table he made a comment to Suzanne's teasing about seeing the two of them holding hands while walking across the parking lot on the way to Jason's and her apartment. Jack sheepishly admitted it had been a long time since he had held hands with a woman and it felt nice. This brought smiles to the faces of everyone. Later that evening when they were alone back at her apartment, Janice told him his earlier comment about holding hands with her had endeared him to her and her family, that it had made her heart sing.

Jack beamed. "Hearing you say that makes my heart sing, too," he replied.

Rather than have the ladies cook, Jason hosted all of them at another fashionable restaurant for Thanksgiving dinner. Jack was attentive and charming during the times they shared meals and relaxed with family in Jason's and Janice's homes. Everyone told Janice they all thought Jack was a great guy and went out of their way to made him feel welcome.

On the Saturday night following Thanksgiving, Suzanne's mother, Monica, hosted dinner at her home for the family, including Jack who had not made a move to leave for Tennessee. When the meal was finished and they were ready to make their exit, Monica pulled Jack aside to tell him in a stage whisper that Janice was a great person and he should be good to her. She made it clear they all believed Janice had finally found someone who could help her be happy again after the loss of her beloved Clayton. The next day as they were on their way to visit another historic site, her future daughter-in-law linked arms with her and said Janice was visibly glowing when Jack was near or when his name was mentioned, and that it was okay with her if they were sharing a bed. Janice blushed at the raised eyebrows and knowing grin Suzanne gave her. She was relieved Jack was walking on ahead of them with her son and didn't hear the comment or see the expression on either one of their faces—Suzanne with a grin and knowing look, and Janice with one of mortification.

Jack ended up staying with Janice, sharing her bed, and taking side trips with her and members of her family until the Sunday following Thanksgiving when she was to leave to spend the winter in California. He even asked if he could ride along to the airport with her and her son to drop her off. Standing beside the airline check-in desk, Janice finally issued an invitation for Jack to come and spend some time with her in Palm Springs. He grinned with delight at the invitation and said it was something he wanted to do and he would get back to her concerning his travel dates.

"I'll get back to you just as soon as I can find someone to check on the house and boat while I'm gone."

"Try to make it at least over Christmas week through New Year's Eve," suggested Janice. "Belinda and Tom have a houseful of friends for Christmas dinner and always throw a big party on New Year's Eve. I would be delighted if you could be there. I don't want to hide in a bathroom prior to the stroke of midnight on New Year's Eve like I've done in the past to avoid being kissed by someone else's date or spouse. You can continue to stay with me there as long as I do if you want. We will have the house pretty much to ourselves after the holidays. Tom owns a CPA business in northcentral California and tax season will be underway, so he will be too busy to travel to Palm Springs. And Belinda needs to get back to work as Human Resources Director at the hospital in San Francisco, so she won't have much of an opportunity to spend time at the Palm Springs house. I don't plan to come back to Georgia until around the first week in May when the weather warms up on the East Coast. That means you could avoid the cold winter in Tennessee, including all of those snow and ice storms, if you decide to stay longer than a week or two."

"I can't come for the holidays," Jack quickly responded. "I need to be with my family. This will be my first Christmas without Sabrina. I hope you understand."

"Of course I understand. Family always comes first," replied Janice.

Janice's flight across the country was long and tedious without Jack seated beside her. Her recently happy heart was feeling less of the music associated with love with each passing mile separating them. As a couple, married or not, wouldn't she be considered a part of his extended family? They had even talked about planning to spend time south of the border in Mexico when they applied for their passports, and again during the Thanksgiving visit. This made her wonder if he had been planning to visit Mexico by himself or with someone else, especially with his hurry to get the passports prior to her issuing the invitation to join her in California. Who was he planning to have as a travel companion if the invitation to join her in California had not been forthcoming at the last minute? Why had he been so insistent they get passports when she had not mentioned him joining her in California at the time? *Stop being so suspicious*, she chided herself. *Jack has made it clear numerous times he thinks we are good together. Doesn't that count for something?*

Christmas Eve, the following week, and especially New Year's Eve were dismal for Janice. She did her best by dressing festively for the occasions for the sake of her family and friends and putting on a happy face, but inside she was miserable. New Year's Eve was exceptionally depressing. This had been a time when she and Clayton always celebrated their wedding anniversary while attending parties. She felt so depressed that a few minutes before midnight she escaped into her bedroom to close and lock the door. She stayed there until the sound of horns, cheers, and noisemakers lessened in order to avoid contact with anyone who might try to kiss her. She envisioned Jack sitting all alone in his recliner back in Tennessee with a glass of homemade wine in his hand feeling just as miserable as she was.

Janice's spirits soared dramatically when Jack called a few days after New Year's to say he was coming for a sixteen-day visit the middle of January, and would she mind checking on accommodations in Mexico? She was so happy to hear his voice she didn't ask what he had done to celebrate New Year's Eve or let him know how miserable she had been without him.

Checking on motels in the nearby Mexican Baja, she found the rates charged by motel and hotel operators for decent accommodations were higher than expected. This made her hesitate. Janice didn't know if Jack's finances could stand that sort of cost, and she didn't want to come right out and ask him. While they had agreed to share any travel expenses if they took trips, that would still add up to a lot of money, even for just a long weekend. In addition to transportation, food, and entertainment, the cost would end up being more than $1,000 for a three-night stay on the beach. It was high season in Mexico as well as in

Southern California. Already steep prices were the seasonal norm and always soared even higher during the months of January, February, March, and April. When, in an e-mail, she casually mentioned the costs involved, she sensed by his response that he changed his mind about making the trip south of the border. She assured him there were lots of things they could do in the Palm Springs area, if the weather cooperated. "It has been an unusually wet and cool winter," she informed him, "but I'm sure I can come up with other activities you will enjoy."

"I'll bet you can come up with lots of things we can enjoy," Jack suggestively replied in his next e-mail. "I'll leave the planning part up to you."

So far the weather was proving to be among one of the rainiest periods on record in years, along with lower than normal temperatures. Jack kept telling her he was okay with whatever they did while he spent time in Palm Springs. "I'm more interested in the local culture and scenery, and of course spending time with you," he assured her. This is when Janice began dedicating more and more time to researching activities for them to do during his stay. This meant hours searching different web sites on the computer and asking friends for their suggestions, but she didn't mind. What mattered was Jack would be there with her.

They could hold and touch each other in ways only lovers can experience. "Maybe I can even talk him into staying longer," Janice whispered to herself more than once during the intense computer search for activities. It has been said ignorance is bliss. In this case no truer words could have been spoken.

CHAPTER 6

Jack's scheduled arrival time at the Palm Springs International Airport on that cool, overcast January morning turned out to be later than expected. Jack had called Janice to let her know as his plane waited for an open gate. She received his call at the same time she was approaching Arrivals in an Uber. Rather than asking the driver to continue circling the airport, she decided to let him go on his way; she'd call another driver after picking Jack up. It was a good thing she made this decision. She sat in the terminal and waited until Jack made his appearance, more than fifteen minutes later than the new ETA he had given her over the phone. He didn't bother to let her know he decided to stop and purchase coffee on the way through the main terminal before walking to baggage claim to meet her. Janice spotted him first among the large crowd near the carousel and approached him. He gave her a quick kiss and hug. They waited another fifteen minutes before the carousel began to move, disgorging bag after bag of similar size and shape. This allowed his bag to travel past them, making it necessary to wait until it came around a second time. Jack seemed excited to be in Palm Springs. He said he was looking forward to learning more about the gay community, which he called "the other side." Janice assured him he would have plenty of opportunity to do this since several of her gay friends were trying to get them tickets to a cross-dressing show at one of the gay bars; and they would also join them for the Monday night, two-for-one dinners at the local casino buffet. Jack mentioned in an e-mail he sent just before he left Tennessee that he had come down with little bit of a cold and had gone to the doctor early on Saturday morning before his scheduled Tuesday flight departure. He failed to let her know it was more than just a little cold. He actually had lower left lobe pneumonia, and he had been on massive doses of antibiotics every six hours. He told her this in the car on the way back from the airport. Janice immediately changed their downtown lunch plans and decided she'd have a driver take them home. She would serve him homemade chicken noodle soup and ham sandwiches she'd prepared as a backup, should he be too tired to go out to eat.

Jack ate lunch, then said he needed to take a nap. He stretched out on the huge silk-covered beige living room sofa and promptly went to sleep for several hours while Janice sat quietly reading nearby. He awakened in time for dinner, which Janice prepared.

Dinner was followed by a quick tour of the 3,200 square-foot house. Outside, she showed him the large, pergola-covered backyard patio, the open, manicured lawn, gardens, the salt water pool and its seating area, a fire pit, bubbling fountain, privacy hedge concealing a stucco wall, black olive trees, and more flower gardens. The pool, lawn and gardens were immaculately cared for by a gardener on a weekly basis. A housekeeper took care of the interior cleaning on a weekly or bi-weekly basis, depending on whether anyone was in residence.

Jack was impressed with the luxurious surroundings. "My house looks like a dump compared to this place," he commented. "But then you already know I haven't done much redecorating since Sabrina died."

"Are you hinting again that I should do some redecorating for you?" asked Janice. Jack smiled and nodded, affirmatively. "Your house is lovely," continued Janice, although during the time she spent there she assessed it was in dire need of a loving touch and a thorough cleaning.

"It wouldn't take a whole lot to make it cozy and charming." She made this comment knowing Jack had done little other than remove Sabrina's belongings and perform minimal lawn work. She remembered the strong odor emanating from the kitchen range left by skillets filled with old bacon grease sitting in the oven and the spilled food encrusted on the refrigerator shelves. She couldn't help but notice anytime she'd prepared a meal for them. She wanted to clean things but felt it wouldn't have been the right thing to do at the time. She was concerned that Jack might have taken offense. She felt these issues could be easily addressed later when their bond as a couple was more firmly established.

That night they retired early to the large master bedroom, complete with his and hers walk-in closets. Expansive sliding glass doors out into the backyard patio and pool covered one entire wall. Only occupants who wanted additional privacy needed to close the floor-to-ceiling green silk drapes, not that it was necessary due to the six-foot, stucco fence surrounding the property. The mirrored wall and duel marble bathroom sinks were separated by a large expanse of counter space. The bath tub could easily hold two, as could a glass and tile walled, walk-in shower. The cherry wood sleigh bed was king-size and covered in luxurious linens. The TV was hidden in a massive, matching, multi-drawered cherry wood chest that towered upward within a foot of the vaulted ceiling. A polished writing desk and upholstered chair occupied another wall of the 30 by 40-foot main bedroom. A red divan with foot rest, the kind you would expect to see in a 1930's movie set, sat off to the side of a glass-enclosed fireplace next to built-in, floor-to-ceiling shelves where a variety of expensive plates, books, and other art objects had been arranged. A small table sat beside the divan where new books were stacked, waiting to be read.

While they were preparing for bed Jack said he was afraid he might give her the same "bug" he had if they got too close to each other. At his insistence, this resulted in each of them lying apart on his and her sides of the king mattress, as far away from each other as they could get.

This sleeping arrangement continued for the next three nights until Janice told him there was little chance of her getting sick due to the antibiotics he was taking. Jack didn't object when Janice told him she had waited almost two months since they were last together to remove his white T-shirt and cotton briefs and send them to the foot of the bed like she had done in the past. Jack eagerly agreed and said he was all too willing and ready for this to happen. The remainder of his stay found them making love every night using touch and words of endearment for the remainder of his visit.

There was no doubt Jack was recovering from pneumonia. His dry, hacking cough lessened substantially with Janice's attentive care, the antibiotics, and well-prepared healthy foods; not to mention the long leisurely walks in nearby Ruth Hardy park on those sun-filled days when temperatures reached the mid-sixties by late morning. By day six of his visit, Jack said he felt well enough to explore more of the area.

"I didn't fly all the way out here to California just to lie around on the couch and sleep all day," he declared following the breakfast of French toast, fresh orange juice, and crisp bacon Janice prepared for them.

"But you are recovering from pneumonia," she replied. "I was concerned there could be a problem when you told me in an e-mail while you were still in Tennessee that you had been outside in the cold washing those wine carboys on the deck with temperatures hovering in the 30s. You should have told me it was more than a simple cold. The trip could have been delayed until you got well."

"I know it was a dumb thing to do and I should have told you," replied Jack contritely. "I didn't want to leave a mess without cleaning it up. The airline tickets were already paid for and non-refundable. Plus I didn't want to miss seeing this part of California. Almost as an afterthought he added, "And I didn't want to disappoint you."

This is when Janice remembered he seemed compulsive by frequently sweeping the floor in his living room when she had spent time there. The slightest trace of dirt tracked in had been immediately met with the broom and dust pan or a handheld vacuum cleaner. This type of reaction made her wonder if he had a compulsive side that didn't include the kitchen stove or refrigerator. But just as she had done before on other issues, she brushed those thoughts aside. He was here in California. The pneumonia was getting better by the hour, and that is what mattered. They would be hugging each other and making love every night while sharing a bed instead of her hugging a pillow as she had been doing before he arrived and would continue to do after he left.

Janice presented Jack with the opportunity to visit several wineries in the mountainous Temecula area north east of Palm Springs, since Mexico was no longer an option. But the weather and the price prevented them from doing so. Jack cringed at the thought of paying $85.00 or more per person for a day trip tour and lunch. "All we would see in this drizzling rain are dead grape vines and wine kegs," he commented. "I would rather go see a movie and eat popcorn."

Jack was content to go out for lunches at a variety of local restaurants, enjoy her dinners prepared at home, do a little shopping, take walks, watch television, nap every afternoon, and make love every night. During the beginning of week two of his visit, though, he did agree to take a ride up the mountain in the world-famous rotating Tram. The Tram rose 8,500 feet to a restaurant and gift shop located at the Palm Springs summit of the San Jacinto Mountains. Jack was completely enthralled during the twenty-minute ride up and down, as well as with the rugged, snow-capped mountains as the couple walked around on the windswept perimeter terrace. To his credit, he did pay for their lunch.

When they visited the gift shop Janice could not resist buying Jack a gaudy hat with a bejeweled crown fastened to the front. This was the symbol on the cover of one of his redneck humor books. "You can wear the hat at signings when you feature that book," said Janice. Jack appeared to be delighted with it and said he couldn't wait to show up at a friend's home in Tennessee wearing it, a trench coat, dangly earrings, and a scanty Speedo to reflect what he thought was the gay image of Palm Springs. They both had a good laugh at the thought of how this conservative couple would react. He would later tell her he had, in fact, done this and they thought it was a hoot.

Janice's daughter had already booked a flight to San Francisco, 130 miles from their condo in Petaluma, to come to Palm Springs over the weekend before she knew Jack was coming to visit that same weekend. This caused some anxiety for Jack. Janice assured him her daughter was okay with him being there and sharing a bedroom with her. "Belinda wants us to be happy," said Janice. "She and her husband lived together before they were married, just like my son is doing with his girlfriend." Jack finally said he was comfortable with her answer.

As it turned out, it was not an issue for them or Janice's daughter. Her daughter used one of the guest rooms and a bath located across the house from the master bedroom of the sprawling house. Separated by a sitting room, the fire place, and open living and dining room, that part of the house had been designed to ensure everyone's privacy.

Belinda rented a car at the airport, so Janice and Jack didn't have to rely on using Janice's Uber account they had been using before Belinda arrived. Belinda took them to downtown Palm Springs the first morning of her visit. They enjoyed a late breakfast at a lovely little French restaurant. Belinda insisted on paying for their meals. Then came some sightseeing and shopping in the downtown area's vast array of small shops because Jack said he was looking to purchase some new clothes. Janice thought he would choke when he saw the prices in one of the men's shops, so they drove to a department store known for more moderately priced clothing in a mall five miles away from the downtown area. Jack did purchase a couple of T-shirts that were on sale.

The next day they took a drive through the hilly, sand-covered desert to the area known as Whitewater, due to the rapid runoff stream coming down from the mountainous area northeast of town. The weather was nice enough that they could walk around the lake and take pictures of the fast-running stream featuring young salmon and spectacular mountain views. Again, Belinda insisted on paying for their meals. Jack did not object.

The following day they all piled into Belinda's rental car to go to what is referred to as "down the valley" so Jack could see the really expensive shopping area on world famous El Paseo Drive that attempts to rival Rodeo Drive in Beverly Hills. It was obvious Jack had no desire to shop there.

The whirlwind weekend ended Sunday night at a well-known night club, Vickie's of Santa Fe, for some lively jazz music, drinks, and a light snack-type dinner to top off Belinda's last night. To his credit, Jack picked up the modest tab for all three of them; this was his first offer to pay for their meals since Belinda had arrived.

Janice and Jack had joined several of her gay couple friends for the evening buffet at the local Casino both Monday evenings during Jack's visit. This gave him an opportunity to meet several more of her gay friends and a few relatives. They all appeared to cordially accept Jack and he them. Janice also took him to eat at many of her favorite restaurants throughout his stay, usually for lunch since it was less expensive. She paid for most of the meals, even though the agreement was to have been 50/50. Jack didn't object to her paying, nor did he reach for the checks when they were presented. She also paid for a majority of food at the grocery store as well and cooked their dinners, including one that she prepared Japanese style. It was complete with sake served in thin, decorative, porcelain cups she had purchased as soon as she knew he was coming to California. She did this because Jack had mentioned he enjoyed spending time in Japan when he was in the Marines. It was her nature to give people what they enjoyed, expecting little or nothing in return.

He was absolutely thrilled with the male-female impersonator show at the gay bar and their walks in Ruth Hardy park on those days when the weather cooperated. Jack made it no secret he was thoroughly enjoying himself throughout his visit. He kept telling Janice he didn't want to go home, but felt he had to go. He had to soon help judge entries in the writing competition.

Janice didn't understand his reasoning. It was January. The contest award presentation ceremony wasn't scheduled to take place until the end of April. Elaina, not Jack, was in charge of the project as the vice president of the writers group. Janice encouraged him to sign up for automatic bill paying and to let his friend who was checking on his house and boat know that he wanted to extend his trip. Janice would have been more than happy to pay the small fee the airline would charge to change the date of departure. But she couldn't convince Jack to stay any longer, for reasons that remained unclear to her at the time. By this time she loved and trusted Jack implicitly, so she didn't push for answers.

When the sixteen days were coming to an end it was with a heavy heart, at least on the part of Janice, when they parted with an embrace and a kiss at the airport. Jack told her he would be looking forward to her return back east the first week of May. Janice cried when she returned to the empty house to face what would be 48 days without him. She had made the decision to return to Tennessee in mid-March instead of early May because she missed Jack so much. Would he ever know she kissed his picture every night before turning out the bedside table light after he left? Or that she hugged the empty pillow where he had laid his head next to hers? There were even times when she cried herself to sleep because she was missing him so much. The thought he wasn't missing her never entered her mind since his e-mails often said he missed her, too. But was that declaration nothing but a bare faced-lie? That question would remain unanswered until early April.

CHAPTER 7

It was true that Janice missed Jack, but she also felt the strong need to unpack her belongings at the house she had rented in Tennessee back on the first of November before making the trip to southern California. She made the decision to move back to Tennessee months ago when her son announced he and Suzanne were getting married. His new wife wanted to live in Florida near where she had lived before she met and married Jason. The decision for them to move back to Florida had been made months before Janice and Jack had any thoughts of entering a romantic relationship. Janice had no interest in returning to Florida, or for that manner, continuing to live in Georgia after Jason, Suzanne, and Monica left the area. She could see no reason to continue living there without any family or close friends. Coupled with her love for Jack and being reunited with those who had become dear friends back in Tennessee, she made the decision to move back to the mountains. The fact that Jack appeared firmly entrenched in the picture served to reinforce her decision.

She had no idea the time would come when someone would accuse her of "hauling ass" back to Tennessee just to be near Jack. Nothing could be further from the truth. That decision had been made when Jason and Suzanne announced their intent to move to Florida and prior to Jack asking her out to dinner. She would admit, though, the time spent at Jack's house, him staying at her apartment in Georgia over Thanksgiving week, and the sixteen days he spent with her in California did play a significant part in the final decision to return to Tennessee. Janice knew she would have still made this decision even if Jack were not in the picture. The fact Jack kept telling her they were "a good fit and he wanted her in his life" only added to the feeling that she had made the right decision.

The e-mails between Janice and Jack continued hot and heavy after Jack left California. It persisted daily, sometimes more than once daily, through mid-March with him telling her he was missing her, too. He said he was delighted when she let him know she was coming back to live in Tennessee earlier than expected, adding he would be waiting to pick her up at the airport as soon as she returned. "Just e-mail me the particulars and I'll be there," he responded.

Janice had to admit she was disappointed when he did not send her a Valentine card in response to her sending a funny one to him. She didn't expect one of those mushy hearts and flowers cards expressing undying love when the one she sent to him was silly. Jack did express he felt badly that he did not send her a card but gave no reason for not making the effort. Hurt, Janice let him know this made her feel that she was not his Valentine but just a friend with benefits. His next e-mail stated he didn't feel that way about their relationship and that she was more than a friend with or without benefits. Janice foolishly chose to believe him.

"You have to stay at my house for at least the first few nights when you get back to Tennessee," he said an e-mail soon after Valentine's Day. The he added, "I want you to stay even stay longer, at least until we get you unpacked and settled." But in the next sentence he added, "I hate to let you know I will have to leave soon after you get back. I have to fly to Florida two weeks after you return. I am going to the Everglades for a week to do some research on a book. My publisher and her husband, who spend the winter there, have invited me to stay with them and show me around the area. They have promised to introduce me to some of the local, colorful, swamp-dwelling people who are to be the basis of the book."

"Don't worry about it," she replied. "You do what you need to do," wrote Janice in a return e-mail. "I'll be working on getting settled in my new place while you are gone, but we have to plan something to celebrate St. Patrick's Day. I get back on Tuesday night. That means I will be there in time for the traditional celebration of corned beef, boiled potatoes, cabbage, and green beer on Friday, March 17. You pick the place. And I will plan on taking you to the airport for the Florida trip," she added.

"I'm sure I can come up with something for St. Patrick's Day," he assured her in his next e-mail. "If taking me to the airport will be inconvenient for you, I can make other arrangements."

"Are you kidding about it being inconvenient? I would love to take you to the airport," she replied.

"Then it's all settled," he wrote back within minutes.

It seemed like forever for Janice as the days turned into weeks before her flight back to where she believed a new and happy life awaited. She loved Tennessee and the people who lived there, many of whom had become dear friends who had given a lot of emotional support during and after her husband's terminal illness. It was one of the few places she truly felt at home. She was also looking forward to meeting and getting to know more of Jack's family and friends, including his family members living in Virginia.

Janice had never wanted to leave Tennessee in the first place. She was convinced by her children she could not continue living alone in the house nestled in the remote mountain-side. The move to Atlanta became a decision she regretted with every passing day. This pressure, and the fact that Jason was planning a move to Florida following his marriage to Suzanne, was when Jack encouraged her to return to Tennessee.

With his encouragement and that of family and friends, Janice began to make the move, at least for the spring, summer, and early fall months. She still planned to spend winters in California, with the hope that Jack would join her for all winter months moving forward. At this point, they were now openly considered a couple by family and mutual friends.

She knew she did not want to live in Florida, even with Jason and Suzanne planning to live there after their marriage. It was hot and humid with lots of disgusting bugs and destructive hurricanes, in addition to the many memories of years spent there with her beloved Clayton. She loved Tennessee and she loved Jack, even though she wanted to live apart from him until she was completely sure he was the one she wanted to spend the rest of her life waking up beside every day.

Although she found it difficult to find suitable housing in and around Kingston, Tennessee, she was able to find a small home to rent with the help of one of Jack's realtor friends. At the time she had not given any serious thought to moving in with him. She felt that such a live-in arrangement would be a little too soon following the death of his wife and would give reason for people to talk.

His home on the river was lovely in spite of the need for updating, but she knew he needed more time to grieve his wife's passing in spite of him repeatedly telling her he had moved on. She, too, needed space, having lived alone for the past six years. That, and she felt they didn't really know each other well enough to live under the same roof on a long-term basis. In addition to those issues, she wasn't sure if she wanted to get married again or live with a man without the benefit of marriage.

"Too many complications if I were to move in with him," she told her daughter when Belinda brought up that possibility. "I could stand to possibly lose a lot of money in the event that I get married again, and if it doesn't work out, where do I go from there? I'm at the max on early Social Security benefits due to your father's generous benefit as his widow. The monthly trust figures will drop significantly if I remarry. I don't know if Jack's financial situation would be comparable. I know that sounds harsh, but I have to be realistic. If I live to a ripe old age I will need those financial resources. We haven't progressed far enough in our relationship for me to be comfortable asking those kinds of questions about his finances. Plus, I'm old school. Living with a man without the benefit of marriage isn't on my radar. I'm really not sure that I'm even ready for marriage." Janice felt immense relief when Belinda backed off.

CHAPTER 8

Jack was still in his nice warm car near the airport, not waiting at the baggage claim area, when Janice arrived late the evening of March 14. She would learn this from his cell phone call letting her know he was circling the airport perimeter in his car, rather than pay the fee to park in short term parking and having to make the walk to the terminal in the cold night air. This meant Janice was forced to struggle with getting her suitcase from the baggage claim area and taking it to the curb to wait until he passed by her way again since cars could not park in front of the terminal for security reasons. Of course he was apologetic when he did pull up to the curb to help place the suitcase in the car's trunk. But the fact remained he had not made much of an effort for her comfort on the chilly and windy March evening. It didn't seem to register with Jack she was stepping into 38 degrees from the sunny 97-degree day she left behind in Palm Springs early that afternoon for the flight back to Tennessee—a shock to her system to say the least. It would have been easy for her to let him know she wasn't pleased, but she held her tongue, not wanting to create any unpleasantness so soon after her return.

It was after eleven p.m. when they arrived at Jack's home. Janice announced with a wide yawn that she was tired and needed to go to bed. Jack soon joined her in the bedroom to take her in his arms asking if she was too tired to make love. Not wanting to deny him, she smiled and said she was never too tired for their love making.

The next morning found her preparing their breakfast of bacon, coddled eggs just the way Jack liked them, and buttered toast. She asked Jack to make his coffee since she didn't drink coffee or any caffeinated beverages. She served their food on china she placed on the table and six-chair dining set she had given him to replace the metal table meant for use on the outdoor deck. Jack had moved the metal table inside after getting rid of the pool table taking up the space, when the weather became cooler last fall. Janice offered him the dining set after it turned out to be too large to fit in her new home's dining area. A few days later she gave him the two, matching, slate-embedded end tables and coffee table for the living room space, along with complementing lamps, which were also too large for her new home. She told him she didn't want any money when he asked if she wanted payment. These items replaced old mismatched lamps, barrel chairs, and the metal table. She later added a matching, wrought iron bar when her living room proved to be too small for that as well. The furnishings looked as though they had been specifically selected to be placed in Jack's rustic, water front house when, in fact, they had been purchased for her large Georgia apartment. She did jokingly say she would like to visit the items once in a while. This was when he mentioned that she needed to consider moving in with him.

She hesitated before answering. "How about we talk about that possibility closer to the time when I am due to renew my lease?"

"When is your lease up?"

"The first of November. I have to give a 30-day notice if I plan to move," she replied. "That will give us spring, summer and early fall to see if that's what we want to do." Jack reluctantly agreed they should wait until then.

The ten days Janice ended up spending with Jack after her return from California consisted of a flurry of activity between him overseeing yard workers at his home and them making trips back and forth from her house to do some unpacking in the late afternoons. Between these activities there were lunches when she was introduced to his friends. "I wanted you to meet them before I'm scheduled to leave for Florida. That way you will have someone to contact should you need anything," he offered.

Goosebumps ran up her arms when he reminded her of his trip to the Everglades. Not only was she going to miss him, she knew the area he would be staying could be dangerous due to the overabundance of alligators and a variety of tropical snakes and spiders.

Janice had not been invited to join them, but she tried to convince herself that she didn't mind. She knew Jack would be busy gathering information for the book and wouldn't have much time to spend with her even if she had gone with him. To reassure him it was all right that she wouldn't be accompanying him she said, "I still have my new quarters to finish getting in shape while you are away." This was something she intended to attack with gusto after he left. "I want my home to be a cozy and comfortable setting during the times you will be with me." Jack gave her a look that left the impression he was looking forward to those times. On the other hand, she wasn't exactly sure how they would work out such visits but assumed things would fall into place as more people became aware of their relationship.

On the Thursday evening before Jack was scheduled to leave for Florida the following day, he held the weekly writers group meeting at his home instead of the library. Janice, who was still staying at his home and sharing a bed with Jack's blessing, prepared snacks. Only one couple in addition to Elaina arrived, for a total of five people. Janice knew from past experiences there were anywhere from a dozen and sometimes more people who would usually attend these meetings. She thought it was a little strange there weren't more people in attendance. When they finished the meeting and began enjoying the wine and snacks, she heard Elaina mention to the other couple she was planning to take Jack to the airport the following day.

When she heard this comment Janice turned to Jack and gave him a questioning look.

He responded by quickly saying, "Elaina was just a backup in case you didn't make it back in time from California to take me." There had never been a question about Janice coming back to Tennessee in time to take him to the airport, or she would have called to let him know. The look Elaina gave her when Jack said Janice would be taking him to the airport was one she instantly recognized was not a friendly one! After everyone left, Janice confronted Jack.

"I need to know where I stand involving the relationship between you and Elaina. I have the feeling, by the look on her face in regard to the airport transportation issue, along with what transpired on St. Patrick's Day, there is something I need to know about going on between the two of you!" Jack's face turned beet red and he started to give his usual response that Elaina was just a friend he was grooming to take over as president of the writers group. It was obvious Janice wasn't buying this explanation because Elaina had already, more or less, taken over the writers group. "Before you say anything more, you need to know I am aware Elaina and you spent time together in your sauna while I was in California, and you attended Christmas dinner at her home rather than join my family in California. This is in addition to the time you invited her to accompany you to a New Year's Eve party when you declined my invitation. She made sure I knew how much fun the two of you had at the party in an e-mail she sent to friends she knew would contact me while I was still in California. I should have confronted you at the time, but I believed it when you kept telling me we were such a good fit, that you missed me, and she was just a friend, so I let it go. I am also aware the Christmas dinner took place at her home after she was able to convince her husband to go visit his relatives without her over the holidays. She bragged to certain people that she did that in order to get him out of the house so she could enjoy having Christmas dinner with you. She actually bragged about it to people she knew would let me know. I can't believe I was stupid enough that I chose not to make an issue of it until now. But once again, I believed and trusted you when you said she was just a friend!"

Jack's demeanor became defensive as he began to nervously pace around the room, obviously trying to think of a way to justify what had taken place between Elaina and him and placate Janice. "And how would you know those things?" he challenged, seeming to ignore what Janice just told him regarding Elaina's e-mails and what mutual friends had told her. "You were 3,000 miles away spending the winter in California. Maybe if you had been here in Tennessee I wouldn't have had to go elsewhere for Christmas dinner and had you as my partner to escort to the New Year's Eve party! I think your imagination is working overtime!"

"Are you deaf?" exclaimed Janice. "I just told you Elaina e-mailed several friends and me with the particulars, and she knew those friends would fill me in! The fact remains I do know, so don't try to deny it! Aren't you forgetting something? I invited you to come to California to spend time with me over the holidays! Are you trying to tell me Elaina wasn't being truthful when she sent the e-mails? When I invited you to join me in California, you told me you wanted to be with your family over the Christmas holidays since it would be the first year without Sabrina. You made it clear that was the reason why you couldn't join me and my family in California! Since when is a "friend" considered family?"

Jack continued to respond as though she had not spoken. "I keep telling you Elaina is just a friend," Jack insisted. "I have repeatedly told you I'm only grooming her to take over the writers group! You don't have any reason to be upset. She only used my sauna to sweat out a cold. I admit it was stupid on my part to have joined her wearing nothing but my bathing trunks, but nothing of a sexual nature happened. You know you don't have anything to worry about in the sex department. You and I are a good fit," he continued to strongly insist.

Even though Janice suspected his manner, combined with her information, belied innocence in his relationship with this woman, she still did not want to believe he was lying. Hadn't she spent a week with him at his home after the fundraiser when she had driven through the night to help him through the heart tests? Hadn't he spent the better part of a week in Georgia with her over Thanksgiving while visiting her and her family? Hadn't they shared a bed? Hadn't he recently spent sixteen days with her, again sharing a bed, in California? Hadn't they just spent nine days together, living the life a married couple would? Hadn't he asked her to move in with him? She tried to remember but couldn't count the number of times he had and continued to tell her they were such a good fit and Elaina was only a friend. Although she hated confrontation Janice knew it was time to clear the air once and for all. The issues involving Elaina needed to be settled, or else the relationship with Jack was over! She was not about to share him on an intimate level with that disgusting, slutty tramp!

"If Elaina is just as a friend as you claim, you need to give her a call right now here in front of me on speaker phone and let her know, in no uncertain terms, we are more than just friends! It's that or I'm out of here! If you refuse you can take me back to my house and it's over between us!" insisted Janice.

Jack pleaded with her not to go, continuing to try to convince her that he and Elaina were just friends, and that he wanted Janice, not Elaina, to be a part of his life on a long-term basis. Janice wasn't buying his explanation and

Jack knew it, even before Elaina left his house after the meeting.

"I need to give her some time to drive home," said Jack. Never having been confronted on issues such as these, he continued to pace while stalling for time to think about how best to handle being called out.

Half an hour passed as the tension mounted between them and he continued to focus on Elaina's reaction to being informed she was not taking him to the airport. "It was just a misunderstanding on Elaina's part about her taking me to the airport. She thought it was a done deal that she was going to take me," he insisted. "It's my fault. I didn't make it clear you would be taking me and she was just a backup in case you changed your plans and didn't make it back from California in time."

Janice could feel her heart pounding like a trip hammer. She knew Jack's heart had to be pounding the same way, but she kept insisting he had to call Elaina and make it clear they were now a couple, or she was leaving and their relationship was over. "That is all well and good about the airport *misunderstanding*, but that doesn't explain the other encounters like the sauna, the dinner without her husband, the New Year's Eve party, or the night you invited her to join us for dinner on St. Patrick's Day, and again when you invited her to dinner at your home while I was obviously staying here with you! If there was nothing going on between the two of you, you must explain her hostile behavior toward me and refusal to eat what I had prepared while insisting she hadn't been invited to dinner?" retorted Janice. "If she wasn't invited why did she come to your house? I will admit a long time ago—and she was married—I did hear her make a comment about wanting to be your friend with benefits. At the time I thought she was joking. I did think there was something going on between the two of you after her last couple of e-mails detailing your mutual activities, but I was foolish enough to believe you when you said the two of you were just friends. And, if you recall at the second book signing, it was you who said she was just a friend when I didn't even consider asking for a relationship status when the two of you shared a table. I know you heard her tell me she wasn't invited to dinner when *you* were the one who invited her on that Monday night back in March, and that it was *me* who betrayed *her*! You just stood there like a bump on a log and said nothing!"

By this time Janice's voice had taken on a higher and louder pitch. Jack kept denying he had heard this conversation between her and Elaina, but she knew otherwise and said as much. "How can you deny hearing that conversation? I didn't imagine you were standing right there beside me when it took place! You need to make that call to her right now, or we are through!"

This is when Jack picked up his cell phone and made the call, figuring this course of action would convince Janice he and Elaina were not involved romantically, but he didn't think through what he was doing, or he would have used another tactic.

When Elaina picked up, he didn't waste any time stating, "Elaina, I'm calling to let you know Janice and I have taken our relationship to the next level. You need to find someone your own age."

The comment he made about her finding someone her own age should have sent an immediate signal to Janice to let her know her intuition was right on target. There was definitely something going on between the two of them! And if that weren't enough to send up a red flag, Jack was dumb enough to place the conversation on speaker phone so Janice could hear Elaina's response.

"Your relationship with her won't last!" said Elaina in a hysterical voice. "Age doesn't make any difference. She's controlling, and you are a free spirit." She paused briefly before asking, "Is she listening to our conversation?"

"She's right here and we are on speaker phone," said Jack in response to the question. "Then you need to step outside onto the deck and close the door so we can talk in private," ordered Elaina. It was not a request or suggestion. It was a demand.

To Janice's dismay Jack took the cell phone outside onto the deck, closing the sliding glass door behind him. This move prevented Janice from hearing what transpired between them. She knew this wasn't the right thing to do on his part and that she should leave immediately. But at the same time, she had no way to leave safely. Jack had driven them from her house to his house in his car, leaving hers in her carport when they returned from more unpacking at her house earlier that afternoon. It was at least eighteen miles to her house. Much of the distance consisted of narrow, tree-lined roads without lights, with three miles on I-40. Janice knew walking was not a viable option. In the moment she couldn't think of someone to call to come and get her at this late hour without making a scene and airing what could be considered dirty laundry.

When Jack came back into the room five minutes later he was all smiles. He told Janice that Elaina said she was good with his decision to move forward in his relationship with Janice. He was so convincing Janice had the feeling she was, once again, on solid ground with Jack. That feeling began to evaporate when Jack told her he had invited Elaina to dinner the following Monday evening to discuss taking over the financial end of the writers group and to prove they were just friends. Janice blanched at the news Elaina was coming to dinner at Jack's house. Blinded by love, she wanted to believe Jack when he insisted there was nothing going on between himself and Elaina beyond a mutual interest in the writers group activities. He closed the distance between them to take her in his arms and tell her once again what a good fit they were and that he wanted her, not Elaina, to be in his life on a permanent basis.

He just stood here in front of me and told Elaina he wasn't interested in having a relationship with her, Janice reasoned to herself silently. Wanting desperately to believe Jack was telling the truth, Janice stayed the night with him and they made passionate love. As planned, she took him to the airport the next evening after both of them spent the afternoon at her house continuing to unpack her belongings. Jack appeared to be upbeat while helping with the unpacking process until it was time to make the drive to the airport.

"I really hate to leave," he announced. Janice said she would miss him but understood the reason he had to go. They ended up having a nice dinner at a restaurant near the airport before she dropped him off at departures and headed back to spend her first night alone in her new home. After spending the past ten nights sleeping next to Jack, the bed seemed cold and empty. Waking up without him next to her was even more unsettling on Saturday morning. A premonition swept over her as she was preparing to eat breakfast alone. It could best be described as an overwhelming feeling something she couldn't quite define had changed between them. It was not a good feeling.

"I'll call you as soon as my plane lands in Florida," Jack had told her when he kissed her goodbye on Friday night at the airport. But he didn't call.

The cell phone call came late Saturday night to tell her he was sitting around a campfire on a bale of hay while listening to the swamp dwellers play bluegrass music. When she mentioned she didn't hear any music, he said the band was taking a break. He further explained this was the group he had come to study for his next book. There was no apology or explanation as to why he had not called the night before beyond that of, "Sorry I didn't get around to calling last night. I've been busy with my publisher. She and her husband have been showing me all of the places that could prove to be useful and introducing me to the people she thinks would be beneficial to writing the book. I'm tired and it's only Saturday." Jack didn't have much else to add to the conversation. Janice thanked him for calling and told him to have a good time, but not so good a time that he brought home any social diseases. He laughed and said she didn't have to worry about that in light of his "condition."

"I miss you," said Janice in closing. Jack said he was missing her, too. Normally, hearing his voice would be comforting. But it was not comforting on this night. If asked, she could not have told anyone what was different between them, yet she knew something was up. She was waiting for the other shoe to drop. She wanted to know what prompted the uneasy feeling, but at the same time, she didn't want to know. Janice was in love, and she believed that when love was involved, there should be trust. And at the moment, she was forced to admit she did not have a feeling of trust.

It might have been a mistake when Janice decided it would be best not to call Jack during the week he spent in Florida. Or it could have been providence looking out for her. It wasn't an easy decision, but she convinced herself he would be too busy doing research to spend time engaging in conversation, or else he would have called her. He did not call again until the following Friday morning after his plane arrived at the Atlanta airport on the layover to change planes for the last leg of his flight. That brief call was to make sure she would pick him up at the airport when his plane landed. She wouldn't learn he had found time to call friends during the week until he let it slip during a later conversation. He didn't know Elaina also made sure Janice would hear about his calls to her through a mutual acquaintance with a reputation of being a blabber mouth. In her heart she felt certain this was Elaina's way of letting her know she was far more than just a friend where Jack was concerned. Being in love, Janice wanted to believe Jack was being faithful and truthful.

On Thursday before Jack's scheduled arrival in Tennessee, Janice made a trip to the grocery store to stock up on foods she knew he liked. The bill ended up at $212.62. Many of the foods she chose were not on the list of things she ate. She made choices of foods in an effort to keep from elevating Jack's already elevated A1C blood levels following the June stroke last year. He had worked hard to lower the blood level from 7.5 to 6.3. At the same time she felt she couldn't deprive Jack of the things he liked to eat, even if he still needed to lose a few more pounds. Carefully reading labels kept the salt, fats, and sugars as low as possible and still provided tasty treats and meals for him.

Janice awakened at 7:00 a.m. with a heightened sense of anticipation accompanied by a positive attitude on that early Friday morning in April. Jack was due to return that afternoon and planned to spend the night with her before heading to his home using the car he had left parked in front of her house while he was gone. A car that prompted a nosy neighbor to let her know she had seen it. She put aside her uneasy feelings and hummed as she showered, washed, set her hair, and carefully dressed in one of Jack's favorite outfits. While doing so, she planned for the dinner they would share. She allowed herself to be happy. She focused on the fact he was planning to stay with her that night instead of focusing on the misgivings that continued to lurk in the back of her mind. The arrangement for him to spend the night had been decided before he left for Florida. He said he would be tired following a long day that would start very early the morning of his scheduled return. Janice was happy to agree that spending the night with her made sense, along with the anticipation of having him lie there beside her throughout the night after making love.

She washed the bed linens and made up the bed they would share, then vacuumed and dusted. She was proud of the comfortable home she had made. There continued to be the nagging feeling in the back of her mind regarding his involvement with Elaina. She knew those thoughts kept her from making a commitment, even though she believed wholeheartedly that she loved Jack. She did her best to shake off the nagging feeling he was not totally committed to her. When she allowed herself to think about it, she had to admit she had not heard him say the word *love*. He often used, "We're such a good fit." That should have been a clue about his true feelings.

Two hours before his flight was due to land, Jack called again. "I'm in the Atlanta airport about to board the flight home. See you in about an hour and 45 minutes." He made no mention regarding anticipation of spending time with her after the week's absence.

"I'll be there. I am really looking forward to seeing you," said Janice. "I'll meet you in the baggage claim area."

"Okay. See you then," he replied. His voice had been matter-of-fact, not like someone who missed her and was anxious to spend time with her again. Janice overlooked his lack of excitement, writing it off to fatigue as the result of the early morning departure from the airport in Florida. That thought was in addition to what she believed must have been a terribly busy week gathering information for his next book.

Just as she said she would, Janice was there waiting at the airport baggage claim area, but there was no sign of Jack. She walked around searching for him among the throng of other passengers waiting for their luggage. Then she then sat down in one of a row of blue plastic seats to wait for him near the baggage carousel. The baggage delivery system had not started moving after the last flight. She watched it stop after unloading bags from the flight preceding Jack's flight and it had not yet resumed rotating. He finally came sauntering along, his attention focused on the carousel rather than looking for her.

She spotted him and walked up behind him. "Hello weary traveler," she said as she tapped him on the right shoulder. He turned and gave her a half-hearted smile, but no kiss or the hug she was anticipating after him being gone a full week. Janice did her best to maintain a casual demeanor as they chatted about his trip while they waited for his luggage, but her heart was heavy. It took an effort for her not to show disappointment at his cool reception. She asked if he eaten lunch during the layover in Atlanta. He said no. She had not eaten either, so after retrieving his luggage she drove to a nice local chain restaurant where she had eaten before they became a couple. They both ordered a bowl of chili and some cornbread. He ordered iced tea while she drank water. He seemed completely at ease as they continued their conversation about his week in Florida. He didn't ask how her week had gone. After they had eaten and she paid the bill when he didn't offer, she tossed him her car keys as they approached her car in the parking lot.

"You drive. You don't like the way I pull into traffic," she joked, recalling the way he chastised her on that day in Knoxville. Jack caught the keys and mumbled something inaudible under his breath.

Jack was all smiles at her house and complimented on the manner in which she had decorated her home while he was gone. He didn't hesitate to open a bottle of blackberry wine mutual friends had brought and left sitting on the bar. He poured two glasses and handed one to Janice, who was now allowed one drink a day. He then took a seat in the only reclining lounge chair and made himself comfortable by adjusting the elevated footrest and back support. Then he opened a notebook taken from a beige manila folder he had leaned against the chair earlier. Then he asked Janice to listen while he read the few pages he had written on the proposed book while she sat nearby on the sofa. Janice found the manuscript vague and disjointed but didn't say so since she knew it was a first draft. She offered several suggestions concerning descriptions of the tropical surroundings. She had offered this information because she had visited the Everglades on several occasions.

She was tired and the wine was beginning to make her feel sleepy as 6:00 p.m. approached. Jack's response to her input was dismissive. He said he wasn't hungry for the meal she had planned, and that a salad would do for dinner.

Janice prepared and served the salads while Jack continued to sit and watch TV until it was time to eat at the kitchen table. As they ate Jack began to voice the fact he was no longer sure how he felt as to where their relationship was headed. She felt a lump the size of a golf ball form in the pit of her stomach. It grew larger as the two of them finished their salads then settled into bed for the night not long after they ate. Fearful of what his response might be, she didn't ask him to be more specific about where their relationship was headed; nor did she snuggle up against him like she usually did. Instead, she told him he should get some sleep after the long day. She turned away from him in bed and snapped off the table lamp's soft glow, leaving them in total darkness. She knew for sure something had definitely changed in their relationship but had no idea what prompted the change.

In a matter of minutes Jack asked her to turn over and hold him. Against her better judgment she did as he asked. He held her tight against his chest and said he wasn't meant to sleep alone. They didn't make love but clung to each other throughout much of the night just as they had done months earlier during their first, non-sexual, intimate encounter. She now had the feeling it had been a big mistake staying at his home following the heart stress test, and that it had all been a mistake. If he was aware, he didn't let on that he knew she shed silent tears that soaked into the pillow they shared.

"I have to get up early and go meet some people at the library to sort through the contest entries sent there by students for the writing competition," he announced toward morning, as they lay there awake, side by side. "Elaina said she didn't have much of a response when she asked for help. I don't think I'll need your help. I'll call you if I do," he said before drifting back off to sleep. This statement confirmed what she had been told. He and Elaina had been in contact while he was in Florida. Otherwise, he would not have known she was not getting any response to her request for help from club members in the judging process.

Janice was caught off guard during the night when she tried to slip away from him in bed. Without saying a word he wrapped both arms around her and held her tightly against his chest before letting her go. Had the circumstances been different she would have responded in a loving way, rather than turning away from him to lie awake heartbroken until dawn.

They were both up and out of bed at 6:00 a.m. on that Saturday morning. While Jack showered and dressed Janice prepared breakfast and tried to portray lightheartedness when Jack entered the kitchen. He ate everything on his plate with his usual gusto and drank two cups of coffee.

When it was time for him to leave for the library he hugged and kissed her. "I'll be bringing some of my things to leave here when I come back later tomorrow," he told her with a seductive grin. "You should do the same the next time you come to my house." This conversation should have raised her spirits, but it didn't. The uneasiness of his comment about the uncertain direction of their relationship during last night's conversation while they ate their salads continued to plague her. She could not shake the uneasy feeling that became more intense while she took care of clearing the breakfast dishes, cleaning the bathroom, and making the bed they had shared after he had gone.

That was the last she heard from Jack the remainder of the weekend. She gave some thought about e-mailing or calling him but decided against it. "He said he would call if he needed my help," she murmured. Instead of dwelling on the fact she hadn't heard from him, she drove to a furniture store later that Saturday afternoon to purchase another chair for the living room. "He will call me if I'm needed," she kept trying to convinced herself. The chair task accomplished, she returned home and prepared leftovers from what would have been their dinner last night, which she ended up leaving untouched. The lump in her throat would not allow her to swallow.

On Sunday afternoon, and still not hearing from Jack, she decided to visit a couple of dear, elderly friends living in a nearby town. She had known them for fifteen years. She took them out for an early dinner and stayed to talk with them longer than she had planned. It was easy to check her cell phone and know Jack had not yet called or e-mailed her. She felt it was too late to call or e-mail him when she returned to her home and anyway, he had a key if he returned, as he had indicated he would yesterday. As she lay alone in bed on both Saturday and now Sunday night, she convinced herself Jack was so busy reading and judging student manuscripts he forgot to e-mail or call her. When she awakened the next morning she didn't want to deal with the fact he did not show up during the night or call to let her know he would not be there. She had no way to know Jack was busy, all right. She would soon learn he was apparently busy with more than just reading manuscripts!

Early on Monday morning Jack sent Janice an e-mail saying he had been so engrossed in sorting through the contest entries the entire weekend, and had enough helpers, he didn't feel the need to contact her. Janice responded to his e-mail saying she was disappointed she wasn't one of the helpers, and that she missed seeing him on Sunday night. Without responding to her comment about Sunday night he then wrote that he was headed to the dermatologist this morning for a 10:30 appointment to have a troublesome spot checked and asked if they could they do a late lunch. In what Janice chose to believe was a peace offering, he said he would bring along some of the contest entries for her to judge. At the time, it didn't dawn on her to question why this was necessary if he had not needed her to help during the weekend.

Janice invited him to stop by for some homemade vegetable soup and grilled ham and cheese sandwiches instead of going to a restaurant, figuring it would be easier to talk in a more private setting and learn why he had not shown up on Sunday, had neglected to call, and so on. He responded by saying that would work if she didn't mind having lunch around one p.m. in case he had to wait at the doctor's office. She said that would be okay and set about making the soup as soon as their conversation ended.

It was a little past one when Jack knocked on the front door and she let him in.

"Don't I get a hug?" she asked when he walked inside and past her. She noticed he didn't carry any personal items to store at her home as he'd mentioned Saturday.

"Sure," he replied. He turned to give her a brief, half-hearted hug. He didn't kiss her and quickly walked into the kitchen to take a seat at the table. Janice served lunch, and he talked about the contest entries. He acted as though nothing was out of the ordinary as they ate and continued to chat. "I've got some errands to run," he announced when he finished eating the bowl of soup and sandwich she had prepared.

"Wouldn't you like some fresh fruit and at least a quick cup of coffee before you go?" she asked. She had just bought a three pound tin of his favorite brand of coffee and a pot perked on the counter while they ate the soup and sandwiches. The combined fresh strawberries, blackberries, blueberries, and pineapple chunks she knew he liked were ready and waiting in the refrigerator, along with a can of whipped cream to top them off.

"I need to make the coffee to go and pass on the fruit," he answered as he glanced nervously at his watch. She watched with mounting anxiety as he prepared the to-go cup he had gone outside to retrieve from his car. Janice noticed it was a cup from a fast food restaurant he often frequented. The cup had not been there when he left his car with her before flying to Florida. When he finished preparing the coffee and snapped the top back on the cup he started walking toward the side door. Janice asked if they were still going to the music session they had planned to attend the following evening. Jack turned toward her with a look on his face she had never seen before. Janice could only later describe the look to a friend as that of pure evil.

"There won't be a music session," he coldly announced. "I've decided I want to be with Elaina! I've always had an attraction to her, even when she was still married, let herself go, and got fat."

Janice looked at him for a moment in total disbelief before she could speak. "How can you stand there and tell me this after sharing my bed, my body, and after you just sat there eating the food I prepared while acting like you didn't have a care in the world?" she asked. "It hasn't even been two full days since you told me you were bringing personal items here and I should do the same at your house! What in the world did that little slut say or do in order for you to make this decision after telling me we were such a good fit and she was just a friend? My god Jack! You spent the night with me on Friday and led me to believe everything was good between us before you left on Saturday morning!"

"I'm sorry," was all Jack could manage. He was not able to look at her. He continued to stand near the door and stare at the floor.

"You aren't sorry, or you wouldn't be doing this," replied Janice. "Oh my God!" she exclaimed. "I feel so dirty! You must have been sneaking around with her all those months you kept telling me she was just a friend and you wanted me in your life, not her! I don't know how I could have been so blind and stupid. I can't believe I ignored what my gut was telling me!"

For several seconds, Jack didn't respond. "There is no reason you should feel dirty. Our relationship has been a good one. You taught me I don't have to have an erection to sexually satisfy a woman."

"Our relationship has taught me to never trust a man again!" exclaimed Janice. She fought to hold back tears, determined not to give him the satisfaction of seeing her cry. "You knew I never allowed a man near me after Clayton died until you..."

Jack cut her off. "Don't go there!" he exclaimed. "I need to get out of here!" He walked closer to the side door leading out into the carport, rather than walk past her and make an exit through the front door.

"Here, take these writing contest entries you brought for me to judge. I'm done with anything connected to you!" declared Janice. She thrust the two packets into Jack's free hand. "I told you at the beginning of our relationship I would not be a party to cheating. I made it clear that if you ever wanted another woman I would get out of the picture as fast as possible, and I meant every word! Now get out of my house and don't ever come back!"

Jack paused. "Can't we talk about this?" he asked. "You have so many good qualities. Don't you think we can be friends?"

"There is absolutely nothing to talk about and no, we cannot be friends! You have made it crystal clear you want Elaina. That makes it evident that you are nothing but a liar and a cheat who has played me since day one! I can't think of anything coming out of your mouth that I would believe after what you've just said! You need to leave *now*!"

Jack continued to hesitate at the doorway as he fumbled with the contest entries in one hand while balancing his coffee cup in the other. "I want you to know I don't feel very good about myself right now."

"You shouldn't feel good about yourself! You lied to me from the beginning and played me for a complete fool!" replied Janice as she proceeded to walk toward him in order to force his exit then close and lock the door behind him. She then slumped down onto a chair at the nearby kitchen table, placed her head in her hands, and began to cry. "Why did he do this to me?" she questioned aloud into the empty room. "He led me to believe we had a future together and all the while he was carrying on a relationship with Elaina, a still married woman the age of his son. All that time, he was telling me she was just a friend. For God's sake, he encouraged me to move back to Tennessee when he learned my son was getting married and moving to Florida and I didn't want to stay in Georgia! He even suggested I consider moving in with him! Did he honestly think he could string both of us along at the same time? I should have listened to my gut. He was lying the entire time. I should have known something was going on between him and Elaina when she e-mailed mutual friends to mention the time she spent with him in his sauna to quote, "sweat out a cold," along with the time he took her to Julian's Super Bowl party while I was in California, telling them what a good time the two of them enjoyed. How could I have missed the signs? I loved and trusted the bastard, and this is what I get?"

Trance-like, a tearful Janice began to wander from room to room for much of the next two days unable to eat or sleep. She could not bring herself to believe the cold and cruel manner in which Jack ended their relationship. "What did I do wrong? Why wasn't I enough?" she kept asking herself. All she could think about was Jack telling her they were such a good fit all those months and he didn't want Elaina, he wanted her. "All I did was fall in love with him and he kept telling me she was just a friend!" she kept saying over and over. She tried to eat on the third day, but the lump in her throat prevented her from swallowing. She would wake up crying multiple times throughout the nights when she did finally go to bed.

She truly loved this man and wanted nothing from him but love and respect. Janice instinctively knew that wasn't the intent of Elaina. More than twenty two years Jack's junior, the same age as his son, Janice felt certain Elaina went about seducing Jack even before her divorce, planning to use his writing expertise and contacts to further her writing career. At the same time Janice figured Elaina didn't realize Jack was planning to use her, because she had told him she had contacts that could help him get a movie deal for one of his books. Janice overheard Elaina tell him that Monday night Jack invited her, the night she refused to eat the dinner Janice had prepared. Elaina had gone so far as to practice the 30-second phone messages (with him listening) that were required by the alleged movie producers to sell them on his book—producers whose names Janice was reasonably sure Elaina had obtained online through the information provided by the publishers of her anthologies. These were people who would expect to be paid to produce a movie if that actually happened, and the odds of that happening were, in all probability, less than zero.

Being a self-indulgent taker, Jack admitted he couldn't resist Elaina making the offer to get him a movie deal. His parting words rang in her ears like a song that keeps playing over and over in your head and you can't get rid of it no matter what you do . . . "There won't be any music concert. I have decided I want Elaina. I've always been attracted to her . . . she is offering me a movie deal . . . I could be making a big mistake, but this is something I feel I have to do."

Janice would keep remembering for a long, long time how Jack had the balls to say, as he continued to stand in the doorway before Janice told him to leave, "Can't we still be friends?" *There is not a snowball's chance in hell we can be friends!* kept playing like a loop in her brain. *You lied to me about your romantic involvement with Elaina. You made your choice, now live with it*, became the saving grace of her next few months, and it allowed her to eventually put the painful ordeal behind her. Janice made it a goal to move on with her life. But even when she moved on, she knew she would not forget Jack and what he had done for a long time, if ever.

Late the next afternoon there was a knock on the side door of her house. Janice peeked out from behind the blue and white gingham curtain covering the door's window to see who was there. She had no intention of allowing Jack back into the house or her life if he was stupid enough to come there after what he had done. She was surprised when there stood Dan, someone who had been doing yard work at Jack's house during the ten days she had stayed there after her return from California. She hadn't had much contact with him beyond preparing lunches for him and another worker. She couldn't help wondering why he was there as she slowly unlocked and opened the door a tiny crack.

"Hi Janice," said Dan. "I just came from working at Jack's house this morning. I was surprised when I didn't see you there so I asked him where you were. He said you weren't there because you were, to quote him, a little upset with him. He said it was personal. The way he was acting and pacing around the room I thought I needed to come by and make sure you were all right." Janice motioned for him to come inside and began to cry.

"Jack came here yesterday, ate the lunch I prepared for us, then dumped me for Elaina Albright," she sobbed. "I had no idea they were carrying on a relationship behind my back. When I asked about her he kept telling me she was just a friend and that he and I were a good fit."

"Oh no!" exclaimed Dan. "What the heck is wrong with him? It is obvious to anyone who has seen the two of you together you are such a good match."

"Apparently not a good enough match," sobbed Janice. "Elaina convinced him she can get him a movie deal on one of his books. She's still married and the same age as his son, for God's sake! I can't compete with that nor do I want to! I can't believe he came here, ate lunch, made himself a cup of coffee to go, then expected me to judge writing contest entries and drop them off at the library where he could pick them up later, when all the while he planned to dump me like yesterday's trash! You tell me what kind of man does that?"

"Gee Janice! It's hard to believe he would do something like that," replied Dan. He stood there shaking his head, a look of total disbelief on his face.

"Believe it, because that is exactly what happened!" declared Janice. "Why do you think he wouldn't tell you what he did? Don't you think he was covering his back side by telling you it was personal? I do. Think about it. If he were to tell you what took place it would definitely not make him look like a good person!"

Dan continued to shake his head in bewilderment. "I think he's lost his mind! He doesn't deserve someone like you. It's easy to see you are a kind and classy lady. I don't know much about Elaina, but from what I've heard from people who do know her, I don't think she has any class." Dan dropped his head to stare at the floor, unable to fully comprehend what had taken place between two people he believed to be so suited to each other. "Janice, I don't know what else to say, but I do know exactly what I'd like to say and do to Jack! You deserve better than that." It was obvious Dan was angry by the expression on his face and the way his arms hung tensely to his sides with fists clenching and un-clenching.

"Please, Dan, don't do anything foolish. You would end up in jail for assault. He isn't worth it," pleaded Janice. "Let Karma take care of both of them. You need the work at Jack's place, so don't cut off your nose to spite your face. They will get what's coming to them when they figure out each one is using the other for their own personal gain. You know, what goes around comes around. Please continue working for him and take every dollar you can from him with my blessing. Thank you for your concern for my well-being, but I will survive once I come to terms with having been played the fool."

Janice resisting the strong urge to let Dan know Jack had made fun of his heat stroke-related disabilities behind his back. Jack was using Dan just like he had used her and planned to use Elaina but knew she couldn't prove it at the time. She felt Dan would have to learn the hard way, just as she had learned, without her help, what a snake in the grass Jack was. *Jack doesn't yet realize Elaina is planning to use him is poetic justice*, she thought. But knowing this didn't lessen the intense emotional pain she was feeling at having been taken advantage of and coldly dropped by Jack for this tramp and her empty promises. She did take comfort in knowing Elaina was in for disappointment when she had to deal with the fact Jack was totally impotent and had no intention of a surgical intervention enabling him to perform in the bedroom as he had probably promised her he would eventually do. Janice was aware Elaina was angry with her husband's inability to satisfy her sexually; something she more than once, unashamedly, broadcast to anyone who would listen. Plus, Janice correctly guessed there was not the limitless amount of financial resources Elaina thought Jack had at his disposal.

Two days later Janice could hardly believe her eyes when she turned on her computer to find an e-mail from Jack. He was asking for her to take a look at what he had written concerning the book he had allegedly been researching in Florida. He wanted her opinion. This outraged her. "What in the hell is he thinking asking me to give an opinion? He must be out of his friggin' mind after telling me he wanted that little tramp Elaina! He doesn't deserve a response!" Later that day she changed her mind. She wrote, "You are to remove my name, address, phone number, and e-mail address from your files. Immediately! You have some nerve asking me to comment on your writing after dropping me for that disgusting piece of trash! Are you so stupid that you don't realize Elaina is promising to get your book made into a move in order to get your help in getting her books legitimately published? Are you so enamored with someone your son's age to foster a belief she will participate in a long-term romantic relationship with an impotent old man? Stop and think! She's still married! She is 22 years younger than you! You are not the man I thought you were. You are nothing but a self-serving liar and cheat who used me from day one! Just wait until she realizes you only want to use her in an effort to have a movie made and she becomes aware that you are impotent and have no intention of having surgery to solve that problem. She will drop you like a hot skillet, and you will end up a lonely, impotent, old man, especially when people learn what you have done to me. I would have been there for you no matter what life sent your way, but you blew it! Don't bother to respond. You are blocked on my cell phone and the computer."

Janice considered signing the e-mail using the code name they had shared when she'd believed they were in a committed relationship. This was done in case someone read their e-mails before they were ready to let people know. But at the last minute she decided against using it. The name was based on a Roman goddess responsible for peace and tranquility. That name definitely no longer fit the way she felt toward Jack. Janice fully realized she was being unkind to mention his age and impotence, but she was in no frame of mind to care. She had been used and hurt made and felt better lashing out. Soon, though, she found herself, once again, in tears.

She was so upset she rashly contacted her publisher and told her not to proceed with the latest novel Jack had helped her edit. She then called her son in Florida and tearfully told him what had taken place. "I can't stay here and watch those two," she cried. "We travel in the same circles here in Tennessee, and I can't bear it! You have to help me make a move to Florida."

"What! I thought everything was going great between the two of you," exclaimed Jason.

"I thought so, too," replied Janice. "I was wrong! Terribly wrong! I have been such a fool! I believed Jack. He kept telling me that bitch was just a friend and we were a good fit. I stood there and listened to part of a speaker phone conversation between the two of them with him telling her we had moved on to the next step in our relationship and she needed to find someone her own age." Janice could barely speak because she was crying so hard. "What he did and the way he did it makes me feel so stupid and dirty! All of the signs that she was more than just a friend were there. I can't believe I blindly chose not to see them. I have been such a stupid fool!"

"Mom, listen to me! You are not a stupid fool, and you have done nothing wrong. You fell in love with him and he is obviously a conman. I work to expose conmen every day in my job, and he's really good at conning people. He had me and everyone else who came in contact with him fooled while he visited in Georgia over Thanksgiving. We all thought he was a decent honest man. I'll start working on getting you a place to live here in Florida if that's what you really want to do. But you need to take some time and think this through. You got settled back in Tennessee only three weeks ago."

"I can't stay here and watch this play out," insisted Janice tearfully. "I loved and trusted him. It hurts too much. I can't believe I was so stupid not to have acted more forcefully on the signs he was lying before it came to this. I didn't want to believe he was such a low down son-of-a bitch while she pretended to be my friend and had the gall to say I betrayed her! Would you believe she told me I betrayed *her* when she came to Jack's house at his invitation for dinner and refused to eat what I had prepared? Jack just sat there calmly eating dinner and saying nothing while she verbally unloaded on me. To top it off, after she refused to eat, she just sat a across from me at the table staring daggers while sipping iced tea after mouthing off! After I finished pretending to eat and cleared the table, she had to know I sat in the living room and could hear her giggle, flirt, and convince Jack she had contacts that could help him get one of his books made into a movie. At the time I would have bet money she had no such contacts. She isn't even a legitimately published author beyond poorly written anthologies, the lowest form of published writing, in my opinion. I am certain she plans to use him to get published legitimately, and he plans to use her with the hope of getting a movie deal. I can only imagine what went on between them when he spent the weekend with her after spending the night with me when he came back from the Florida trip! I wouldn't be surprised to learn she joined him in Florida while he was supposedly researching the book. He certainly didn't have much of a rough draft to show me when he came back! "

His mother's sobs broke Jason's heart. She was a strong woman who had always been faithful to his Dad. He knew she believed Jack's and her relationship had become a committed one. To hear his mother in such distress made him want to find the bastard and set him straight. But at the same time, Jason was well aware this was not a viable option. He knew such a confrontation could end up with him going to jail on assault charges.

"Mom . . . Mom! Listen to me!" implored Jason. "How could you have known he would stoop so low? None of us knew. We all thought Jack was on the up and up," he insisted. "That's why people like him are known as conmen. They have no regard for anyone but themselves and what they want. People like him and that woman will do or say anything in order to get what they want, so don't be so hard on yourself," he pleaded.

"I'm sorry to have unloaded on you, Jason," said Janice as she tried to regain her composure. "But I have to get out of here. I just can't stay here in Tennessee and watch her make a fool out of him."

"I think he's already made a fool out of himself, but all right Mom, I'll start looking for a place for you. It will probably take a week or more. You know you are more than welcome to move in here with Suzanne, her mom, and me. There's plenty of room in the new Florida house."

"Thanks for the offer, but I need my own space. You already have a mother-in-law living with you. No house, even a big one like yours, has enough room for three grown women in one kitchen, even if they happen to like each other." Jason did not make an effort to argue with her. He knew what she said was the truth.

That same day after the call to her son, Janice tearfully took down the pictures she had so carefully hung on the walls. She removed dishes, pots, and pans and began to repack the rest of her belongings as Easter week approached. She knew she didn't want to be alone for the holiday—not after Jack had taken her to see the church where they were supposed to attend services and enjoy the community potluck meal afterward in the church social hall. She had already missed the dog rescue group fundraiser they were planning on attending together, and she would miss the award ceremony for the winners of the writing competition, something she had heavily invested time and money into over the past six years. Even during the two years she had moved away to Georgia, she had continued to sponsor scholarships in Clayton's name. She was supposed to present an award she sponsored to an underserved individual who showed promise as a writer. It hurt to know Elaina would take her place at these events, and probably in Jack's bed, without contributing a dime.

This prompted Janice to pick up the phone and call her son again two days later on Palm Sunday afternoon. "Would you mind if I flew down to Florida in order to spend Easter week at your house?" she asked. "I don't want to be here alone or with anyone I know. There will be too many questions asking why Jack isn't around if I join friends. I can't handle answering questions right now. It's that or me sitting here alone."

"Mom, you know you are always welcome to come here," replied Jason. "I think I've already got a couple of places lined up for you to take a look at, too. I would really like for you to see them while you're here instead of relying totally on my judgment. My friends are helping me look. They are sorry you've had to experience what this man has done. Keep in mind almost all of us have been dumped at one time or another. One girl I had been dating on a regular basis told me out of the blue she was mad at me and she ended our relationship without telling me why! To this day I still don't have a clue what I did wrong. You just don't have any idea what motivates some people."

"I know exactly what's motivating Jack. It's the promise of a movie deal and he's flattered someone the age of his son is interested in him on what he believes to be a romantic level. She is looking for him to promote her writing and she thinks he has deep pockets. It's that or she has a daddy complex. He can't see she is planning to use him, and she's unaware he plans to use her to further his ambitions. I've already checked flights and found an airline with the best rate at $178.00 round trip into Ft. Lauderdale. Spending Easter week with you guys will give me some time to lick my wounds and clear my head. Will you book it on line for me? I'll pay you back when I get there."

"Sure. I'll get right on it and get back to you with the flight numbers and departure schedules. I hope they still have seats. This is Palm Sunday and you want to fly two days from now on Tuesday. I'll try my best, but that's a really tight turnaround time, so I may not be able to make it happen."

"One airline still shows empty seats on the internet advertisement I just saw on the computer," insisted Janice. She spent the next half hour nervously pacing around in the living room where packing boxes permitted while she waited for Jason's response. He was able to book the flight, but he forgot to inform the airline travel site Janice would have luggage, and she would need a boarding pass. Janice wouldn't know this until she checked in at the airport. It would cost her an additional $50.00 for one bag and $5.00

for a boarding pass at the ticket counter. She didn't care. She just wanted out of "Dodge," no matter the cost.

Unsure who to ask for a ride to the airport, she called Dan since he told her to call him if there was anything he could do. He was gracious enough to take her to the airport, return her car to the attached carport of her house, and return the following week to pick her up. This would greatly reduce the possibility of someone breaking into or stealing her car if left in the airport parking garage for a week. Truthfully, she was in no emotional condition to be driving.

For once, Janice was glad to have a very talkative female seatmate during a flight. The constant chatter by this woman regarding her health issues kept Janice's mind off her troubles for the hour and 45-minute flight that didn't even serve water or a small package of peanuts without a significant charge.

Just as planned, her son was waiting in the baggage claim area at the Ft. Lauderdale airport when she arrived. Her daughter-in-law did not accompany him. She was surprised to learn Suzanne had facial and chin reduction plastic surgery early that morning and was recovering at their home with her mother's help. Jason kept telling Janice what happened between her and Jack was not her fault during the hour long drive to his home. He didn't understand that words did not help, so she decided to remain quiet and let him talk as the now unfamiliar landscape rolled past the car window, leaving her with a feeling of despair. Janice had no idea she would be stepping into a hornet nest instead of the healing environment she envisioned involving her own emotional trauma. If she had she known what lay ahead, she would have been more than happy to spend Easter Sunday alone and even eating a microwaved TV dinner rather than deal with what was about to unfold.

WHAT THE HEART WANTS

PART 2

CHAPTER 9

Traffic was heavy on I-95 during the drive north to her son's new home situated on a lake in a gated community near Stuart, Florida. What had been a four-lane highway was now six lanes in each direction. Many of what had been familiar landmarks to Janice years ago while living in the area were no longer along the busy interstate. There were even fewer familiar sights as they approached the area where her son's new house was located. What had been flower and vegetable farms had given way to a modern high school campus, a community college campus, a hospital, shopping centers, and exclusive housing developments. This was just the beginning of what turned out to be very confusing to her. She felt as though she was being transported to find herself in the middle of an foreign country instead of an area she and her now deceased husband once lived for almost twenty years. Janice had not been expecting everything to be the same as it was seven years ago, but she also did not expect so many drastic changes that left her feeling totally overwhelmed.

They arrived at Jason's home late that afternoon to find Suzanne in pain, not having taken the prescribed pain medication her doctor had ordered. She was wrapped in a bathrobe and sitting on the family room sofa in front of the TV. She had an ice pack under her chin and a cold compress above her eyes. Janice leaned over and kissed her on the shoulder and said hello. She responded with a groan. Suzanne's mother, Monica, got up from a nearby chair to come forward to give Janice a hug. What was meant to be a comforting gesture on her part caused Janice to start crying, something she had vowed not to do.

"Oh Monica!" she sobbed. "This has been such a shock and I am so hurt. I had to get away and clear my head."

Monica let her continue to cry while embracing her, patting her back and telling her what happened was for the best. "He's not worth it. It's his loss," Monica kept saying over and over. Janice knew what she was saying was true, but her words didn't take away the hurt. She honestly believed her life was in a shambles because she loved and trusted a man she thought she knew, and that somehow, what had transpired was her fault. She struggled to regain her composure while her son escorted her to the bedroom she would be using, then on a tour of his lovely, new, four-bedroom home to distract her.

Janice let her son know she thought their house was beautiful. It had plenty of room for most of Monica's furniture along with that belonging to Jason and Suzanne. As sad as she felt, Janice was pleased her son had been able to purchase a comfortable home. He had given his ex-wife almost everything they owned six years ago when he filed for divorce after spending twelve miserable years enduring her whining and demanding ways. The divorce had not surprised Janice. In fact, she was surprised it hadn't happened years earlier. Her name, Joy, did not reveal her true nature until after she had a wedding ring on her finger. Then her self-centered, demanding personality quickly emerged to become more and more pronounced over the years Jason stayed with her.

The next morning Janice found it comforting to sit in the large, screened back porch of Jason's home overlooking a lake. It gave her time to think about what she wanted to do with the rest of her life. She knew she could not continue to make a home in Tennessee and watch a man she once loved made a fool of by that scheming little bitch who pretended to be her friend. Nor could she consider forgiving Jack for the cruel way he tossed her aside after his deliberate lies. Janice decided she fully intended to find a place to live in Florida near her son and new daughter-in-law during her week's stay.

She liked the first apartment her son took her to see. "I don't need to look any farther," she told him. The leasing agent took little time in coming up via computer with the financial and credit check information required to allow Janice to know she had been approved to live in the gated community. The next stop was at Bank of America to set up a checking account and make the necessary deposits for natural gas, electric, and automatic rent payments to be deducted from the checking account.

It was disheartening a day later when she learned she had been given the wrong address for her apartment. A power company representative called late the following morning to say the address given to her by an office staff member was for the leasing office and not her apartment. Not being aware this error occurred, Janice had also given this address when the bank account and credit card was established shortly after leaving the leasing office. The bank was called immediately, but apparently not fast enough. They had already issued a credit card and ordered checks with the incorrect address, making it necessary to tackle the situation with everyone again. This was not a good start to a new life. In the meantime, the bank had a large portion of her monetary assets, and she had no access to funds beyond counter checks and some identification numbers since she didn't believe in using an ATM card. Her mail would end up being sent to the leasing office until the appropriate change of address could be made to various companies and friends who had been contacted. This would require Janice or Jason to go to the leasing office to pick up Janice's mail until she actually moved into the apartment; and that wasn't scheduled to take place for two weeks following a complete renovation. "Good luck on the apartment renovations taking only two weeks," she told her son.

The area where the apartment complex was located no longer proved to be familiar to her. Her son didn't seem to understand her confusion. This helped her make the decision she could not move to Florida. This turned out to be a decision that would be re-enforced by two more events.

Easter Sunday in Florida dawned cloudy and cool accompanied by drizzling rain. Her daughter-in-law couldn't make up her mind if she wanted to attend church services. Her elective chin surgery was still in need of an elastic cloth support to her chin. Her eyelids were puffy and discolored from the surgery to remove excess skin she felt blocked her vision. Pain medication offered minimal relief. Members of her family from New York were visiting the area. This included her only brother, his wife, and their two children. Suzanne did not get along with her brother and sister-in-law for valid reasons. They insisted they had a right to come and see the new house Jason recently purchased to make sure their elderly mother, who was also living there, was being given good care in pleasant surroundings. At first Suzanne said she didn't want them coming there, but then relented and decided she would go to church, regardless of her appearance and level of pain. She also allowed her brother and his family to make a brief visit immediately following the service, as long as Jason and her mother conducted the tour.

Everything seemed to be tense but under control while they were all sitting in the same pew at church, even though Suzanne did not speak to her brother, his wife, their daughter, or their son. After the service it was agreed upon through conversations with Jason and Suzanne's mother and brother they would follow them to the new home, take a look around, and leave.

Suzanne's mother and Jason, as agreed, took them on a tour of the house while Suzanne paced around in areas where they were not present. Janice remained seated on the back porch to stay out of the way. When it was time for Suzanne's brother and family to leave, they came out onto the back porch to tell Janice goodbye. Suzanne followed them, and to everyone's surprise, she unexpectedly hugged her brother. Everyone thought the healing process between them had started after the inspiring church sermon presented by the pastor that morning. They left the porch and started to walk across the expanse of the open floor plan to end up in the hallway near the front door. That's when Janice, still seated on the back porch, heard Suzanne screaming obscenities, followed by a commotion caused by loud noises, as though someone was pounding on a wall.

It turned out Suzanne had grasped both sides of her sister-in'-laws face and began slamming her head against the wall. When Jason was able to pull Suzanne off the terrified woman, he suffered resounding blows to his face and chest by Suzanne. Suzanne, her brother, sister-in-law, niece, and nephew were all screaming obscenities at one another while her family members made a hasty exit from the house! "Get the f... out of my house and never come back!" Suzanne screamed at the top of her lungs to her retreating family.

Janice, having dashed from the back porch to see what was happening, was appalled by her daughter-in-law's behavior, and said as much. Then Suzanne, in spite of Jason trying to calm her, turned away from him to begin verbally attacking Janice in an obscene manner. Janice held her tongue, allowing her to continue briefly before responding.

"I'm sorry Suzanne, but I have never been a witness to anything like the behavior you just displayed toward your family members! I find it hard believe what you just said and did to your family! Furthermore, I will not allow you to speak to me this way!"

"Well you better get used to it or get the f. . . out of my house with the rest of them!" Suzanne screamed like a mad woman.

Before this episode, Janice and Suzanne had been the best of friends, enjoying a loving relationship like that between a mother and daughter. They shared meals, chats, and shopping trips together. Janice loved her daughter-in-law and thought the feeling was mutual. Suzanne's outburst left Janice in a state of shock. Jason intervened by taking his mother's arm and leading her out of the main house and into the attached garage.

"I need to get you out of here so she can calm down," Jason told her. "Come on Mom, let's go get some lunch."

Janice had been grocery shopping the day before, planning to prepare a traditional baked ham meal for their Easter dinner, but the unfortunate circumstances did not allow her to make the necessary final preparations. She was softly crying in a state of total disbelief when she got into her son's car and they drove to a nearby deli. During the drive there Jason kept offering apologies for the behavior of his wife. Janice sat in the front passenger seat continuing to cry silent tears with little to say.

Once seated in the busy deli they ordered soup and sandwiches and planned to order food to take back to Suzanne's mother, who insisted she remain behind at the house. She was hoping to calm her daughter. The soups had just been delivered to their table when Jason's cell phone alerted him there was a text message from Suzanne. It read, "I'm looking for your gun, and I'm going to kill myself!" Jason's face paled as he read the message aloud to his mother. "It won't take her long to find the gun," he said. "What do I do now, Mom?" asked her obviously shaken son.

"You don't have a choice. You have to call 911. She is threatening suicide and her mother could be in jeopardy as well," said Janice. Jason stepped outside the deli to make the 911 call, knowing the police would be able to arrive at the house before he and Janice could make it back there, and he was right. Two black and white squad cars were sitting on the street in front of the house when they arrived approximately ten minutes later. The police dispatcher, who had remained on the line with Jason, instructed him that he should park away from the house, and both he and his mother should remain in the locked car for their own protection until given the all-clear signal by an officer. Jason ignored the instructions and pulled into the driveway, intending to enter the house as he pressed a button that opened the garage door automatically from inside his car. "Please, don't go in there!" cautioned a fearful Janice. "She could have found the gun. In her current state of mind she could shoot you, the officers, both of us, and her mother. She can't possibly be in her right mind!"

"You stay here in the car and lock it," replied a determined Jason. "She won't shoot me or her mother. She has had other blowups, just not as bad as this one is turning out to be."

Janice had only witnessed one other outburst by Suzanne. That instance involved a police officer neighbor living in their same apartment complex in Georgia. This happened when he took in one of the stray cats as a pet that she had been feeding. But that encounter had been mild compared to what Janice witnessed today. This time there was no doubt that Suzanne was totally out of control.

Janice was in a state that could only be described as near panic as she watched her only son calmly walk through the open, two-car garage and on into the house. Another officer, a female, soon arrived to enter the house through the front door without knocking. About half an hour later Suzanne exited the same door with her hands cuffed in front or her. She was flanked by the two male officers, and the female officer followed close behind. She was then placed in the backseat of a patrol car. It was clear to Janice, as a former psych nurse, Suzanne would be Baker Acted into the psychiatric ward of a nearby hospital. The Baker Act allows the holding of a person threatening harm to himself or others for 72 hours without their consent while a mental evaluation is done to determine the next step of care.

Suzanne saw Janice sitting in Jason's car as she was being led down the sidewalk toward the police cruiser. She raised her handcuffed hands and extended the middle finger of her right hand in order to shake it toward Janice and silently mouth the words, "Screw you!" Jason stood in the open garage doorway, watching this take place with a look of pure anguish and defeat on his face as his wife was placed in the squad car and taken away. Janice closed her red, swollen eyes and looked away, unable to bear the anguish on her son's face.

"You can come back inside now Mom," he said when Janice continued to sit in the car in a state of disbelief. She was able to slowly unlock the door, get out, and go inside with a feeling of numbness throughout her body and mind; not unlike the numbness she felt when Jack announced he wanted Elaina and not her.

Suzanne's elderly mother was standing outside her bedroom door sobbing uncontrollably. Janice managed to step forward and give her a hug but could not find the right words to convey her feelings. She was thankful Suzanne's brother and nephew returned to the house, trying unsuccessfully to comfort Monica. Suzanne's brother turned to Jason and told him he had done the right thing by calling the police. "Suzanne has had problems for years," he continued while looking directly toward Janice. "We didn't know what to do when she acted out, so nothing was ever done." He then shocked Jason and Janice when he stated he suspected Suzanne was also a closet alcoholic. Monica nodded her head in agreement to this statement. Several minutes later they left with a distraught Monica, insisting she spend the night with them. This gave Jason and Janice an opportunity to sit quietly on the back porch and pick at sandwiches Janice had the deli place in to-go boxes. The two tried to process the day's events.

"You know you will have to go to the hospital admissions office to give them Suzanne's medical history and insurance information, so you need to give the admissions clerk a call," stated Janice. Jason nodded, gave a dejected sigh, and made the call. As suspected the clerk wanted him to come to the hospital emergency room as soon as possible to complete and sign their forms.

"I guess I need to go," he said. "Will you be all right here alone Mom?

"I'll be all right. You need to go take care of your wife," Janice insisted. "I would offer to go with you but seeing me might upset Suzanne even more."

It was five o'clock in the afternoon when Jason left the house to head for the hospital. Three hours would pass before he called to let Janice know the emergency staff was allowing him to stay with Suzanne. It was almost midnight before he returned home after she was taken to a room on the psych ward and sedated for the night. Janice waited up for him, knowing full well she would not be able to sleep until she knew her son was safe and emotionally okay.

She didn't know what to expect when the automatic garage door opened and Jason entered the house through the laundry room into the family room. It was obvious he had been through the mill. His face was drawn and haggard; his eyes were swollen. Janice knew without a doubt he had been crying. "Suzanne is scared and angry with me for calling the police," said Jason wearily in response to the questioning look from his mother. "I've never seen her act quite like she has been acting today. I don't know if she's an alcoholic. I've never seen her drink to excess, even when we go out to a bar or a party."

"Closet alcoholics seldom drink to excess when others are present unless the disease is completely out of control," said Janice. "They drink in secret so nobody knows. That way they don't have to admit to themselves or anyone else they have a problem. They don't become slobbering, out of control drunks until they are well along in the disease. At least that much appears to be in her favor since she apparently hasn't made it to that stage yet. But you need to check the house thoroughly to find where she has hidden her stashes. There is usually more than one hiding place, so look everywhere. You did the right thing, son," said Janice in an effort to reinforce what Suzanne's brother had said. "She needs help, a lot more help than any of us can give her. We are all too close to the situation to be effective."

That night Janice lay there awake, praying Suzanne would not be able to con the psychiatrist into letting her come home too soon. When rational, Suzanne could be extremely convincing and charming. Two days later, just as Janice suspected, Suzanne was able to talk the doctor into letting her come home instead of extending the 72-hour stay or receiving further treatment beyond her promise to see a psychiatrist. She was scheduled for release late on Tuesday evening, and Janice was relieved to know she was scheduled to fly back to Tennessee early on Tuesday morning. The two of them would not have any contact.

This did little to ease her fear that Suzanne could harm her son, even though he assured her his hand gun was now in a locked safe and Suzanne did not know the combination. On the drive to the airport Jason also let his mother know he did find stashes of alcohol hidden in various places throughout the house. Janice was aware her daughter-in-law's outrageous behavior could have been caused by symptoms associated with not being able to sneak drinks during the time she could not eat or drink fluids prior to the plastic surgery; along with knowing Janice might easily discover her alcoholism. Suzanne was aware her mother-in-law worked at a drug and alcohol rehab unit early in her career when working as a nurse.

Janice felt certain there were other underlying serious mental issues as well. Suzanne had once told Janice that she experienced profound verbal and physical abuse, broken bones included, at the hands of her ex-husband. This part of her life occurred before she got up the nerve to divorce him, and she met Jason a few years later. There had been no professional help between the divorce and marriage to Jason.

Janice dreaded what she would face upon the return to Tennessee. Not only were there all of those packing boxes stacked everywhere, she also had to face being reminded of the places Jack had occupied, especially the bedroom they had shared, and know the plans they made would not happen. This was in addition to worrying about the safety of her son and what would become of her daughter-in-law. This prompted her to spend the remainder of her time in Tennessee attempting to sleep in the guest bedroom each night. She could not sleep in the bed she and Jack had shared.

Many of her possessions were packed to get ready for the move before she left for the Florida visit. But there were still odds and ends remaining. She couldn't seem to get motivated enough to finish the task at hand. The moving truck and packers weren't scheduled for arrival until the end of the month when Jason could take time off work to come to Tennessee and oversee the move. Hopefully, Suzanne would be under psychiatric care and more stable by then. This knowledge allowed her to think she had plenty of time to prepare. She knew it was time for her to break the news to her landlord that she was moving out early and why. He and his wife had been nice to her. She dreaded making the call. Janice was aware she would have to buy out the remainder of her rental contract, but she was prepared to do that rather than face the distinct possibility of being in awkward and painful contact with Jack.

The landlord was very understanding when Janice broke the news by phone. He came to her house a short time later, not for the payout check, but to offer moral support.

This is when she learned he had gone through a similar situation of being betrayed. He told her his first wife cheated on him after a 26-year marriage, and he felt the need, just as Janice was doing, to make sure there was plenty of distance between them. He then made the comment, "That woman who came to join us for dinner on St. Patrick's Day made some comments that led me to believe there was something going on between your friend Jack and her . . . like the suggestive way she mentioned giving him a massage when he said his muscles were hurting, the way she ignored you by directing her conversations toward him, and how she made such an issue of ordering the same meal he ordered." There was no getting around the fact the woman her landlord was referring to was Elaina. Janice swallowed hard, but she didn't cry.

"Please don't let what this man has done taint how you feel about men," he told her. "There are a lot of nice guys out there, and I'm sure you will find one of them."

Janice merely nodded in response rather than let him know that for her, none of them would ever stand a chance to prove they were nice guys. She felt certain she could no longer trust any man after what Jack did.

Looking back at what transpired Janice could not help wondering why Jack invited Elaina to join them for dinner on St. Patrick's Day and not had the courtesy to mention it to her. He knew her landlord and his wife would be joining them because she asked him if that would be all right, and he said it was okay. He didn't tell her he invited Elaina until he saw her enter the restaurant and start looking around for their party. Just as she had done at the two meetings at Jack's house, Elaina did not acknowledge Janice's presence except to stare daggers her way throughout the evening. There was no mistaking she was batting her eyes in a flirty manner toward Jack and directing her conversation toward him from across the table as though Janice weren't seated right there beside him.

To say that evening was uncomfortable would be nothing less than a gross understatement. The atmosphere was such that it prevented Janice from eating her meal. She did move food around on her plate to give the impression she was eating in an attempt to make her guests feel less uncomfortable at what was obviously taking place. Once the evening ended, Elaina gave Jack a lingering hug and kiss on the cheek before she left. On the way to the car Janice asked him why he had invited Elaina to join them and failed to mention it to her until the last minute.

"I knew she was going to be alone, and I have already told you I'm grooming her to take over the writers group. End of conversation!"

Jack made it clear he didn't want to talk about it anymore. He drove to his house even though Janice insisted she wanted to be taken to her house. She did this even though going there at this late hour would mean boxes stacked on the beds would need to be moved in order for her to have a place to sleep.

Janice could not help remembering when Jack said, "It's late, and you don't really want to go back there. The house is still in disarray. I keep telling you there isn't anything going on between Elaina and me! What else do I have to do to prove it? You are staying at my house. We are sleeping together. I have introduced you to some of my friends. What is it with you? It isn't like you to be the jealous type."

Janice remained quiet throughout his verbal rampage. She didn't want to fight with Jack. It reminded her of the fights that took place between her parents when she was a child.

That night when they went to bed Jack insisted Janice lie close to him with her head resting on his shoulder, but he made no effort at further contact, not even a goodnight kiss, and neither did she. The next morning he was all smiles as if nothing out of the ordinary had taken place between them the previous night. Janice now regretted the fact she went along with his behavior rather than face more arguing.

"I should have known," Janice lamented to her landlord. "He has been playing me all along, and like a fool, I believed him."

"There is no way you could have known. You don't think like he does. I can tell you aren't the kind of person who treats others the way he treated you. I've been a landlord for a very long time. I know people."

While grateful for her landlord's attempt to show understanding, it didn't help sooth Janice's feelings of being a failure as a woman. She felt stupid for not having listened to her gut. She should have acted more quickly on the signs Jack was not being honest with her. It didn't help when her daughter, Belinda, called later that same day from California. After talking with her brother, Belinda was upset about what had taken place regarding the Florida visit. "Mom, why didn't you call and tell me what went down involving Suzanne's crazy behavior?" questioned Belinda.

"I'm sorry I didn't call you, but you are so far away and everything has been such a mess. I couldn't bring myself to make the call and upset you when there was nothing you could do about it. Forgive me," offered Janice. Belinda then expressed understanding.

"Jason filled me in. I am so sorry you had to experience that on top of what had happened with Jack. I don't know if it helps to know he fooled me just like he fooled the rest of us," said Belinda before continuing. "Mom, are you sure you want to move to Florida? I know you don't like the humidity or bugs, and everything has changed a lot since you and Dad lived there. With what Jason has told me, he will have his hands full taking care of Suzanne and dealing with her family. You have made a lot of friends here in

California during the winters you've spent at the Palm Springs house. You can stay there until you find suitable housing, and that should be easy. I know you want your own place. There are apartments and condos out the wazoo in and around the area where you would want to live. I can get right on it to find one for you."

"I don't know what to do," said Janice with pure anguish in her voice. "All of the details are in place for me to make the move to Florida. Your brother has gone out of his way to help me make them. I'm approved for housing in a lovely gated community in Palm City not far from where your dad and I once lived. The only thing left to do is for me to sign the lease. I've moved money into a bank account there. A date for the utilities to be turned on has been confirmed, and a moving company is already arranged and deposits are made. I don't think it would be right for me to back out now."

"But Mom, are you happy with this arrangement?" countered Belinda.

Janice felt she had to be honest and admit moving to Florida wasn't what she really wanted to do. The apartment she was scheduled to move into, while lovely, was smaller than she wanted. The location was completely foreign to her due to all the changes that had taken place in the area. Her daughter-in-law had ordered her out of their home in a fit of rage and not made any attempt to apologize since the incident. Her son was facing what would more than likely prove to be a long recovery process involving his wife that could end up in divorce if she refused to cooperate with treatment. Janice knew she was not equipped to deal with all that drama on top of her own health issues and emotional distress. At the same time she felt an obligation to her son for all the work he had done to make the move there as easy as possible.

"If you aren't happy with moving to Florida, you should definitely reconsider. You, of all people, should know life is too short to be living where you are not happy," insisted Belinda.

"No, I am not happy with the Florida decision, but I can't let Jason down. He has put a lot of time and effort into helping me, and it wouldn't be fair," she continued to insist.

"Mom, you won't be letting Jason down. He told me he wants you to be happy, no matter where you choose to live, so think about it. Between the two of us we can make whatever you want happen."

"I don't know what I want, except I do know I do not want to continue living here in Tennessee," said Janice through tears. "How could Jack do this to me? All I did was fall in love with him and try to help him deal with his wife's loss and find happiness again. I stupidly believed it when he told me that little tramp, Elaina, was just a friend, when the entire time he was lying through his damned teeth!"

"Mom, how many times do I have to tell you that you are NOT stupid? Jack had us all fooled," insisted Belinda. "You need to think about the fun you did have when you and he spent time together and move on with your life. Chalk it up to a learning experience. I'll call you again in a day or two after you've had time to think about what I've said. Just keep remembering Jason is going to have his hands full with Suzanne, along with her mother and the rest of her family. Jack is history. We both know it will not be easy, but you can do it!"

After she hung up Janice sat and cried for the better part of an hour, remembering those nights she had allowed Jack to touch her body, she his body, and how dirty, used, and betrayed she now felt. "God, please forgive me," she pleaded. "What I allowed to happen was totally wrong!

CHAPTER 10

Janice spent the next three restless days and nights mulling over what Belinda had said. Then she called to let her know she would change plans and make the move to California instead of Florida. "I hope Jason won't be angry with me for making this decision after all he has done."

"Mom, he won't be angry with you. In fact we talked again this morning and he said he knew you really didn't want to make the move to Florida. He was going along with you, just like you have gone along with him in setting up the arrangements for your move there. How soon do you want to fly out here to California and take a look at apartments or condos?"

"Today," answered Janice bleakly. She knew full well that would be impossible, but she hoped her answer would relay the message of just how ready she was to leave Tennessee.

"Mom, get serious. I need some time to find suitable properties where you might want to live. Plus, airline ticket prices will be sky high on such a short notice. Give me two weeks."

Janice was miserable at the thought of having to wait two weeks before leaving Tennessee, but she agreed it made more sense to wait. This meant she would have to make a trip to the grocery store for necessary food. She hoped she wouldn't run into Jack, who often shopped at this same store. The market had a high-end coffee service in the little café located just inside the entrance. Being seen there might mean answering questions from friends about why Jack was no longer around. Dan knew what had taken place, and she felt certain he would talk to mutual friends.

Although painful, Janice let her good friends Mary and her husband Harold know what Jack had done. She believed Jack was counting on her not to say anything to anyone about his behavior, just as she had remained silent about their budding relationship, or about Elaina's outrageous behavior. Janice decided she would tell everyone who asked exactly what had taken place with no holds barred. She figured they should know Elaina's true nature and that Jack wasn't the man they all thought he was.

"I'm going over to his house to scratch his eyes out!" declared her friend Mary. "Don't let him and that little slut run you out of here! Why, you just got back to Tennessee and got settled! We all love you and want you to stay."

"Please, Mary, don't do anything stupid. I appreciate your support, but he isn't worth upsetting you. Should you attack him, you would end up going to jail. Please understand. I can't stay here and watch the two of them engage in the things he and I would have done. It would destroy me more than it already has. I'm going to start over by moving to California in two weeks."

"What's this about moving to California? I thought you told me you were moving to Florida."

"Florida was the original plan, but Mary, as you well know, plans can and do change. I really don't like the idea of returning to Florida to live. I have too many memories about living there when my husband was alive. Most of the friends we shared there have moved on with their lives. As a single, widowed woman I would be viewed as a fifth wheel. And there is the issue of my daughter-in-law's mental illness. That, and the humidity for most of the year can be really terrible, not to mention there are hurricanes and bugs everywhere! I have family and friends in California. And don't you dare remind me they have earthquakes out there." added Janice.

Mary kept quietly sipping her wine for several minutes while she mulled over what Janice had just said to her. "You have a point. Maybe it is best for you move to California, but you have to allow Harold and me to visit. You know I grew up not far from where you spend winters out there, and I need a reason to keep fighting this illness that threatens to kill me. I need the hope of visiting you out there to keep me going."

Janice could not resist giving Mary a hug. "You know you are always welcome to visit, but please give my daughter and me a little time to find a place for me to live and get settled. I don't want to live with her and my son-in-law year-round. They don't need a mother and mother-in-law living in their home full time, especially not while I'm an emotional train wreck. My son-in-law is starting to think about selling his business and retiring. I know he and Belinda have dreamed of making their home permanently in the Palm Springs house when Tom retires in a year or two."

"I didn't know Tom was close to retiring," said Mary. "Your daughter is only in her early thirties. Tom can't be that much older, but now that you mention it I do seem to recall you telling me that Tom is a lot older than Belinda. He doesn't look or act his age, but even then he will only be in his early fifties at the most." She smiled and went on to say, "I guess it's better to be an older man's darling than a young man's slave, as the old saying goes."

"When I said *retiring*, what I meant was he will be running his business by computer and won't need to be in the office very much . . . if he doesn't find a suitable buyer."

Mary sensed Janice was somewhat embarrassed by her comments regarding the age difference between her daughter and son-in-law, resulting in Janice feeling the need to defend her daughter's choice of a husband, so she turned the conversation back to Jack. "What in the world was Jack thinking? Didn't he know when he had it good by finding someone as loving and loyal like you?"

"Obviously not or he wouldn't have done what he did. Jack has his own agenda and doesn't care about me, but let's change the subject, please. That man has made himself history in my life. Now where is that strawberry ice cream you said you had for dessert?"

Janice ended up giving Mary and Harold many items she felt she could not take with her to California. In return they provided dinners and lots of moral support. Harold went so far as to accompany her, with Mary's blessing, to say goodbye to her musician friends for the second time—the first time being her goodbye when she moved to Georgia two years earlier. They were all shocked when she revealed the reason she felt she had no choice but to leave so soon after returning to Tennessee. She squared her shoulders, took a deep breath, and even though she knew it was going to be difficult, explained. She didn't want to go without telling them why she was leaving.

Saying goodbye to friends who had stood by her during Clayton's illness and death turned out to be more painful than she imagined.

"Jack lied to me about his relationship with an unscrupulous, younger, married woman. He was spending time with her while he played me along by telling me they were just friends," she told them. "I need to start a new life away from here, but you and all of my other Tennessee friends know I will miss you. I hope you understand my need to move away." While expressing their understanding, several of them cried and tried to convince her to tough it out. It was all she could do to keep from crying as she made her exit. Harold drove her back home, where she would live among the painful memories and packing boxes for the next two weeks.

She was able to put the tears on hold until after he left and she was alone to face reality. "Why in the hell am I crying over that son-of-a-bitch?" she asked herself. "He threw me away like a piece of trash!" But deep in her heart, she knew she still had feelings for the man who betrayed her trust. It would take a lot of time to forget him, much less forgive him.

A week before Janice was scheduled to fly to California, she called Dan to ask if he wanted to stop by her place and pick up a custom-made computer wood cabinet he had admired. "You bet!" he replied. She also asked if he could take her to the airport again for the flight to California the following Friday. He immediately agreed.

He arrived the next day in his pickup truck close to lunchtime. Janice warmed up two frozen dinners in the microwave since she knew he was on a limited budget and would probably skip eating lunch. Dan, who finished eating first, excused himself and went into the living room to take measurements of the large piece of furniture she had offered him. He needed to make sure it would fit up the stairs and into his apartment. Janice had just finished her meal when he came back into the kitchen to find her slumped over the table, barely able to speak.

"Janice! What's wrong?" he said while lifting her to an upright position.

"S . . . s . . . stroke," she managed to say pointing to her head with her left hand. She was unable to raise her right hand or arm or move her right leg. "C . . . c . . . call 9 . . . 1 . . . 1." She tried to get up, but her right leg would not support her weight. She continued to try but could not move her right hand, arm, or leg. Somehow, Dan managed to help her into the living room and onto the sofa. "Need cell phone . . . c . . . all . . . my . . . son." She was not able to make the call. Dan made the call after he called 911 in order to get her to the hospital as quickly as possible. He placed the phone up to Janice's ear and mouth where she could barely let her son know she was having another stroke.

"Hang in there Mom. I'm on my way there as soon as I can get a flight," said Jason. He had power of attorney over Janice's medical condition when she could not act on her own behalf. Upon his late-night arrival in Tennessee, Jason found it necessary to call several hospitals in the area to learn where his mother was taken by ambulance, since he was not given this information and didn't know Dan's phone number.

Dan followed the ambulance in his pick-up truck and stayed seated in the emergency room waiting area for several hours while Janice was being treated before he was allowed to be at her bedside. There was no doubt that her speech and the right side of her body were affected. She continued to have no control over her right arm, hand, or leg, and she had difficulty speaking. She was told she was being admitted to the hospital but not until after a CAT scan of her brain was done and read by the neurologist in case it was necessary to transfer her to a more specialized hospital.

The local neurologist determined a transfer would not be necessary, but Janice needed to be kept as a patient. Dan remained seated at her bedside until she was able to let him know it was time for him to leave around five p.m. "Thank . . . you. You . . . are . . . my . . . guardian angel, but you . . . need to go home . . . and . . . get some supper and . . . some sleep," she told him in painfully slow words. Dan smiled.

"I'm glad you are able to speak, even if it is slow. You really had me worried. Do you have any feeling in your arm or leg yet?" Janice was able to tell him she had some feeling, but she still did not have full control over movement on her right side.

"I know . . . what I want to say . . . but some of the words . . . won't come out." She told him.

Dan left, reluctantly, saying he would return in the morning. He said he wanted to meet her children who were about his same age. "I have to meet the kids who dropped everything to be with you," he said. "I've never had anyone to look after me since I was fourteen years old when my old man shot my ma and went to prison. The uncle I was sent to live with by the state didn't want me. He only did it for the money he got paid." This was when Janice realized Dan's interest in her wellbeing was because she had been nice to him.

Janice was taken from the ER to a third-floor hospital room on the cardiac unit around three that afternoon. This decision was made so she could be monitored for heart activity, since personnel were aware of her irregular heart beat problems after pulling up old records showing she had been treated at the same hospital for elevated blood pressure and arrhythmia several years prior. A little past five p.m. she could tell something had changed. The feeling of cotton in her head was less pronounced, and she could put words together without as much effort. The feeling in her right arm and leg were still not normal. She was instructed by her nurse not to get out of bed unaccompanied for any reason.

She was seen again by the neurologist later that same evening around five p.m. He didn't give any indication of what might have happened to her following his examination, but as a former nurse and stroke patient, Janice strongly suspected she was experiencing what is known as a TIA, a transient blockage of an artery in the brain caused by a blood clot. She was hoping the blood thinner she was taking would kick in to dissolve the clot if that was the problem. By the time her children arrived at eleven p.m. that evening, her speech, while still not perfect, and the feeling in her right side had for the most part returned.

When her son arrived at the hospital at eleven p.m. that night, accompanied by her daughter, who met Jason at the Nashville airport after a hastily booked flight from California, the ER admissions clerk told them the room number on the third floor where Janice could be found. She kept repeatedly telling her children she was sorry to have created such a problem for them. They kept telling her she wasn't a problem, but that thought would continue to plague her for a long time. She found it difficult to dismiss how they had both dropped what they were doing and booked flights to be with her at what she knew was a considerable effort and expense on such short notice.

"Mom, do you still want to make the move to California?" her daughter asked the following morning.

"Now more than ever," Janice clearly answered without any hesitation. "I have no doubt this stroke happened as a result of the stress created by what Jack did. Just look at the ripple effect he's had on all of us! I wouldn't even be considering another move and all it entails if he had been a truly caring and trustworthy man!"

"You have to let it go, Mom," said Jason. "You can't change what happened. You have to move on. You can't let what Jack did affect you like this. You are a strong woman. I know you can make a fresh start."

"Easier said than done," mumbled Janice. "I just want to get out of here. Hospitals are dangerous places!"

"The doctor wants you to have an MRI tomorrow to make sure there isn't any more damage to your brain that didn't show up on the initial CAT scan," said Belinda. "If that's clear, we've been told you'll be discharged. We've also been told you are dehydrated and your blood urea nitrogen is elevated," Belinda replied. "You need to drink more water to help thin your blood. The nurse told me they plan to administer an electrolyte-balanced IV later tonight."

"I don't need or want an IV! I've been drinking plenty of water," insisted Janice, even though she knew that probably wasn't true, especially during the past few days since her return to Tennessee from Florida. "I know I have good insurance, but I don't like the idea of the hospital taking advantage of it when I am perfectly capable of drinking more water!"

Jason smiled. "I can see you are getting back to being your spunky self, Mom." Janice could only hope he was right in his assessment.

"Are you telling me you are refusing the IV?" the nurse asked later that night.

"That would be a definite yes," answered Janice. She couldn't believe it when the nurse continued to prepare to administer the IV. This was after Janice made it clear she didn't want it. The nurse shook her head and proceeded to place a plastic bag filled with clear fluid on an IV pole at the foot of the bed before leaving the room in a huff. "What a waste," Janice mumbled as she turned over in bed and prepared to go to sleep after sending her kids to spend the night at her home.

The next morning Janice felt she was stable enough to at least go wash her face at the hospital bathroom sink before her kids returned. Against advice, she proceeded to slide out of bed, testing to see if her right leg could hold her weight. Satisfied it would hold her with a little support by placing her hand on the wall, she hesitantly walked into the bathroom, shut the door, and began washing her face. Refreshed, she was sitting up at the side of the bed trying to eat a low salt, low cholesterol, diabetic, heart diet breakfast that was left on her bedside table while she was in the bathroom. At least that is what the scrap of paper said that had been placed on the tray. She couldn't believe the tray featured a container of orange juice (she was a diabetic), an artery-clogging blueberry muffin, four fried sausage links, a large serving of scrambled eggs, a half pint of skim milk, and a cup of what she assumed was regular coffee. She had told the admitting nurse she was a diabetic, and that she couldn't tolerate caffeine, not even decaf tea or coffee, due to her ongoing heart problems. She left the muffin, orange juice, sausage, and coffee untouched. She finished the last bite of the tasteless glob masquerading as scrambled eggs and began drinking the skim milk when her children arrived. They, too, were surprised at what was served.

"Help yourselves to the orange juice, coffee, muffin and sausage," she offered. "I no longer eat things like that, even on a good day." Both of her kids declined.

The hours of waiting for the MRI to be done seemed long for the three of them. Two staff doctors came into the hospital room around 11:00 a.m. to tell Janice they felt she needed to take a cholesterol-lowering medication. She refused, citing studies that show such medications have not been proven to prevent heart attacks or strokes, but that they do present a multitude of other problems. One of the doctors then mentioned there was a newer version, but it caused severe diarrhea by sending fats out through the bowels. "That's all I need, messing my pants when there isn't a bathroom close by," said Janice under her breath. But rather than say so loudly she added, "I think I'll stick to doing a better job of controlling fats in my diet. By the way, since when are sausage and blueberry muffins on a low cholesterol diet and orange juice on a diabetic diet? Those items were on my breakfast tray. I do not eat things like that."

Both doctors shrugged their shoulders and had no comments. Lunch wasn't much better: iced tea had been substituted for the coffee. The tea looked enticing, but she had no choice but to believe it also contained caffeine, so she didn't drink it. The grilled chicken sandwich was served on a large white bread bun slathered with what looked like mayo. Janice ate the steamed broccoli and the chicken without the bun. She left what looked like chocolate pudding topped with marshmallows.

It was one o'clock in the afternoon before an orderly appeared to transport Janice via wheelchair to the MRI room. She lay on a table, and they placed a pillow under her legs. Her head was kept in place by hard plastic pieces firmly clamped against her temples. The technician gave her disposable ear plugs to help reduce the noise that would be created by the scanner. She asked if Janice wanted a wash cloth to place over her eyes. She said that would be nice, but the washcloth never appeared.

The procedure took approximately twenty minutes. Janice was instructed not to move during this time. All sorts of loud mechanical sounds could be heard as microscopically thin slices of her brain were bombarded and recorded on film to reveal any further damage. Next was the wait for the neurologist to interpret those images and explain results to Janice's doctors who would then explain her condition to her. During much of this wait time, Janice sat on the side of the hospital bed back in her room with her left leg and bare foot extended on the mattress and her right leg dangling off to the side. Her children sat at the foot of the bed.

"What's wrong with your left foot?" asked a concerned Belinda. "It's badly bruised."

"Oh that," said Janice. "I dropped a heavy packing box on it yesterday morning before Dan arrived. It hurt a lot, but I kept on working and didn't bother to check for any damage under my tennis shoe."

It would only be after she returned home that she realized the accident could have caused a large clot or multiple clots to travel to her brain. The blood thinner was not able to handle the clot(s) until hours later due to so much bruising at one time.

Her foot and toes stayed black for a few days, then blue, followed by a sickly yellow and green after several weeks. Three weeks after the incident there were still traces of bruising on all of the toes of her left foot, but Janice had feeling in them, and there was no foul odor to indicate infection or gangrene. *I need to remember to mention the bruise to my new cardiologist when I find one in California, as a possible cause for the stroke symptoms, after I get settled,* she told herself.

At the time Belinda mentioned the bruised foot, Janice cautioned her not to say anything to anyone on staff at the hospital for fear it could prolong her stay despite everything having returned to normal. Nobody at the hospital seemed to have noticed the bruising. Since her stroke symptoms had lessened dramatically, she was concentrating on her upcoming flight to California five days away.

Four hours following the MRI another doctor came to her hospital room to let Janice and her children know there had been no obvious additional damage to her brain. "You can go home just as soon as the nurses get your discharge papers together," he told her. "There is nothing more we can do since you are already on the blood thinner. We could tell you to add aspirin, but that would totally knock out your body's ability to form a clot in the event of an injury or surgery. Do you want to take that risk?"

It didn't take Janice long to say, "That is a risk I'm not willing to take. I live an active lifestyle, and I don't want to give it up. I have too many things I still want to do. I'm in the process of moving to California and getting my next novel published."

"I can't say that I blame you for refusing the aspirin," replied the neurologist. "I don't think I would be willing to take that risk either, but I had to offer you the opportunity. When and where in California are you headed?" Janice told him Palm Springs in five days. He looked surprised, smiled, and raised his eyebrows. "I've heard it's a nice place to live. Good luck to you on the move. I don't suppose telling you to wait a little longer before flying would be taken seriously, so I'll just advise you stay well hydrated, watch your diet, move around on the plane, and find a good cardiologist as soon as you get there," he cautioned before leaving the room.

It took another hour before Janice was discharged, followed by a twenty-minute wait for someone to wheel her to where her son parked his car at the back entrance of the hospital.

"Where do you want to have dinner?" he asked as soon as she and Belinda joined him for the ride to a restaurant then home.

"I don't care which restaurant we go to, as long as I can get some decent roasted chicken and a salad," said Janice.

"I can't have the processed meat sandwiches and pizza I ate in Florida. You saw what that hotdog did to my ankles, Jason." Janice's ankles had ballooned to twice their normal size after one hot dog. She didn't want to make Jason feel guilty for serving those types of foods, so she ate them without any comment, but now she felt he needed to know foods like those may have contributed to the stroke. She wasn't just being a picky eater.

"I'm sorry Mom. I should have known better than to serve that junk," replied Jason. "But since Suzanne had just had her surgery, followed by her breakdown, I figured they were easier than any of us trying to prepare regular meals."

"Don't worry about it," replied Janice. "When I'm at someone else's table I eat what is served. I could have said no thank you. I just know I need to get back on the straight and narrow when it comes to food. I only mention it now so you don't think I'm a picky eater."

Janice was aware there were only two local restaurants open where she could get a decent meal as it approached seven p.m., and both of them closed at eight on Sundays. She had shared meals with Jack at both of them. The thought of eating at either one was not pleasant. *Don't be silly*, she told herself. *Choose one.* She chose the one where they had shared barbecue ribs, with enough left over for a second meal at Jack's house later. She imaged Elaina sharing a meal with Jack. The knot in her stomach grew larger when the waitress led them to the same table she had shared with Jack. *Just sit down and order*, she told herself. It was hard to swallow the baked chicken breast and coleslaw, but she managed to eat most of it. Her children had no idea of the turmoil going through her head by being there. They thought she was just tired after not having slept will at the hospital. Neither one of them could totally dismiss the cruel way Jack had broken up with Janice as a factor in what happened to their mom, but they kept such thoughts to themselves, knowing that saying anything would upset Janice more.

When they returned to Janice's house later that evening, both kids helped pack some miscellaneous items in boxes Jason had thought to purchase at the local home improvement store. They gave up on any more packing when they ran out of boxes. This gave Janice a chance to ask them to go out into the enclosed storage area located at the back of the carport. "I want you to go through the boxes out there and toss out anything you don't think I will need in California, especially pictures. I can't stand looking at pictures! There is a large trash can in the corner of the carport. Forgive me, but I still can't handle looking at pictures taken when your dad was alive. Pick out those you want and put the rest in the trash. That part of my life is over just like this one."

Unfortunately, the kids left an open box of pictures sitting on the kitchen table. On top of the pile, a large colored picture and several smaller ones of her now dead husband Clayton lay where Janice could clearly see them. He was barbequing hot dogs and hamburgers on the backyard grill for friends who stood in the background, friends she'd had to say goodbye to for a second time. Upon observing the pictures Janice burst into tears and left the room. Her children let her cry in the living room for several minutes before they followed to apologize.

"We're sorry, Mom," said a distraught Belinda. "We'll get rid of the pictures. We didn't know you were coming back into the kitchen or we wouldn't have left them where you could see them." Janice felt terrible at her reaction of seeing the pictures and went to bed where she cried herself into a fitful sleep.

Belinda had an early flight back to California the following morning. Jason took her to the airport. He returned an hour later to stay with Janice until Tuesday afternoon, which is when he would need to drive the rental car back to the same airport for his flight to Florida. This left Janice alone until Thursday afternoon when her flight to California was scheduled to depart. She was apprehensive at the thought of being alone during this time, but she didn't let Jason know.

"I'll be all right," she kept whispering to herself. "It's only going to be a day and a half before I start a new life."

WHAT THE HEART WANTS

PART 3

CHAPTER 11

Belinda made Janice's plane reservation to California. Dan dropped her off curbside and left to take her luggage to the gate to have it weighed, scanned by security, and checked to its final destination of Palm Springs, California, via a layover in Denver, Colorado. Only five days post-stroke, Janice assured Dan she could handle what needed to be done without his help.

"We're all going to miss you," said Dan. "I hope to visit you soon in California."

"I would be delighted for you to visit," replied Janice. "Thank you for everything." She felt tears sting her eyes as she waved goodbye. She watched him pull away from the curb, knowing she may, in all likelihood, never see Dan again.

Airline personnel had been notified that, due to the balance and walking problem that persisted as a result of the first stroke, Janice would need a wheelchair to make the trip through security and down the long hallway to the departure gate. The attendant behind the check-in desk called for a wheelchair that did not arrive for 45 minutes as Janice sat in the hallway waiting area. "It's a good thing I allowed plenty of time before the flight was scheduled for departure," Janice groused to a fellow passenger also waiting for wheelchair assistance.

The transportation attendant was nice and apologetic when she did finally arrive. She was even more apologetic when Janice handed her a five dollar tip for her help. Janice spent the better part of another hour sitting in the wheelchair waiting to be taken down a ramp to the door of the waiting aircraft.

With difficulty, she made her way down the aisle by grasping seat backs to get to the seat indicated by the stewardess. It turned out to be the wrong seat, and she had to move a row back amid unkind remarks of the person who arrived late and was assigned to the same seat. Janice was able to keep from lashing out at this insensitive individual while contritely smiling for his inconvenience. He responded with a stiff nod.

Janice arrived at the Denver airport a little more than three hours later. On this flight, her seat companion did not engage in conversation but instead played video games on his phone the second the passengers were given the all-clear to use them. Janice brought along a book she wanted to read, so she was grateful she did not have to small talk.

Her daughter, too, had requested a flight that did not involve stairs en route to the connecting flight. This was not the case. Janice found herself facing a long stair-like ramp located on the tarmac instead of an enclosed sky bridge into the terminal. There was nobody waiting with a wheelchair at the bottom of the ramp. "Guess there's no time like the present to see if I can make it into the terminal," she muttered.

Slowly, with the aid of a cane, she made her way across the cold and windy tarmac to inside the terminal. Three men wearing airline company shirts and vests were standing around talking at a kiosk located just inside the door. None of them offered to help her gain entrance through the heavy glass door. She politely asked where the requested wheelchair could be found. "My connecting flight leaves in an hour and I'm sure it leaves on another level at the other end of the terminal," she informed them. One man called for a wheelchair. She was then told to take a seat in the cold and drafty hallway and assured that someone would be there in a few minutes.

The men continued talking among themselves. When fifteen minutes passed, Janice called her daughter to let her know she was going to miss her flight if someone didn't show up in the next few minutes to help her. She did so after she spoke with the three men for the second time and they did nothing but tell her someone would be along shortly to assist her. Another fifteen minutes passed without any one showing up.

This prompted Janice to make another call to her daughter and exclaim out of character, "My flight leaves in 30 minutes, and the three bozos standing here talking don't seem to give a damn!"

"Sit tight, Mom. I'll get in touch with the airport administrator's office and find out what's going on," said Belinda, a professional woman who was accustomed to giving orders and expecting them to be promptly carried out.

Several more minutes passed with no wheelchair in sight when a man who appeared to be in a supervisory capacity joined her and the others. "What's going on here? Why isn't there a wheelchair here for our customer?" The men hemmed and hawed around saying they had repeatedly called for one, which was not true. One call had been made. The man appearing to be a supervisor got on his radio and a short-heated conversation ensued. Soon, someone appeared. The departing flight was on another floor at the far end of the airport, just as Janice had told the three men. They made it just in time before the plane's door closed. Within minutes the flight rolled backward onto the runway with the help of a mule, turned, and made ready for takeoff.

As the plane sat on the tarmac waiting for takeoff clearance, Janice called Belinda on her cell phone to let her know she had made it. Belinda said she had just gotten off the phone with someone in charge. Janice never learned what transpired between her daughter and the person on the other end of the phone. She was left to assume Belinda, a long-time customer of the airline in question, was given information that her mother had made the flight. Their call had to be terminated due to takeoff before Belinda could share more information. Janice didn't see any reason to bring up the subject again after arriving safely in Palm Springs.

It was after ten p.m. when a tired Janice arrived at the Palm Springs International Airport. This time a transportation attendant was waiting with a wheelchair on the sky bridge platform just outside the plane's cabin door. He took her to baggage pickup and waited to remove her suitcase from the carousel. He then wheeled her curbside where she waited for her daughter, who arrived by car minutes later. Janice could think only of what a difference this was compared to her experience in Denver.

Janice was exhausted but too tired to go to bed when they arrived at her daughter's house. They talked for almost an hour before she retired. Belinda kept telling Janice that what Jack did wasn't her fault, that she should consider her time with him as fun, and that she should move on with her life.

Rather than rehash telling Belinda how she was feeling after being so coldly rejected by Jack, she agreed with her. It was 1:00 a.m. Pacific Standard Time, 3:00 a.m. Central Standard Time. Still on Tennessee time, Janice awakened at 6:00 a.m. (9:00 a.m. back east) to begin the search for a place to live, but this would not happen for several hours. Her daughter, a hospital human resources director, had business she needed to attend to via computer and phone before they could go out for a late breakfast then begin their day.

As it turned out, suitable housing was less readily available than her daughter anticipated. Most of the listings were for one-bedroom, short-term vacation rentals, not the two-bedroom, long-term, first-floor apartment with private laundry facilities that Janice was seeking. The few long-term rentals available in her price range were small; most were in the range of 700 to 850 square feet. Janice felt cramped in the 1,000 square-foot house she rented back in Tennessee, so she didn't see the smaller homes as options. After looking at several locations, one apartment looked promising at 1,186 square feet, but it had a kitchen sink so badly scarred it had deep black scratches showing through against white porcelain, which was totally out of character for the property. The arrogant condo manager steadfastly refused her offer to have a new sink installed at her expense. He said it would set a precedent for the entire condo complex, and he knew the owners would not permit this to happen for fear other residents would want him to replace their sinks.

"I don't think I can live with that sink. It's disgusting," Janice told her daughter and him. "No wonder this apartment has been shown online as available for quite some time."

Janice finally gave up looking and settled for an apartment listed as a downstairs unit in a gated, boutique apartment complex. The complex consisted of six units in each of the twelve two-story buildings. The apartment was a 985 square-foot, two-bedroom, two-bath space, and living there would mean getting rid of even more of her furniture and belongings. Luckily, there was an additional room for storage, albeit small, that contained a stackable washer and dryer. It was right outside the main apartment for her exclusive use.

Janice was glad, in a way, that she had given away all of her large pieces of furniture and sold her relatively new full-size washer and dryer at a considerable loss. She knew her large furniture would never have fit into the allotted space. She was not enthralled at the prospect of having to do laundry in an outside enclosure with no A/C when temperatures often exceeded 110 degrees in the summer and dropped to the mid-twenties in the winter. At least it was a private laundry room. She would learn private laundry facilities were considered a rare luxury in Palm Springs, even in upscale facilities. Her monthly rent was just under $1,500 a month plus utilities, with an additional maintenance fee of $10.00 per month to cover the cost of possibly changing burned out lightbulbs and the A/C filter once every three months. Her rent per month in a 1400 square-foot apartment in Georgia was $350.00 less and included a full size washer and dryer inside the apartment.

"Welcome to California!" exclaimed Janice.   Belinda grimaced, but had little to say. Janice couldn't help thinking about her landlord in Tennessee who mowed the lawn, changed the A/C filter every three months, and put enzymes into the septic system without any additional charge. Shortly after she moved in, he even installed a new dishwasher and garbage disposal without raising the monthly rent. Janice shuddered at the thought of watching her hard-earned savings shrink, but she still could not come to terms with the idea of living in a city where she might come in contact with Jack and Elaina. That possibility was more painful than she was willing to endure. The wounds were too deep and brought up past traumas for Janice, like the time her first love, at the age of eighteen when they became engaged, cheated on her with her best friend. Perhaps the root of most of the pain was the little known fact that Janice had been repeatedly molested as a child by someone who should have protected her. Her mother knew what was happening and did nothing to stop the abuse. Even after she sought intensive therapy as an adult, these experiences continued to affect her.

In her mind, men were not to be trusted, even more so after what Jack had done. She blamed herself that she had let down her guard. He convinced her he was an honorable man and they had a future together. She blamed herself for selling her mountainside home and moving to Georgia, then back to Tennessee. *I should have been able to ride it out like my friends wanted me to and stayed in Tennessee,* she tearfully told herself on many occasions. But at the same time, her heart knew to continue living in Tennessee was not an option she could live with for the rest of her life.

Having spent six winters in Palm Springs, Janice now preferred the company of gay men, many of whom lived in the area. They did not hit on her and they treated her like a princess. They were safe. She rejected the offer of one gay couple who wanted to introduce her to one of their straight, widowed friends. "I will never trust a straight man again," she declared. This was in spite of them telling her they had known him for years and he was a decent and honorable man. "I don't care if he's the spitting image of Jesus," she responded. "The answer is no! I don't want to meet your friend as a possible partner. He may be the exception to the men I've met, but I am never going to be up for having my heart broken again!"

"Never is a long time," replied her friend Mathew. "Let's wait a while and see if you change your mind."

Janice wanted to say *that will happen when hell freezes over and pigs fly*, but she didn't say so. She didn't want to hurt her friend's feelings any more than she already had by refusing his kind offer.

The next unexpected blow hit Janice when she found a letter in the mailbox sent from the hospital in Tennessee where she had been treated for the second mini-stroke just prior to the move to California. The letter stated doctors and nurses had decided she was held overnight for observation and had not been formally admitted! This meant she was responsible for all charges, and that Medicare and her supplementary insurance company would not cover the horrendous cost. Janice panicked. She was never given this information at the time of treatment, nor were her two children.

The letter arrived on a Saturday and the hospital business office was closed on the weekends. In a state of shock, Janice called her daughter and left a message. When Belinda did not respond for several hours, Janice called Jason in Florida and read the letter to him. "Mom, don't panic. It sounds like a form letter. Some idiot probably keyed in the wrong codes. The doctors told Belinda and me you were formally admitted. I'll take care of it," said Jason. His reassurance didn't help. Janice continued to panic. "What if I do have to pay? This will bankrupt me!" she cried. "Nobody told me I was being kept for observation or I would never have allowed them to take me to a room on the floor! They have observation areas in the ER if that was all I needed."

"Mom, the doctors told us you were admitted. There was no doubt you had another stroke," insisted Jason. "Belinda and I will take care of it on Monday."

Janice cried after they hung up. She had heard rumors that some hospitals pulled this type of a stunt when they thought they could get more money from the patient than they could get from insurance companies who routinely prorate charges. She had reason to believe she was in for a rough time from the billing department. She was aware hospitals keep an army of attorneys at their beck and call. How could she, a widow, hope to win a legal battle against such odds?

It was past noon on Monday, California time, when Janice e-mailed her daughter in San Francisco at her workplace. "Any news concerning the situation back at the Tennessee Hospital? Plus, I've not heard anything from the apartment complex stating I've been approved to live there," she wrote. She had also heard nothing from her son, and it was now past five p.m. in Tennessee. The business office in the hospital would be closed. Panic set in again, so instead of waiting for an e-mail response, Janice decided to call her daughter.

"Mom, I've been extremely busy with work," said a harried Belinda. "I've sent all of the information the leasing agent asked for regarding your apartment. Jason and I will talk with the business office at the hospital tomorrow. It's past now past five p.m. in Tennessee. There won't be anyone available to help us. Everything will work out. Be patient." Her daughter's words did little to ease the increasing panic Janice was feeling at the possibility of owing thousands of dollars and having no place to live. She felt frustrated and like she was at the mercy of her son and daughter, both of whom were treating her as though she were a child.

"Maybe I am being childish," Janice said aloud after the conversation with Belinda ended. "But darn it all, I've been through a lot this past month. I've been dumped for a sleaze ball of a younger woman by someone I thought had feelings for me. I've given up three homes, said goodbye to long-time friends, and had a second stroke. To top it all off, I'm merely existing by staying here in my daughter and son-in-law's home, living alone in limbo while waiting to know if I have a permanent place to live! And now I'm left to wonder if I owe thousands of dollars in hospital bills. And if that isn't enough, Jack's new love interest keeps taunting me with e-mails calling me nasty names and accusing me of using my money to buy Jack's affection. I do use my money to help those less fortunate than myself, but buying friendship or affection is something I've never felt the need to do!" She suddenly found herself in the midst of another tearful meltdown. "Dear God, what have I done to deserve this?" she questioned. "All I did was be stupid enough to fall in love with someone I trusted, and God, you tell us love is the most important thing in this life! Why didn't I listen to my head instead of my heart?" she sobbed. It took the better part of an hour before Janice could get her emotions under control and admit to herself that she had been used by an unscrupulous man and equally unscrupulous woman. "I will never trust anyone again, especially another man," she vowed once more.

The week passed with no resolution of the hospital bill or the apartment. That wouldn't come until the following Tuesday when her daughter called her.

"Mom, the problem with your new apartment lease is the fact the leasing agent doesn't know how to get into the secured e-mail to review your financial information. I'm sending her instructions how to do this as we speak. She sent me a copy of your lease with the wrong dates, and I've asked her to correct them. As for the hospital, I will set it up for both of us to get on the phone line and speak with someone in the billing department to see what that letter is all about."

Several minutes later, someone from the hospital business office came on the line to inform them the person who could help was not due in that day, and they needed to call back tomorrow. Next, a call was placed to Janice's secondary insurance company since contacting Medicare was not an option due to long wait times and Belinda's busy schedule. The lady at the secondary company was helpful. She contacted the hospital and spoke to the person Janice and her daughter had just been told wasn't in. This took a long time as they waited on their phones for answers to finally learn that the government required a letter in order to waive the charges. The lady assured Belinda that Janice was in no way responsible for any charges associated with her recent hospitalization. No apology was offered by the hospital employee. Learning she didn't owe the hospital money didn't erase the fact Janice spent four days thinking she could owe thousands of dollars.

"Well, at least I won't have to file for Chapter 11 any time soon," said Janice, trying to find a bright side to the fiasco. "Now we just have to figure out if I have a place of my own to live."

"Mom, you know you have the necessary resources that will qualify you to live there, and they already know your credit score is in excess of 800. Stop worrying! You know you can stay at our Palm Springs house until you get the word you can move into the apartment," replied her daughter.

Just as Janice said before, it was easier said than done for her not to worry. Nothing had gone according to her expectations since Jack dumped her for Elaina. She had no reason to think that would change any time soon. But big changes loomed on the horizon for Janice, in ways she could not even begin to imagine.

WHAT THE HEART WANTS

PART 4

CHAPTER 12

Through e-mail and phone calls from friends in Tennessee, Janice learned that Jack had wasted little time in his quest to use Elaina. Similarly, Elaina wasted no time trying to convince Jack that if he put up cash required for production costs, she could help turn his book into a movie.

She wasn't surprised to learn Jack's next move was to take Elaina on a road trip to meet his son in another state, in an effort to make her feel as though he would be the answer to all of her heart's desires. Elaina had no way of knowing that Jack had been planning to make this trip for several months in order to deliver a family heirloom rocking chair to his son. Jack told Janice he no longer wanted it in his home because it reminded him of Sabrina, his deceased wife. Janice had no doubt Jack simply wanted to make Elaina believe it was a special trip planned just for her, when in fact it was a trip designed for her to help him maneuver the heavy chair into his car, take turns or do the driving, and to have someone else to cover expenses, after the way he had not paid tabs while visiting Janice in Tennessee, Georgia, and California. Janice knew that had she continued to be a part of Jack's life, it would have been *her* helping to load the chair, driving part or most of the way, and picking up the majority of the tab for meals and gas. She felt an overwhelming since of relief now that she was able to think more objectively about Jack without the benefit of love's rose colored glasses. This forced her to realize, beyond a reasonable doubt, Jack had shown his true colors as a conman and a taker who put his needs and desires ahead of anyone else's.

Janice also received word that Elaina continued her ruse to make Jack believe she could help him get one of his books made into a movie and that she found him physically attractive. Janice was given this information by a friend who thought it would make her feel better if she knew what was happening. This knowledge broke Janice's heart, even after having been lied to and used by Jack.

Years later, another friend told Janice that Elaina was able to convince Jack to spend literally thousands of dollars on a movie that had yet to be produced. The friend went on to say she knew Elaina had spent Jack's money on a new car and expensive jewelry for herself just before she dumped him (when she became aware his money was about to run out). Elaina had also told Jack, and many others, how Jack was not able to satisfy her sexually, and that is what prompted her to leave him for greener pastures.

According to the informant, this left Jack an emotionally drained, financially drained, lonely old man, just as Janice had warned him would happen five years ago when he chose Elaina over her. Janice found herself thankful when enough time had passed that old fiends no longer kept her in the loop of what was happening in Jack's life, until she received a phone call out of the blue. It was Dan. He called to give her an update on Jack's unfortunate circumstances.

"That's too bad," said Janice when Dan let her know Jack was in bad shape and often cried for her.

"He made his choice when he chose Elaina. What am I supposed to do about it now? I've moved on to make a new life in California, a life that does not and will not include him!"

"Janice, I know Jack hurt you. It has been very hard for me to make the decision to contact you, but I know you aren't the kind of person to turn your back on someone who is in dire need. Jack really needs you," insisted Dan. He continued talking before Janice could respond. "After suffering a mitral valve failure a little more than a year ago, which required more surgery after a full blown heart attack, he has spent the last year in a rundown old nursing home where people are forced to rely on Medicaid to pay the bill. Every time I visit I find him slumped in a chair and staring at the wall. He cries and asks for you. I have to admit I've been tempted to give him your address and phone number. His son has all but abandoned him since Elaina and her friends scammed him out of his money. Jack is barely hanging on in a place that's not fit for a dog to live, let alone a human being! I'm not a doctor, but I know he is not getting the medical help he needs. Won't you please reconsider and try to forgive the past and help him? I know you once had deep feelings for him," pleaded Dan.

"That was a long time ago. He made his choice. I told you I've moved on with my life," Janice firmly told him. "It has taken me a long time to pick up the pieces. I certainly do not want a repeat performance involving the humiliation and pain Jack caused when he told me he wanted that tart Elaina. Well, he got what he thought he wanted. Too bad he had to learn the hard way what a piece of trash she is! In my opinion he has nobody to blame but himself for the way things have turned out for him!"

"Your reaction surprises me. I thought you might consider giving Jack a second chance. Sorry to have bothered you," said Dan, fully prepared for her to terminate their conversation.

"Please allow me to turn the tables and ask, if you were in my shoes, would you forgive someone who repeatedly lied to you and took away your sense of trust and self-worth without a second thought?" asked Janice. Dan had to agree he would not be able to forgive such an individual. "Then I strongly suggest you not judge me or have such unrealistic expectations when it comes to me forgiving Jack. I went through a living hell! My life was literally turned upside down! I loved him and would have stood by him for whatever life would have sent his way, and he knew it. Yet he chose to take up with the likes of Elaina. I was so distraught by the cruel way he ended our relationship I felt

I had no choice except to move clear across the country! Do you think it would have been easy for me to stand by in Tennessee and watch this play out while Elaina made a fool out of him? Please don't call me again regarding anything to do with Jack. That part of my life is in the past. I intend to leave it there!"

"I think you've made your point," said Dan. "I won't mention him again, and I hope you still consider me a friend." Janice couldn't miss the sadness she detected in his voice, but she wasn't about to reconsider her position regarding any future contact with Jack. The hurt he had caused her ran too deeply.

"Sorry if I came on strong, Dan. Please know I still consider you a friend. I have no problem with you. I will always be grateful for your help, but I must insist that you not call me again with any reference to Jack."

The more she thought about Jack's circumstances over the following days, Janice could not help but find herself reacting to what Dan said about him living in a sub-standard nursing home after having suffered another mitral valve replacement and major heart attack. *He's broke and Elaina left him. Dan believes him to be suffering from what everyone thinks is some sort of a mental impairment. He keeps calling out for me. Dear God, won't you please tell me what I should do!*

These painful and disturbing thoughts kept playing over and over in her head, rendering her sleepless for the next three nights. She kept trying to convince herself she didn't owe Jack Fairchild anything. Hadn't he made it painfully clear when he chose to be with Elaina with no regard for Janice's feelings?

After several more sleepless nights, Janice made the decision she had to at least fly back east to Tennessee to assess his condition, along with his living arrangements, in order to make sure he was getting the medical care he needed. If not, maybe she would provide financial assistance to upgrade his room and care without his knowledge of where the money came from. "After I make this trip to Tennessee I can truly put him out of my heart and mind," she whispered to herself while making the airline reservations. She could only hope going back to Tennessee would make it possible to deal with the painful memories that plagued her from time during the five years since their breakup.

Janice found the rundown nursing home located in rural Tennessee just as Dan had described it. It did not take long before she would learn Jack was housed in a drab room painted battleship gray among those reserved for Medicaid patients who lacked the ability to pay for their care. His room was no larger than a broom closet, which he shared with another patient. It was furnished with two single, metal, hospital beds placed about three feet apart, an old narrow dresser placed between the beds, and two recliner chairs covered in cracked vinyl shoved tightly against the wall. A single window, lacking a drape and in need of washing, overlooked the employee parking lot pockmarked with potholes. The poor condition of the exterior of the two-story building revealed peeling, light green paint as she approached in a rental car. It made her wonder if there had been any state inspections recently, if ever.

That thought intensified when her nose was assaulted by the smell of stale urine and feces mixed with the odor of boiling cabbage and potatoes upon entering the unlocked, windowless, double, metal entrance doors. The smell was so strong it made her gag. It took several minutes before a nurse or aide, Janice couldn't be sure which, approached from down a long, poorly lit hallway. The heavyset short woman was not wearing a uniform. Janice would not have known she was an employee without spotting the plastic nametag pinned haphazardly to her ill-fitting, gray polyester blouse.

"Kin I help ya?" she questioned.

"I'm here to visit Jack Fairchild," responded Janice.

"Foller me," said the 50-something, poorly groomed woman. Janice was not surprised when the woman did not ask for her name or identification and did not offer her own name. Janice was surprised and appalled at the number of people, many dressed in worn out, mismatched clothing or threadbare hospital gowns, who were tied with sturdy cloth straps to their wheelchairs lining the hallway. Some were drooling and staring off into space. Some were talking to people only they could see. There were puddles of urine on the floor accompanied by the strong smell of feces. As she passed by, frail hands reached out and tried to grasp her hand or pull at her clothing. Some begged to be taken back to their rooms, and some called out the names of people she assumed were their relatives or children. The sight brought tears to her eyes, and she longed to reach out and help these poor unfortunate souls. But Janice knew there was little she could do for them at the present time. She needed to concentrate on locating Jack and checking on his condition. *I'll make calls to the proper authorities when I return to California*, she silently promised.

Jack was sitting in one of the ancient recliners wearing only a faded blue cotton hospital gown covered with what appeared to be coffee stains. Dried food cascaded down the front of the gown. A thin, yellowed, cotton blanket covered his lap and legs. Cheap, black, rubber flip flops covered his exposed feet, which made it easy to see his toenails were in need of trimming. His beard and moustache, once his neatly trimmed pride and joy, grew wild like that of a homeless street person without access to a shower, scissors, or a mirror. Bits of dried food were clinging to the hairs around his mouth. His head was bowed and his eyes were closed. When the aide entered the room with Janice, he looked up with the vacant stare people often associate with dementia. The aide warned her about what she would find on the walk to the room, but Janice was still unprepared for the pitiful sight that met her eyes. She couldn't believe this was the same man she had once believed she loved with all her heart.

"Don't be surprised none if he don't know ya," the aide warned. "He does have some good days. We kin only hope this is one 'o them. It breaks my heart when he keeps callin' out the name 'o somebody by tha name 'o Janice. Don't none of us know who she is or where she lives. Iffen we did, we would git in contact her wit her 'n let her know he's here. Ya wouldn't happen ta know who she is and how ta git in contact wid her, would ya?"

"I'm Janice. Jack and I knew each other a long time ago. I just learned he was here in this nursing home a week ago. I live on the West Coast, in Palm Springs, California, to be more specific."

The aide took a closer look and her jaw dropped as she became excited. "Are ya tha Janice Crenshaw whose books have been made into movies fer TV?" the obviously star-struck woman gushed. "I seen most 'o them movies 'n read 'bout everthin' ya have wrote. Oh, I cain't believe ya are standin' here right in front 'o me! I gotta go let everbody know you're here!" Janice hesitated in her response just long enough for the aide to continue in an accusing voice, "Now don't ya go tryin' ta deny it! I seen ya on a couple 'o them TV talk shows, so I know it's gotta be ya!"

"Yes, I am that Janice Crenshaw, but please, don't tell anyone." begged Janice in alarm at the thought of several people rushing into the small room. "It could impact Jack in a bad way if a lot of people rush in here all at once, and that's the last thing I want to happen. If you have one shred of decency and care about his wellbeing, please don't tell anyone I'm here. I need to speak with the nursing home administrator and Jack's doctor immediately. I want to take him home with me where he will receive good care." The aide raised her eyebrows in a look of total surprise.

"Are ya sure ya wanna take him home wit ya?" she questioned. "Jest look at him! He's nothin' but a total mess!"

"If you must know, he and I were once lovers, but that was many years ago," answered Janice impatiently. "If you tell anyone I said that I will deny it and so will my publicist who has the ability to make you look like a complete fool and have this awful place shut down! You don't want that to happen, do you?" The woman's eyes opened wide as she shook her head before she answered.

"I don't want no trouble 'cause I need this here job. I got six hungry kids ta support. We don't have no charge nurse on duty today so ya need ta stay here whilst I go call his doctor and tha administrator," she said. "I promise I won't tell a soul ya are here, but ya have ta promise me signed copies 'o all yer books. After all, we belong ta the same sisterhood with ya once havin' been a nurse. I know 'bout that from readin' yer bio in one 'o them books."

Janice knew she had to continue to play the part of a powerful benefactor in order to get Jack out of this terrible place as quickly as possible. When the aide scurried off to make the calls, Janice was left alone with Jack, his roommate having gone to play bingo in what served as the all-purpose dining and activity room. She gingerly took a seat on the edge of his rumpled, unmade bed and reached out to gently touch his left arm. Jack looked up and opened his eyes. A look of confusion slowly replaced one that could be interpreted as possible recognition. "Janice? Where have you been? I've been asking for you for what seems like forever."

"I've been busy working, but I'm here now," she replied quietly. "You and I are going to take a helicopter ride to my house in California where you are going to live from now on. Is that all right with you?" Jack nodded affirmatively. "You and I were once good friends, and we lost touch."

Jack continued to study her face while trying to remember why this woman was so important to him. He suddenly began to smile. "It's coming back to me. The mountains. I remember the mountains and that king-size bed!" Copious tears began to roll down his cheeks. "You really are Janice?" he questioned in wonder. Janice could not contain the tears spilling down her face when she reconfirmed her identity and his memory from long ago.

"I know we've both changed since we last saw each other five years ago," she told him. "Time and life has a way of doing that . . ."

Jack interrupted her and continued to speak. "I remember that other woman . . . I can't remember her name . . . I do remember she took all my money then left. I thought you left me, too." The distraught look on his face was heartbreaking.

"Shhh . . . You don't need to think about her anymore. I'm here now. I have never stopped caring about you, not even for a moment," declared Janice. She had to admit that while she didn't like him much after what he had done in such a cruel way, she continued, in the deep recesses of her heart, to love him.

"I love you," replied Jack fervently as he reached out to take her hands in his. "You say we're going to take a helicopter ride to your house? I don't think I've ever had a ride in a helicopter before . . . have I?"

"You were always adventuresome, so you could have flown in one," she replied. "Do you remember trying to eat raw salmon with capers and cream cheese on a bagel at Sherman's Deli in Palm Springs after you told me you wanted to try new things at every opportunity? I could tell by the look on your face at the first bite you regretted that decision, but you ate it." Janice mentioned this episode in an attempt to jog his memory.

"No," was all Jack had to say as he continued to intently study her face with a look of pure wonder. If he remembered the mountains, that was at least a starting point for him to remember the pleasant times.

After meeting with the nursing home administrator and Jack's doctor, both men agreed Janice could take Jack home with her. They would deal with the state authorities should any questions arise. This decision was made after she produced a "donation" in the form of a large check that was to be used to clean up the nursing home and hire competent help.

Janice didn't waste any time using her cell phone to call her assistant, whom she'd hired after her move to California and subsequent financial success as an author, to make arrangements for the helicopter, along with a car and driver to transport them to the Tennessee and Palm Springs airports. She'd also asked for a limo service to transport them to her elaborate California home when they arrived in Palm Springs. "Oh, and we will need a full time male nurse to meet us upon landing," she informed her assistant.

The nursing home doctor warned her she may face opposition from Jack's son who was now his legal guardian, even though he never visited his father. "You do understand he will be discharged to your care against medical advice?" he questioned. "That means Medicaid may not pay for his care for the remainder of this month."

"I think my generous donation will more than cover any charges Medicaid does not pay," Janice responded with a frown. "Would you be so kind as to send someone in here to help me prepare for Jack's departure?" It was not a question, but a demand—polite but still a demand. "The helicopter will be at the airport in about an hour, so that doesn't leave us a whole lot of time."

"I will take care of it right away," answered the administrator.

The helicopter flight from Tennessee to California was unremarkable as flights go. Stops at several small airports along the way to refuel proved uneventful during the seven hours of actual flight time interspersed with short walks, the purchasing of snacks, and rest room visits while the refueling processes was taking place. Jack seemed to alternate between awe over the scenery below when airborne, staring at Janice, and napping. When he was awake, he insisted on holding her hand and kissing it from time to time to reassure himself she was really there and this was happening.

"I remember this place. At least I think I do," Jack excitedly told her as their flight landed at the Palm Springs International Airport. After helping him out of the helicopter, the male nurse Janice had requested took Jack by wheelchair across the open tarmac toward the terminal. She trailed along beside them with her suitcase and the few items Jack needed that she had purchased in haste while his discharge papers were being completed at the nursing home. It upset him when she told him she was going shopping, but she reassured him she would be back before the paperwork was finished.

"You will remember a lot of things once you get proper medical care and some decent food," said Janice upon their return to California. "New medicines and therapy are available to treat your memory problems and heart condition. I'm sure you will love the meals my housekeeper, Bernice, can whip up at a moment's notice. I intend to make sure you get whatever you need no matter the cost!" she declared. The adoring look Jack gave her served to start rapidly melting what had become a cold, walled-off place in her heart.

"Can we stay at the house in the room with the big bed and glass doors that go out onto the patio next to the pool?" asked Jack. His comment gave Janice added hope something could be done to bring back Jack's ability to fully remember the time they spent together in that room. She felt he was doing a remarkable job of describing the bedroom where they spent those magical sixteen days more than five years ago.

"The house and grounds you remember belong to my daughter and son-in-law, so we can't stay there, but I have a house almost like theirs not far away," replied Janice. "I'm sure you will like it. It has a nice pool, too." Jack nodded and settled back against the soft, black leather limo seat and closed his eyes for the ride to Janice's mountainside home. She sat across from him studying the face for which she still had feelings in spite of how much he had hurt her. As he began to softly snore, tears threatened to spill down Janice's cheeks. "What a waste of what could have been the best years of our lives," she bitterly said to the male nurse sitting on the seat opposite her beside Jack. "I know I can't change what happened in the past, so I need to focus my concentration on what happens from now on."

"That is the only way you can move on," the nurse assured her. "I've witnessed so many people get a chance to make things right. They don't take it, and that is a darn shame." Janice knew he was right. At the same time there was no doubt in her mind that she would never forgive Elaina. That nagging voice in the back of her head could not help wondering if she could fully forgive Jack enough to resume intense feelings of love she once felt. *Do I still love him, or do I feel sorry for him?* These were the thoughts going through her mind.

It was not an easy road for Jack to regain his memory or his health. Janice was surprised the day he questioned why she was willing to help him after the hurtful way he had treated her. Janice was patient in telling him that was all in the past, and this was a new day in their lives. At first, with her encouragement, Jack started to remember little things from the past, but he couldn't remember what he ate for breakfast or if he had even eaten breakfast on some days.

The doctors assured Janice this was not uncommon, especially when serious medical or emotional trauma had taken place. Jack was hurt and used by Elaina and then suffered through the mitral valve failure, its replacement, the heart attack, and the terrible existence in the nursing home.

But with proper medication, healthy food, and therapy, along with Janice's continued attentive care, Jack's mental and physical status did improve over the following year. That isn't to say there weren't gaps in his memory and emotional bumps in the road causing both of them to become frustrated and exchange cross words. To think otherwise would be foolish. There were more verbal outbursts on Jack's part than hers, which required patience as she helped him recall the good times they had spent together. Jack's frustration grew even more intense when he began to remember Elaina, how she had used him for her own gain, and how she played a major part in scamming him out of his money before she left him. Janice knew progress was being made when Jack was able to remember and voice regret that he chose Elaina.

"What I did to you is inexcusable," he lamented tearfully. "By the time I figured out I made the wrong choice, my money was gone and so were you. I didn't expect to ever see you again, but I never gave up hope. All our friends turned their backs on me and wouldn't tell me where you were. I would have tried harder to find you, but

I had another heart attack when the heart valve failed. This required more surgery. I ran out of money, so I couldn't afford to hire private investigators. Oh Janice! I am so sorry. I was such a thoughtless and selfish fool!"

"You have to let go of what happened. You can't change it. I can't change it. You need to move past it. We're together again, and that's all that matters," insisted Janice. She wished she had a sweater when it felt like a cold wind blew through the open window to surround her, even though it was a sun-filled, 85-degree, cloudless California day. She shut her eyes and took a deep breath. *Dear God, help me, help us,* she silently prayed as she continued to feel the real sudden chill overtaking her body. *I act and sound like my kids did when they kept telling me to move on when you dumped me.* "Did I just say were together again and that's all that matters?" She softly questioned.

"I hear what you are saying, but . . ." Jack started to say before Janice put her arms around him then placed the index finger of her right hand across his lips. He stopped talking, laid his head on her shoulder, and started to cry in earnest. Heartbreaking sobs racked his still frail body. She, too, began to cry silent tears as she led him into her bedroom. She calmly insisted they lie down on the bed beside each other and take a nap. He didn't protest when she continued to hold him tenderly until his tears subsided and he fell asleep. Sleep eluded her. She slipped out of bed without disturbing him and headed to the pool-side patio through the sliding glass door. It was peaceful sitting there while the breeze fluttered the table umbrella and whispered through the palm trees; it was the perfect landscape she needed to give serious thought as to what would become their future.

Jack was pleasantly surprised two months later in early May when Janice asked him to marry her. "I thought you would never ask," he replied as a wide grin spread across his tanned face. "I thought about asking you, but I know I messed up big time, and I don't have anything left to offer you. I never thought you would forgive me for what I did, let alone want to marry me."

"That makes two of us who thought this day would never come," said Janice with a wry smile. "But the heart wants what the heart wants, and my heart wants you. How about it? It's Leap Year so I'm asking you to marry me. I'm being practical as well. This will allow you to be placed on my medical insurance plan. Plus, as your wife, I can help make decisions for any future medical care, should the need arise. That is in addition to the primary fact that I happen to love you and want us to spend the rest of our lives together," she added before bending down to give him a gentle kiss on the cheek.

Janice was aware they would have to petition the court back in Tennessee to have Jack's son removed as his legal guardian before they could proceed with wedding plans. His son had not hesitated in taking the steps necessary to have his father declared mentally incompetent in order to sell his riverside home and yacht and be appointed his father's legal guardian. Once the guardianship was granted, he sold everything, took the money, and ran. Janice knew it could be a lengthy legal battle to have him removed, but it was a task she could now well afford and was willing to take, but only if Jack agreed.

"The first thing we need to do is have your doctor certify that you are mentally competent and capable of entering into marriage. I'm sure that won't be a problem any longer. Next we need to take legal action against your son to have him removed as your guardian. Are you up for taking such an action?" Jack dropped his head to stare at the patio stones. It took several minutes of deep thought before he gave his answer.

"That's a pretty hard decision regarding my son," he began. "He is my flesh and blood, even if he did take advantage of me . . . , but you are right. He abandoned me after Elaina and her friends took my money. He sold all of my property then left me to rot in that hellhole of a nursing home without so much as a backward glance. I don't deserve you, but yes, I want us to get married. And yes, I want to take whatever legal action is necessary against my son to get him removed as my guardian."

Thankfully, Jack's son did not object to being removed as his father's guardian when Janice offered him a check for $10,000 dollars and promised they would not sue him for restitution of the money he took from the sale of Jack's property. "Don't even think about asking me or your father for any more money," she admonished when his son asked if she would be willing to up the ante. "If you do you will find yourself in prison for falsely convincing a judge your father was incompetent so you could rob him. You need to understand I have the contacts and finances to make that happen."

"You won't get any argument from me on that count," Stephen assured her. "The old man and I never did see eye to eye, and I'm sure he will be glad I'm out of the picture."

Theirs was a simple wedding ceremony by California standards, held under a grove of ancient gnarled acacia trees in Ruth Hardy Park on that late May afternoon, two years to the day since Janice rescued Jack from the nursing home. The wedding attendees consisted of mutual friends from Tennessee Janice arranged to have flown to Palm Springs and put up in a hotel, several of her local gay couple friends, a justice of the peace, Belinda, Jason, her grandson, and their spouses. White satin ribbons were tied to surrounding tree trunks by her children, and white lace table cloths were placed on picnic tables arranged into a 'U' shape. The ribbons and wedding cake topped with the traditional bride and groom were the only decorations requested by Janice. She wore a simple, pale blue, cotton dress, its full skirt reaching to her ankles, silver-accented open-toed, low-heeled shoes, and pale pink nail polish.

Jack wore the same, now frayed and faded, blue floral, Hawaiian shirt and khaki Bermuda shorts he had worn the day he let her know they were no longer a couple and he wanted Elaina. Tearfully, he told her he wanted to wear this outfit so he could turn back time and make things right. She carried a bouquet of yellow, long-stemmed roses, her favorite flower, provided by Jack who now received Social Security benefits. A catered picnic arranged by Janice's family followed the wedding ceremony. Janice's son and daughter served as attendants while her grandson and his wife looked on. People walking their dogs in the park offered congratulations when they became aware a wedding was taking place. Those who came forward out of curiosity were invited to partake in the festivities, the food, the elaborate four-tiered wedding cake, and beverages. It wasn't long before there were an additional dozen or so people, unknown to them before that day, enjoying a variety of sandwiches, salads, cake, coffee, and iced tea at the wedding reception. Everyone could feel the love between the happy couple and see, without doubt, that Jack couldn't keep his eyes off Janice, nor could she keep her eyes off him.

They spent their wedding night in the same bed they had shared when he visited in California now more than eight years ago. When she thought about it, Janice found it difficult to accept the fact it was that long ago since they spent those wonder-filled sixteen days exploring each other's bodies and talking about the things they planned to do together in the future.

Janice's daughter and son-in-law were gracious enough to spend the night in a local hotel so this step back in time could take place in the same location. At their ages and with Jack's medical history, love-making was a challenge, but they were rewarded with a satisfactory experience with many more such nights to follow over the next two years.

Two years of wedded bliss passed quickly before Janice made the final decision to seek legal action against Elaina and her conmen. This decision occurred not long after Jack suddenly passed away from another heart attack, leaving Janice to become devastated once again. She didn't care if the statute of limitations for seeking financial restitution had expired when it came to Elaina's actions. She didn't want monetary payment. Her books and movie scripts had taken off. Money was not the issue. She wanted to make Elaina's life a living hell by pressing charges of fraud and elder abuse. She hired a private detective to find her and help with the prosecution of those who had taken Jack's dignity and money and deprived them both years of happiness.

It didn't take long before the private investigator was able to locate all of them. They were operating scam after scam on unsuspecting widowed or unhappily married male writers living in other states. According to the investigator,

Elaina continued using the same tactics she had once used on Jack with promises of love, fortune, and fame if the current man cooperated financially in allowing them to make a movie from one of his books. However, the investigator failed to let Janice know Elaina and her friends had become aware he was hot on their trail. They fled like rats on a sinking ship. His excuses didn't hold water in her estimation. Janice ended their arrangement by firing him and hiring a reputable lawyer.

"Elaina is going to regret the day she ever laid eyes on Jack or me," declared Janice. "If she thinks I spent money buying a relationship with Jack, what does she think I'll do with my money in getting justice?"

When they discussed the possibility of going after Elaina while Jack was still alive, Jack asked if she really wanted to pursue finding and prosecuting Elaina, since so much time had elapsed. "What you think?" she replied. "That bitch robbed both of us. Thieves like her deserve to go to jail, and I aim to make that happen or die trying! I want her to feel the pain I felt when . . ." Her voice choked and she could not finish the sentence.

Jack hung his head, indicating he had nothing more to say on the subject except, "Do what you need to do. I will cooperate in any way I can."

WHAT THE HEART WANTS

PART 5

CHAPTER 13

Janice's heart needed and wanted love, but it wanted revenge even more after Jack died. She became more determined than ever to seek every possible legal avenue to get it. "I'll show Elaina Albright and her miserable cronies what money can do!" she announced to the team of prominent attorneys she hired after firing the incompetent investigator. "She once accused me of using my money to buy friends and Jack's love. If Elaina thinks I used it to buy friends and love, what does she think I'll spend to get justice?" she told lead attorney Percy Evans, just as she had told Jack in a prior conversation before his untimely death. "Mr. Evans I want you to do whatever it takes to put her and her scumbag friends in prison where they belong. Send me the bill! I don't expect to be compensated for what they have taken from Jack money-wise, but when it comes to Elaina, I want her to spend time in prison to think about what she did to Jack, me, and any others she has scammed over the past five years!"

"It may not be as easy as you think to go after Elaina." cautioned Percy. "People like her move on as soon as they get wind someone is on to them. The private investigator you hired has, unfortunately, forced the hand of her group to move on after they realized they were being tailed. His poor surveillance skills led them to scatter like rats on the proverbial sinking ship. While I am reasonably sure they will regroup at some point, especially since they have figured out it's a source of easy money to scam writers who want to gain fame and fortune. But until we get more reliable information as to their whereabouts, I cannot stress enough that the case will be difficult. Then again, it's to our advantage they likely won't give up scamming foolhardy people." Janice cringed at hearing the word 'foolhardy', a word that described Jack when he was taken in, but she knew what Percy said was a fact. "Right now we don't know where this journey will take us," he cautioned. "I do know we need to hire a more competent investigator, and that could cost you some big bucks."

"I thought I made it clear I don't care what it costs!" declared Janice. "They have to pay for what they have done. They cost Jack and me what could have been five wonderful years together. Five long friggin' years! Jack's state of health when I found him in that deplorable nursing home didn't leave us anywhere near enough quality time together after I rescued him. Would you believe he lingered there without proper food or care for an entire year before I learned where he was?" She was shaking with rage and in tears by the time she finished speaking.

"Easy there, Janice," implored Percy, handing her a neatly pressed, monogramed, white linen handkerchiefs.

"We will do our best to find Elaina and her friends. And when we do, they will go to prison for fraud and possibly elder abuse if they continue to be engaged in the same sort of scam. You do realize the statute of limitations for getting any money has run out regarding her scamming Jack?" he asked. Janice said she knew, but insisted they had to proceed. "I am relatively confident we will be able to come up with some other charges, like evading the authorities and elder abuse for starters, since we have reason to believe she and her accomplices are still engaged in the same type of scam on older men," continued Percy.

"You had better be right," declared Janice. "I'm placing my trust in you. And that isn't easy for me to do since you happen to have the misfortune of being a man."

At that comment Percy grimaced. "You can be sure my team and I will do our best on your behalf," he replied. "My mother was scammed a few years ago by someone like these people. It didn't involve a movie deal, but it did involve a lot of money. Those people are now rotting in prison. Does that tell you something?"

Janice nodded, but she still didn't know if she completely trusted Percy or not. "Just because you successfully prosecuted the crooks who scammed your mother doesn't mean you will be successful with these miserable creeps," declared Janice. Percy took a deep breath and sighed. He had little doubt he and the rest of his legal team had their work cut out for them, but he declined to make a comment regarding her statement, instead continuing to offer his plan of attack.

"First and foremost, you need to hire Rick Stapleton. He's one of the best investigators in the business. I've had the opportunity to see his work up close. I know he operates in a way that gets results, and I've worked with a lot of them. I warn you, he isn't cheap," said Percy.

"Money isn't an issue, but I want to meet him and pass my own judgment before I agree to give him one dime."

"That won't be a problem," replied Percy. "He's waiting in the outer office. I suspected you would want to meet and evaluate him before any money changes hands, but I took a chance and went out on a limb."

Janice looked at him in a questioning manner. "What do you mean you went out on a limb?"

Percy smiled. "Please let me finish – I have already hired him, and as a result Rick has already successfully done some snooping for us." This statement made the frown on her face disappear. She smiled for the first time since hiring Percy and his legal team.

"That is a smart move on your part to have him come here, but if it doesn't pan out, the dime is on you for what work he's already done," said Janice. "Send him in. I want to meet the man you tell me is one of the best in the business. Talk is cheap. I want action."

"Fair enough," replied Percy. He reached for the intercom button to alert his secretary to send Rick into his office.

WHAT THE HEART WANTS

PART 6

CHAPTER 14

Janice was not expecting to see a tall, well-built, extremely handsome man with piercing brown eyes come through the door into Percy's law office. It was even more of a shock to see him exhibiting the exuberance of a young colt. He was casually dressed in a collarless, green T-shirt with a silly looking penguin embossed on the front and jeans, expensive designer jeans no less. Well-worn brown topsiders, sans socks, covered his feet. It was hard to miss the slight tinge of gray hair at the temples of his dark brown, almost black, curly hair. He had a suntan that could only have been achieved by spending hours on a golf course or at the beach. His lean, muscular appearance assured Janice he worked out in a gym. Janice guessed he was close to her age.

"Hello there Percy, you old barracuda," Rick said as he bounded into the office while extending his hand toward Percy before spotting Janice sitting in a chair to the side of the desk. His attention quickly shifted from Percy to become riveted on Janice. "Well, well, well, who do we have here? Where have you been hiding this lovely creature, you old dog? And here I thought you were just another lonely old man." Percy stood shaking his head in a look of reproach, causing a frown to wrinkle his forehead and tense the muscles around his mouth as he shook Rick's extended hand.

"Rick, this is the client I told you about. Meet Janice Crenshaw Fairchild. Janice, I would like for you to meet Rick Stapleton." Janice merely nodded and did not rise from her chair or extend her hand.

"Well hello there," said Rick in a low sexy voice, a leering smile playing across his ruggedly handsome face. "Where have you been all of my life? You must be an angel who just flew in from heaven because I haven't seen you around here before."

Janice gave him a withering look. "Save the pickup lines for women you meet in bars. You are here for a job interview, not trying to get a date with some bimbo. I want references regarding the work you have done, and I don't mean your mother, other family members, or lonely women. I expect a written statement from at least four of your clients, make that paying clients, to the effect that you have done your job and the expected results were obtained. If you did not satisfy clients' needs, I would like information on why you failed to produce those results."

Rick's self-assured smile quickly evaporated to a look of genuine surprise. "You didn't tell me she's a barracuda just like you! I might have stayed at the club and considered lunch with Lola." Percy's frown changed to a thin-lipped smile.

"I thought you ended your relationship with Lola several months ago."

"I did, but I think lunch with her might have been better than this so-called job interview. By the way, since when do I have to start interviewing for a job with your firm? You know I'm good at what I do."

Percy held up his right hand in a gesture meant to silence Rick. "Janice, would you mind stepping out into the reception area for a few moments, please? I have something I want to discuss with Rick in private," said Percy. Janice reluctantly stood while giving Percy a questioning look. "I promise this won't take long. Then you can join us again," he added when he saw the look on her face.

"All right, but I hope you have another private investigator waiting in the wings. At the moment I don't hold this arrogant, poor excuse for a man in the same regard as you apparently do," replied Janice. As soon as Janice closed the door behind her, Percy told Rick to take a seat. He immediately sprawled out on the expensive brown leather sofa and propped his feet up on the equally expensive cherry wood coffee table in front of him.

"What the hell is going on?" he demanded. "That little bitch just referred to me as arrogant and a poor excuse for a man! Who in the hell does she think she is, Mother Teresa? Just because she's a beautiful woman doesn't give her the right to refer to me as arrogant or a poor excuse for a man! She doesn't even know me!"

"Settle down, Rick!" admonished Percy. "Janice has had a bit of a shock by the death of her husband, Jack, late last year. It's a long, sad story, but you already know it involves some shady characters who took his money under false pretenses, and they probably continue to do the same with other male writers. You also need to know she rescued her husband from an even earlier death, using her money to make sure he had a shot at having a good life, even after he did something you and I know most women would have never forgiven. Before you comment, I want to make it clear that Janice isn't like most women. She's a caring and loving person who was badly hurt. She was able to forgive him, but because she was so badly hurt she doesn't trust anyone, especially men. I can't say that I blame her, especially after what Jack did and the way the investigator she hired before she came to me charged top dollar and did such a lousy job."

"And I'm supposed to feel sorry for her? We've all had our feelings hurt or lost a loved one at one time or another, so please, spare me the tear-jerking details," replied Rick, a bored look on his face as he examined a nail in need of trimming.

"I'm not asking you to feel sorry for Janice, just try to understand where she's coming from. She's the last person to expect pity from anyone, you included. I've had the chance to get to know her while working with her and the other PI, who let us both down. I hasten to add that joker wasn't hired by me. Janice hired him while she was still in a state of shock shortly after her husband's death. We would both appreciate your expertise in continuing to track down this woman, Elaina Albright, and her accomplices. Janice deserves justice, and I aim to do my best to see that she gets it. Do you remember what happened to my mother?" Rick nodded affirmatively. "Well, something remarkably similar happened to Janice and Jack. It cost them not only his money but also his health and years of happiness that he and Janice would have shared. I want you to put on your big boy pants and act like the gentleman I know you are capable of being! Is that clear? Because if it isn't, you can start looking for another law firm to ply your trade, and I will make certain you do not get good references from me! And while you're at it Rick, take your feet off my coffee table and sit up straight!"

Rick slowly removed his right foot followed by his left foot from the coffee table. Percy didn't miss the look of frustration on his face that was made even clearer when he said, "You sure have a burr up your butt today! It's obvious that hostile broad has managed to get you wrapped around her little finger!"

Percy glared at him. "Do not ever refer to Mrs. Fairchild as a hostile broad! You are pushing your luck. I explained her situation. What I need to know right now is whether or not it's possible for you to act in a responsible manner and take on this case? If the answer is no, then consider our business relationship permanently ended. You can pick up a check for the work you have done so far on her behalf on the way out of my office."

Percy made a move toward the intercom, which Rick took to mean that Percy was going to alert his secretary to cut him a check.

Rick scratched his head, rubbed his chin, and then leaned forward. "Percy, you drive a hard bargain. If you didn't pay so well and I didn't like you, I would tell you to go screw yourself. You aren't the only show in this town."

Percy learned forward in his chair, his face exhibiting grim determination, both arms resting firmly on the desk in front of him. "That may be true, but I'm the *biggest* show in this town, and you know it! Please keep in mind that if I put out the word, your ass is grass and I'm the lawn mower! You also need to be aware you are not the only show in town when it comes to good private eyes. So what will it be?"

"Like I have a choice? Man, I have bills to pay just like everyone else. Sure, I'll continue to take on this case as long as I get paid and you keep your client on a tight leash."

"Good. I'll be expecting you to produce or ..."

"I know, I know! My ass is grass and you're the lawn mower. Give me the rest of the gory details so I can follow up on what I've already managed to uncover."

"I think it would be best if you heard the details directly from Janice. Then you might see her in a different light for the delightful person she really is," replied Percy. Rick groaned but had sense enough to keep his mouth shut.

"Shall I ask her to rejoin us?" questioned Percy.

Rick sighed. "Like I said before, do I have a choice?"

"No, you do not have a choice, and I expect you to apologize for the discourteous way you spoke to Janice earlier," insisted Percy.

Rick turned on the charm when he fully realized his job was on the line. "Percy, you remind me of my old man. He was always on my case to be a good boy and sit up straight."

Percy just smiled, sat back in his black leather chair, and pushed the intercom. "Louise, would you please send Janice Fairchild back into my office? And Louise, would you be so kind as to bring us some iced tea, please? I think we could all use a little refreshment about now."

"Right away, sir," replied his secretary.

"Iced tea? For Christ sake man, don't you have any gin, scotch, or bourbon?" exclaimed Rick. "I think I need a real drink right about now."

"Then that's a good reason to ask Janice to join you at the bar across the street after we are finished here. I have it on reliable sources they serve some good snack foods, too," Percy dryly commented.

"You can't be serious! You want me to ask her to join me for a drink and some snacks? You know I never fraternize with my clients," insisted Rick.

"It would be in your best interest to make an exception in this case," answered Percy. Rick knew he had to at least try to do what was asked or he would have to move to a distant state in order to make a living. And that wasn't an option he wanted to consider when it would mean compiling a new client base, finding a home, and making new friends.

There was a knock at the inner office door. "Come in," said Percy. It was Janice followed by Louise carrying a silver tray bearing three, tall, frosty glasses of iced tea, white linen napkins, lemon wedges, artificial sweetener, sugar cubes, and the appropriate long handled spoons. "Just put the tray over there on the coffee table, Louise. Janice, you take a seat on the sofa beside Rick. That will make it easier for you to reach the lemon and sugar," said Percy.

"I prefer to sit in a chair," retorted Janice.

"Awe, come on, Mrs. Fairchild. I don't bite," said Rick. "I'm sorry I spoke to you in such a disrespectful way before. Please forgive me. I promise it won't happen again. Would you like lemon, sugar, or artificial sweetener in your tea? I'll be glad to add … "

"Never mind," replied Janice curtly as she took a seat on the sofa as far away from him as possible. "I am perfectly capable of preparing my own tea."

I'm sure you are, thought Rick. *And I'm equally sure you are capable of a whole lot more.* Percy smiled benevolently as he joined them and sat in the chair where Janice had indicated she wanted to sit. After they took a few sips of tea Rick placed his glass back on the silver tray. Janice continued to hold hers, as did Percy.

"Let's get down to business," said Rick. "Percy tells me I need to hear the details about this case from you, Mrs. Fairchild, so shoot so I can get this show back on the road as fast as possible."

"Let's not be so formal, Rick. I'm sure Janice won't mind if you call her by her first name," interjected Percy. He gave Janice a questioning look. "You don't mind, do you? It seems, I don't know . . . like it would make more sense to be on a first name basis when the two of you will be working closely together on this case. I think it would be nice if both of you could dispense with formality, don't you?"

Janice swallowed hard. "I suppose you are right, Percy." She turned to look directly at Rick, her intense blue eyes causing him to do a double take and shift uncomfortably in his seat. "I do expect to be kept informed on what is being done every step of the way. If using our given names helps in the process, I suppose that would be the best approach," she replied. Rick gave her one of his best disarming smiles.

"You got it, Janice. I'll even let you know every time I use the restroom." She did not rise to the bait in the way Rick had expected her to respond.

"You do that Mr. Stapleton. Just be sure you wash your hands before you make any personal contact with me."

"Don't tell me you've already forgotten Percy wants us to be on a first name basis." he shot back sarcastically.

"Play nice Rick," admonished Percy. "Janice, please fill Rick in on what happened to both you and Jack. He needs to hear it from you instead of from me or reading reports."

It was Janice's turn to squirm in her seat in an attempt to increase the distance between Rick and her. She placed her glass on the tray and said, "I don't think what happened to me is necessary for Rick to know in reference to this case. What happened to Jack is what is important. Elaina Albright persuaded him to spend his life's savings, over $400,000, on the production of a movie to be made from one of his books. I want to point out that money was for production costs on a movie that never got made. I have bank copies of the checks Elaina endorsed to prove she is the one who cashed them and then used the money for personal use and to pay her henchmen. The investigator I hired, before Percy came on the scene, was able to find a paper trail proving she is the one who cashed them soon after Jack deposited them into the account set up for the purpose of financing the movie. He figured out the men she paid to publish her book were the ones who gave her the idea to con Jack into thinking she could help him get a movie deal and make millions. Of course, they expected to be cut in on the deal for any help they provided. She also bought personal items, including a new car and expensive jewelry. When Jack's money ran out she dumped him and moved on to do the same type of scam on at least four unsuspecting, older, male writers we know about. The investigator tracked her to the Miami, Florida, South Beach Art Deco District before she suspected she was being tailed. That's when she and the other two vanished, according to the investigator. He insisted the trail went cold through no fault of his own, and that's why I fired him, hired Percy, and hired you."

Janice didn't know Percy had told Rick the backstory of how Jack had hurt her, how Janice had forgiven him, or how they were married two years after she rescued him from the horrid nursing home. But it was good he had told him because it made Rick's blood boil. These were exactly the type of scumbags he delighted in catching to make sure they didn't scam other people. He was able to control his anger with a practiced deadpan look, with the exception of a barely discernible twitch to his left jaw.

"How soon do you want to leave for Miami, Janice?" he asked, immediately changing his philosophy of never becoming personally involved with clients. "I have a good friend who is a pilot who happens to own his plane. That means we can leave today. All I have to do is give him a call.

If you will make the hotel reservations I will take care of that end. Just so you are aware, I've also been able to track Elaina to the glamorous South Beach Art Deco District. A writer's convention is being held at the Fontainebleau Hotel as we speak. It has been a while since the last investigator lost track of her, and I believe she feels it's a safe bet to return to the Miami area since the convention pickings for another scam are a given. I think we can close in on her once we get down there. I have learned she is presently a registered guest at the Fontainebleau, and I feel confident we won't have a problem nailing her there."

"Give me two hours to get home, pack a few things, and take care of some personal business," replied Janice. "Where do you want me to meet you?"

"Give me your address. I'll give my friend a call to book his services, do some packing, then I'll pick you up for the airport."

Wow, thought Rick when she gave him her address. *That's in the really nice part of Palm Springs. This dame, oops make that* lady, *must really have some big bucks in order to live there.* Rick was not aware of her success as a writer. He had not read any of her books, nor had he seen any of the TV movies based on them. To him she was just another pretty face with a good body and no different from the many the other pretty faces and bodies to be found on the Palm Springs scene. Only, for some reason, he sensed Janice was somehow different from the women he often picked up in the posh bars or clubs for one night stands now and then. He, too, had been hurt when the one woman he loved and trusted, Lola, became romantically involved with his best friend just when Rick was planning to propose to her. Like Janice, Rick was on high alert to avoid any serious involvement with the opposite sex. Known among his buddies, Rick's motto was "love 'em for one night, then leave 'em" after the relationship with Lola ended.

CHAPTER 15

Exactly two hours later, Rick rang the doorbell at Janice's glamorous mountainside residence overlooking the city of Palm Springs proper. Her housekeeper answered the mahogany and etched glass front door.

"I'm here to pick up Janice," he announced. The woman, Bernice Groves, Janice's long-time, trusted cook and housekeeper, gave him the once over.

"Do you have an appointment?" she asked in a tone that could only be interpreted as cool.

"She is expecting me. I'm Rick Stapleton. We are flying to South Florida to work on a legal case." Bernice continued her cold appraisal of Rick before she gave him a nod.

"She did vaguely mention something about a flight to Florida," she replied. "Step inside and have a seat over there in the foyer. I'll let her know you are here." She disappeared up a flight of curving stairs to leave Rick standing there like a schoolboy summoned to the principal's office for breaking the rules.

Janice was closing the zipper on her suitcase when Bernice softly knocked on her door. "Come in," called Janice. Bernice opened the door and entered the large, well-appointed bedroom suite with a mountain and city window view.

"There's a man waiting for you in the foyer. Says his name is Rick Stapleton. He tells me he came here to pick you up for a trip to Miami Beach, Florida. Miami Beach? You didn't tell me you were going to Miami Beach."

Janice had also failed to mention he was very a good looking man who was now dressed in Gucci loafers and designer clothing that made him look like a model who just stepped out of a GQ magazine.

"I'm sorry, Bernice. This just came up a couple of hours ago. You are aware I have been trying to locate Elaina Albright and see to it that she pays dearly for what she did to Jack. Mr. Stapleton is a private investigator who has received information Elaina is in Miami. We need to get down there before she finds out someone new is hot on her trail. I intended to tag along to make sure I get my money's worth this time."

"Not another private investigator!" sniffed Bernice. "Didn't you learn anything by what that other investigator did to you the last time? All he did was take your money! What makes you think this guy is any different?" she exclaimed, indignantly.

"This one is different. My attorney knows him well and he came highly recommend," said Janice. "Besides, it's my money and this is how I want to spend it. I can't sit by and allow that scheming bitch Elaina to get away with what she did to Jack and me!"

"Don't you think it's about time you let the past go and move on with your life? What you are doing will not bring back the time you lost with Jack. Wake up, Janice! As far as I'm concerned, that is good riddance. Why, that man broke your heart. Why don't you accept the fact Jack is gone and he isn't coming back? You gave him back a good life during the two years before his death when he didn't deserve it. You are still an attractive woman who needs to find a new love. Be happy with the time you did have with Jack, if you must, and move on." insisted Bernice.

Janice closed her eyes and bit her tongue before speaking. "I know you have my best interest at heart, just like my children do, Bernice, but this is something I have to do before I am able to move on. There was a time Jack meant the world to me in spite of what he did. I thought I would die when he told me he wanted Elaina and not me. I will admit that for a long time I was so hurt I thought I hated him. At the same time my heart knew deep down that I still loved him. I never stopped loving him, even if my brain thought otherwise for a long time. I owe it to him and myself to do this in his memory."

"I can see there's no point in trying to talk you out of this foolishness," sniffed Bernice in a way to let Janice know she did not approve. "Good luck in Miami Beach. I hope you find what you are looking for and can put this latest chapter of your life behind you and move on."

"So do I Bernice. So do I," replied Janice wearily. "Now if you will excuse me, I really must go meet Mr. Stapleton. He has a private plane waiting and you know how much I hate to keep people waiting, especially if I'm the one paying them!"

Rick had his back to Janice while admiring the painting of a local, snow-covered mountain scene when Janice quietly walked up behind him in the foyer. "Are you ready to go, or are you going to stand there inspecting the artwork?" she announced.

Surprised, Rick jumped at the sound of her voice. Janice tried to soften her approach, but failed when she added, "If you are supposed to be such a top notch investigator, I would think you would constantly be aware of your surroundings and not allow someone to sneak up on you. Would it be better if I were to wear a bell around my neck or squeaky shoes so you know when I'm around?" Her attempt at humor fell flat. Rick took his time slowly turning around to face her.

"I thought I was in friendly territory," he answered. "It looks like I was mistaken in making that assumption. Just don't change the perfume you are wearing and I'll know it's you. Then I can be on high alert for a verbal attack. Then again, maybe I should get a rabies shot, just in case you decide to bite." Rick's demeanor left little doubt he was returning her attempt at humor with thinly veiled sarcasm.

"Don't you think it's about time we call a truce?" asked Janice.

"I don't know what you mean. I'm just standing here admiring the artwork," Rick sweetly replied.

"Oh, come off it!" exclaimed Janice. "You know exactly what I mean. We seem to bring out the worst in each other. We just met three hours ago, and I'm already tired of which one of us can make the more sarcastic remarks. Can't we be civil instead of snipping at one another, especially since it appears we face an eight hour flight together in a small plane and will be spending time together working on this case?"

"I'll do my part if you will do yours," replied Rick. "I'm really not a bad guy when you get to know me. Since you are paying the bills, I'll let you decide where we start the search on South Beach, but I want you to keep in mind that I'm the investigator, not you."

Janice grimaced and nodded.

"Even though it is expensive I've booked us each of us a king-size, non-smoking room at the Fontainebleau Hotel since that is where the writer's convention is being held and also where Elaina is staying. I know she has expensive taste when she is spending other people's money. She proved that to me a long time ago. She is likely to hang out in the bar area at the Fontainebleau looking for an elderly sucker who has lots of money and wants to believe his book will be made into a financially successful movie. That and the sucker will think he has a chance at a fling with her, although unless she has had some plastic surgery and lost some weight, I don't know what any man would see in her, especially naked."

Meow, thought Rick, but he knew better than to make such a comment out loud. It wasn't easy, but he made a concerted effort to limit their conversation during the long flight to comments on cloud formations and the scenery below.

"Your wish to stay at this hotel is my command since you are paying the bill. We're here at the landmark Fontainebleau Hotel in all of its ageless glory," replied Rick as he pulled their rented, shiny black BMW up under the portico-covered entrance of the elegant, well-maintained, beachfront hotel.

I don't know why he couldn't have rented a less expensive car thought Janice. *Guess he knows I have deep pockets.*

They were met immediately by a uniformed bellman wearing a Hawaiian shirt, beige Bermuda shorts, and white, brand name sneakers just like the other bellhops. The sight of his attire caught Janice off guard. It was the type of clothing Jack would have worn, sans the hotel logo. She didn't want to let Rick know how she was feeling so she took a deep breath, squared her shoulders, and said nothing. *If you let him see you in tears he won't respect you, so suck it up*, she firmly told herself.

"Would you like valet or self-parking, sir?" asked the bellhop. "I highly recommend valet parking in our secured garage. We've had a rash of car burglaries in the past couple of months in the open lot," stated the young man as he opened the driver's side car door.

Rick turned in his seat to give Janice an inquisitive look. "It's your dime. Do you want valet parking? I don't really care if some jerk breaks into or steals this rental car. I signed on for their insurance since the extra cost is on you."

"You can't be serious! Of course we want valet parking," she answered icily. She was trying to maintain the image of someone who was in charge of making such decisions when her stomach felt as though it had been invaded by a swarm of honey bees attacking blossoms on a lilac bush.

"Remember the truce," Rick chuckled in a barely audible voice before he exited the car and walked around to help her out, leaving the bellman to retrieve their luggage from the car trunk.

"The lady wants valet parking," he told the attendant, tossing him the car keys.

"I'll take care of it and see to it that your bags are sent to your room, sir," the bellman replied as he handed Rick the claim check. Rick handed him a ten dollar tip before they entered the luxurious doors, opened by a uniformed doorman. Neither Rick nor Janice knew when the bellman said room, he meant just that—a room—not rooms.

"You must be joking!" insisted Janice as they stood at the check-in desk. "I know I specifically requested two king-size, non-smoking rooms when I made reservations by computer earlier today after viewing your site. And those are the type of accommodations that were confirmed!"

"I'm sorry, Madam, but if you read the fine print in our advertisement, we have the option of assigning a room or rooms that may be different than those appearing in the advertisements. There is a large writer's convention going on here in the hotel, along with the annual yacht show down at the marina. We do not have any additional rooms available until the end of next week. Your suite does contain two bedrooms, each with a private bath. There is a living room, kitchenette and bar separating them. Most guests use the second bedroom as a dressing room or to store their personal belongings if they do not expect other guests to join them," said the haughty clerk with a decidedly British accent. "Unless you wish to find other accommodations at a distance of at least 75 miles from Miami Beach, I strongly suggest you take the suite if you plan to be in the area for the next week."

Janice wondered why the bellman accompanying them to their room kept giving them knowing glances as he opened the double French doors and ushered them inside. Her eyes opened wide in a look of total surprise.

The clerk had failed to mention their suite was the honeymoon suite with the master bedroom, complete with a heart shaped bed, rose petals strewn on the carpet throughout the suite floor and on the bed, and foil-wrapped, heart-shaped chocolates on a heart-shaped ceramic tray, accompanying a bottle of expensive champagne chilling in a silver ice bucket, on one of the night stands. To top it off, a mirrored ceiling loomed above the bed!

"What in the hell is this?" she indignantly demanded.

"I think it's obvious, Ma'am," replied the bellman. "This is the honeymoon suite."

"I can see that," she replied. "The only problem is we are not on our honeymoon. We aren't even married!"

"What she means is we aren't married. Yet," interjected Rick. "The ship's captain will take care of that when we set sail in a few days, but we wanted to do some sightseeing and enjoy the yacht show before embarking on the cruise. Now if you will excuse us . . ." Rick handed the man a twenty dollar bill and he left, but not before insisting that he refresh the silver ice bucket as he offered another leering grin.

"What in the world prompted you tell him we are going to get married aboard ship when that is the last possible thing that's going to happen?" Janice sputtered. "What were you thinking? You know we are barely civil to ..."

Rick raised his hand to stop her from continuing. "Think about it. If Elaina is a guest here in the hotel we can almost be assured employees will talk. Elaina could overhear gossip about the couple who isn't married staying in the honeymoon suite and decide to take a closer look. She's probably already on the lookout for someone tailing her, so you need to make an appointment in the beauty salon to have your hair colored at least light brown and cut in a new style, along with checking out the gift shop to buy a pair of sexy sunglasses instead of those gosh awful black-rimmed old lady sunglasses you are wearing!"

"I'll have you know the sunglasses to which you are referring cost $350.00! They are a well-known brand, and for your further information, I happen to like my current hair color and style," Janice informed him.

Rick shrugged his shoulders and threw his hands up in the air in a gesture of defeat. "Look, lady, I'm just trying to make it harder for Elaina to recognize you since she happens to be a guest here! Why don't you just wear a neon green T-shirt with your name in large print in bright purple letters on the back of it? I seriously doubt you have changed your appearance in the last few years and she could spot you in a New York minute!" he exclaimed.

"Remember, we decided not to snipe at each other," chided Janice. "All you had to do was give me a valid reason why you thought I needed to make those changes, and I would have been happy to make them. There is no reason for you to throw in the old lady sunglasses remark!" She hated to admit it, but she had not changed her appearance in years.

"You don't understand the way I work," said Rick. "I am not used to explaining what has to be done. That's why I've made it policy never to fraternize with clients. You need to

313

blame Percy. He insisted I had to make an exception in your case, and for the life of me I don't understand why!"

"So that's what the private conversation was all about back in his office," muttered Janice. "I wondered why Percy insisted I leave the room while the two of you had a good ol' boy talk."

"Your guess is as good as mine as to why he insisted that I had to make an exception for you," replied Rick with a shrug of his broad shoulders. "In case you haven't noticed, there are times when Percy makes decisions only he understands. But I have learned such decisions usually have merit. And that, my dear lady, is why he is one of the best minds in the legal business. Now it's our turn to make the next couple of decisions."

"For starters, I am not your dear lady!" retorted Janice. "It has been a long day. I'm tired and in no mood to make any decisions beyond that of where to have dinner, preferably alone. Then I need to go to bed, alone, and get a good night's sleep!"

"Where you are going to sleep is one of the decisions you need to make. To help you make that decision I'll put it in plain English. Which bedroom do you want? As for dinner, we could order room service if you are too tired to go out. But I think we should go to the bar, have a drink and some snacks, then come back here to the room for a short nap before we hit the nightlife scene and have dinner. I have learned things don't start hopping out here on

Miami's South Beach until ten p.m. at the very earliest. I hasten to point out that if we stay here in the room and order room service we could miss out on the chance to catch Elaina in action. But once again, it's your call."

"If we go to the bar I won't have time to go to the beauty salon for a makeover or buy new sunglasses like you have insisted I need to do." protested Janice.

"Your hair is long enough you could pull it back into a ponytail. As for the sunglasses, in the bar, or at dinner, they won't be necessary, at least for today. I am positive it will be dark by the time we go out for dinner. Problem solved for now."

"Rick, you have an answer for everything, don't you?" replied Janice in disgust. He grinned and shrugged his shoulders. "Don't you know ponytails are meant to be worn by for fourteen-year-old giggly girls who insist on chewing bubble gum and not a mature lady like me? I would look absolutely ridiculous!" Janice replied.

"This is Miami's South Beach. Anything goes here. You will find wrinkled grandmothers with varicose veins and cellulite wearing their tiny bikinis or short shorts. Men, a lot more mature than me, will be dressed in their scanty, bikini brief swimsuits revealing their spindly legs and beer bellies hanging out for the world to see," laughed Rick. "You talk like you're an old woman when you can't be more than 35."

"Don't I wish I were 35 again," said Janice. "Nice try to make me feel better, but I don't think they will be dressed like that at this time of day."

"I disagree about trying to make you feel better. But I have the feeling that if I were, it would fall on deaf ears, so I won't try to defend myself. Just tie back your hair with a scarf, wear an appropriate dress, add some lipstick, and meet me in the lobby bar in fifteen minutes. We have work to do, and it won't get done by us standing here trading barbs! You take the master bedroom."

Rick didn't wait for her to reply. He picked up his suitcase and headed for the smaller of the two bedrooms all the while muttering under his breath. "Damn you Percy! I don't know what in the hell you were thinking when you insisted this woman accompany me on this investigation! My gut tells me she is going to be nothing but a royal pain in the ass!"

"Why is he such an arrogant know-it-all?" muttered Janice as she tied back her long blonde hair with a multicolored blue, Hermés silk scarf that accented her sky blue eyes. Looking in the bathroom mirror she had to admit she didn't look too bad. Actually, with a little blush added to her cheeks and some pink lipstick, she looked fantastic. She also had to admit nobody would guess her age when she put on that cute little blue and white number that had been hanging in the back of her closet for several years that she had decided to toss in the suitcase at the last minute.

Adding a dab of Chanel No. 5 perfume behind her ears and between her still perky breasts, she headed for the hotel lobby bar to meet Rick, who had decided to go on ahead while she changed.

"Over here," called Rick when he saw her get off the elevator and head toward the open bar area. "Wow! You sure look nice. I am glad you took my advice to lose the drab beige slacks and add some lipstick."

When she got closer he added, "And you smell good, too. The ponytail takes off at least ten years."

Janice glared at him. "You could have stopped at 'Wow you look nice and smell good,' but you just can't seem to learn when to keep your mouth shut and leave well enough alone! Is it me, or are you always like this when dealing with women?"

Rick pulled out a chair for her to sit across from him at the small, round cocktail table. "Sit, and since you asked, I'll answer your question, but only after I've had a drink first. What will you have? I'm having a double shot of gin over shaved ice with a lime twist and two stuffed olives." Janice involuntarily sucked in a deep breath as though she had just been punched in the pit of her stomach. "What's wrong?" asked Rick, a look of concern flooding across his face.

"That's the same drink Jack used to order," she uttered in a raw whisper. She immediately hated that she made such a statement, but she couldn't take it back.

Rick winced. "I'm sorry. I didn't realize it would upset you if I ordered gin. I can order whiskey instead if it will make you feel better."

"No. You need to order what you like. You didn't know it was Jack's favorite drink next to his homemade wine. I still have to get used to the idea he's gone."

A scantily clad waitress wearing short shorts and a tight-fitting halter barely covering her double D's approached their table to take their orders. Rick took Janice at her word and ordered the gin. Janice ordered white wine, even though she would have preferred sparkling water with a lemon twist, but felt she needed something stronger. They sat sipping their drinks and casually glancing around the bar for fifteen minutes with little conversation transpiring between them until she spoke up. "You need to hurry up and finish your drink so you can tell me why you seem to be down on women, specifically me."

Rick drained the remains of his drink in a single swallow. "There! Are you satisfied? I am not down on you, specifically. It's just that I don't like to be told how to run my business. Percy is like a father to me, but I resent him giving me orders like my old man used to do. I like women in general, but the one woman who got under my skin managed to cheat on me with my best friend and that makes me a little wary when it comes to the fairer sex. Does that answer your question?"

Janice closed her eyes and sighed softly. "More than you will ever know."

Rick leaned forward in his chair. "Please, don't leave me hanging with a response like that one. I have the feeling you've been hurt, too."

He made this comment even though Percy explained how Jack had hurt her. He hoped she would take this chance to open up and strengthen their bond in a more positive manner. No dummy, Janice immediately picked up on his intent and wasn't about to air what she considered her private dirty laundry.

"You could say that," she replied. "It's a sad story that happened a very long time ago. I have managed to get over it and get on with my life."

Rick snorted a laugh and popped another peanut into his mouth from the crystal bowl sitting on the table. "Sure you have. Is that why you don't trust men?"

"You could say that."

"Why don't you carry a tape recorder tied around your neck so you can play that response every time I ask you a question?" snorted Rick. "I'm not a therapist, but even I can read the signs that you still don't trust men. So get real and clue me in on what happened so we can . . ."

Janice cut him off. "So we can what? Let me get straight to the point and make myself clear. I am not interested in a personal relationship with you or any other man! Not now! Not ever! I made my peace with Jack because deep down I still loved him. Ours is purely a business arrangement."

"I wasn't suggesting anything of a personal nature between us," Rick lied. He was well-aware he would have liked nothing better than to bed this lovely creature. "I am just trying to understand where you are coming from so we can make this case work to our advantage." All the while he was thinking, *Yes, lady, I would like to jump your bones if I didn't think you would cause me bodily harm,* but he didn't say it. "Why don't you finish your wine? It might relax you to the point you can be honest with me. I know you've been hurt, and now you know I've been hurt. My admission is half the battle. The other half is on you."

Janice tilted back her head and emptied the remaining wine into her mouth. She swallowed before she started sputtering and began to point upward toward the open-railed, second-tier balcony of the bar.

"Look! Up there on the upper level! It's Elaina! She is sitting up there having a drink with an older man. I'll bet you dollars to donuts he's here for the writer's convention and he's her next mark! No! Don't turn and stare. Just be casual."

"Are you sure it's her? You haven't seen her in what … seven or eight years? People do change. You could be mistaken."

Janice gave him a dirty look while wiping the spilled wine from her chin.

"I'm positive it's Elaina! I will never forget that slutty tramp for as long as I live! It looks like she still hasn't lost her touch by the way he is looking at her. Why, he's almost drooling. I can hear it now; she is promising him her body, along with the moon and stars and a movie contract if he will put up the cash. And like an old fool, he thinks he stands a chance with a woman the age of his son or daughter."

"Do I detect a note of bitterness in your voice?" asked Rick.

"You could say that," she responded. "Can we leave now? I feel like I'm going to throw up!"

"We could, but not before I make a trip up to the balcony. I think the man with her just might be someone I happen to know."

"Really, you know that man?" Janice questioned.

"No, but she won't know that, and neither will he. It will give me a chance to photograph them and try to get an introduction on tape, for future reference. That way, I will have solid evidence of what she is doing. If I pretend to know that man, she won't suspect why I'm here if we happen to meet again before I manage to get a warrant and collar her. Trust me. I need to do this for evidence," replied Rick.

"How are you going to take a picture without them knowing? And besides, anything she says will be her word against yours."

"Check out the red silk carnation on my lapel." Janice reached out toward the flower.

"No, don't touch it!" exclaimed Rick in a raw whisper as he took her hand and kissed it. "I can activate the fake flower to become a recording device as well as camera. Would you be so kind as to give me some credit for knowing how to get information from a suspect without them knowing what I'm up to?"

"Why did you kiss my hand?" she asked indignantly, quickly withdrawing it from his lips as though the kiss had burned a blister.

Rick rolled his eyes and sighed. "To give the impression of a loving gesture to hide the fact you were checking out the carnation," he whispered. "From now on please do not question everything I do when we are in public. Save it for when we are back in our suite." That said, he got up and casually started to walk toward the curving staircase before he stopped, turned, and went back to stand beside Janice's chair. "Call me on my cell phone when I run my right hand through my hair," he said quietly. Janice could only watch what was about to take place on the upper level and wonder why he made such a statement. She was just about to question him again when she remembered he had just told her she should not question him when they were in public.

With an air of confidence wrapped around him like that of a man of means, Rick approached the cocktail table where Elaina and the unknown older man sat. He almost walked passed their table before he stopped, took two steps backward to do what appeared to be a double take.

"Dave Jackson! Is that you? I haven't seen you in a coon's age, you handsome old devil!"

Startled, the man looked at Jack in total surprise.

"I'm sorry, sir. You have mistaken me for someone else."

It was obvious to Rick the man was flattered at being told he was handsome, so he proceeded.

"Oh, I am so sorry! You are a dead ringer for my friend Dave. Are you sure you don't have a twin brother? Please, allow me buy both of you a drink as an apology for interrupting your evening."

"That won't be necessary," replied the man. "And no, I don't have a twin brother that I know about."

Rick smiled. "Oh, but I insist on buying both of you a drink. That is the least I can do. By the way, what are your names? I love to meet new people. My name is Sam Spade," the first name that popped into his mind. Elaina giggled when she heard the name of the fictional detective.

"Are you Sam Spade, the detective, featured in the mystery novels?" she inquired followed by a sexy pout.

Rick managed to fake a blush. "Gosh no!" he exclaimed. "I write bodice rippers, you know, love stories, or at least I try to write them. My mother was enamored with those detective stories, so she named me Sam. Our last name was Spade. That's why I'm here at the writer's convention. I hope to gain some more pointers on how to get my work published to a larger audience."

"Since you are also a writer, please join us for that drink," offered the man. "My name is Josh Riggins. I write redneck humor. This nice lady is going to help me get one of my books made into a movie. Maybe she can help you as well."

"Wow! That sounds great. Tell me more," said Rick as he pulled out a chair and sat to join them. He could see dollar signs registering in Elaina's eyes as he made sure she noticed the expensive looking Rolex watch on his left wrist. So what if it was a fake and he bought from a street vendor in Paris? *It serves its purpose in situations like these, especially in dim lighting*, thought Rick with a smile.

The split on the side of her skirt allowed Elaina to cross and expose her right leg as provocatively as possible considering she was still overweight. Then she leaned forward toward Rick in a way to allow her ample breasts to almost topple from her low-cut, pale pink, silk blouse. "Why settle for just being published when you can get your book made into a movie? I have the contacts you would need to get that accomplished," she purred.

"Really, you can do that?" Rick asked, wide-eyed, to show an unmistakable interest in what she had just said while openly admiring her cleavage. He was putting on a stellar performance.

"You can bet on it," replied Elaina with a come-hither smile. "But you need to know it will cost you. This does not happen for free. Just ask Josh. I will need a copy of your book for editing by the producer. That will cost you a $100,000 non-refundable dollars for his time. And then there will be other charges, also non-refundable, required by the production staff for the hiring of actors, permits, scenery, and everything else needed. That amount usually starts around $50,000, maybe a little more, as we prepare for production."

At the mention of the fees and charges, Rick drew in a deep breath and shook his head in a negative way.

Elaina backed off, likely afraid she had given too much information and that he might bolt. This prompted her to add, "But just think of how much money you will make when the finished product hits movie houses across the U.S. and foreign countries! You will be making millions of dollars before you know it! But first we need to talk about the details, but not tonight. I've had a busy day and I'm tired." Of course, this was a lie. She needed time to check out Rick's credentials and keep her current mark on the hook without the possibility of him losing interest and backing out.

"Gee, Elaina, do you really think I can make a lot of money?" asked Rick. "That would be just fantastic! I can hardly believe it . . . one of my books made into a movie?" Rick casually ran his right hand through his hair, as if to brush it away from his eyes. In a matter of seconds his cell phone rang.

"Excuse me I really need to take this call. It's important," he said as he started to rise. "Enjoy your drinks. Nice to meet both of you and, Elaina, I'll see you here in the bar around six tomorrow evening to discuss those details you mentioned." He stood to give the impression he was going to leave. "You did say your name was Elaina, didn't you? Sorry, but I'm not very good at remembering names."

"Six will be just fine," she replied. "And yes, the name is Elaina. Elaina Albright. "You don't have to leave," she insisted. "We are thoroughly enjoying your company."

Rick smiled, nodded, and sat back down turning his chair just far enough to make it appear the conversation with the caller was private. "Sorry to put you on hold Harry. I'm having a drink with some new friends . . . only ten million? Go for it, Harry. You know where I keep the check book. Sorry I can't talk more right now. Thanks for taking care of the details for me on this deal. We will talk when I get back to the office next week."

Rick knew he had Elaina's undivided attention even before he snapped his cell phone shut. She had no idea the conversation was directed at Janice, not someone by the name of Harry. "Sorry for the interruption, but I needed to answer that call," Rick sheepishly offered while trying his best to look apologetic.

"Not a problem," Elaina assured him. "Could you be persuaded to take a day trip to the Bahamas with me?" she added as soon as he hung up. "I do enjoy playing roulette, and you strike me as the kind of man who likes to take chances."

Rick continued to look embarrassed. "That would be nice, but I have someone I'm meeting when I go there after the convention is over," he stammered.

"I understand, perhaps another time real soon since we seem to have so much in common. I'm sure we would have a good time," she stated in a low sexy voice. Josh cleared his throat to remind them he was still seated at the same table.

"I'm sorry, Josh, I didn't mean to leave you out," said Elaina as she licked her lips provocatively. "You can come, too. We can take the trip just as soon as you dump your old lady and make things a little more permanent between you and me."

Rick wanted to tell the old man to run for the nearest exit, but knew that was not an option, at least not yet. Instead, he explained he had to meet a friend in the lobby and left.

CHAPTER 16

"Let's get out of here," were the first words out of Rick's mouth when he reappeared at the table he was sharing with Janice on the lower level. She was still sipping on a third glass of wine and starting to feel no pain. She protested their leaving, saying she hadn't finished her drink and that she wanted to know what had taken place with Elaina and the unknown man.

"That's what I'm paying you for," she said in a slightly slurred voice.

"Don't question me! Just follow me out of here and take the elevator to our suite a couple of minutes after I leave. I told Elaina I'm meeting someone in the lobby. I'll meet you in our suite after I find out Elaina's room number." Janice reluctantly did as he asked, but not without feeling like she was being ordered around like a child.

The longer she sat there at the balcony bar with Josh, and the more she thought about the chance encounter with Rick, the more uneasy Elaina became after she saw him make a brief contact with a vaguely familiar woman seated in the lower bar. The lighting was subdued just enough, and the distance made it hard to identify her, so she turned on the charm and told Josh they should call it a night.

"But Elaina, my dear, I thought we would . . ." implored Josh before Elaina interrupted him with a smile then leaned over to give him a lingering French kiss. "We will soon my love," she whispered intimately in his ear, knowing exactly what was on Josh's mind. "But won't your wife wonder about you being gone so long? What happens if she should grow impatient and wander down here to the bar and find us having drinks together?"

"That's easy. I'll just tell her we are discussing the movie deal," replied Josh. "She will be more excited once she knows about all of the money we'll make. By now you must know I'm more interested in a relationship with you than in mere money. Can't we . . ."

"Oh my dear, dear, dear Josh!" exclaimed Elaina with a pout. "She is a woman and as such, she will take one look at me and know there is more to our relationship than a movie deal. I'm in love with you. We will have plenty of time to be alone while she makes her grand entrance on the beach tomorrow afternoon."

Josh snorted a sarcastic laugh. "My dear Elaina, have you ever seen a beached whale try to make a grand entrance? That's my wife!" His demeanor quickly turned to mush when Elaina reiterated that she was in love with him and giggled.

"No I haven't seen a beached whale lately, so I will have to trust your interpretation when it comes to your wife, my sweet." To emphasize her words, she reached out to stroke his cheek lightly with her red lacquered fingernails, knowing full well the type of response it would elicit in the smitten man.

"You, my dear, are pleasingly plump. My wife is a big fat greedy whale!" declared Josh. "You have no idea how much I want to cup your lovely breasts with both hands, kiss them, and make love to you for hours. I may have a few years on me, but that doesn't mean the passion is gone." Elaina did her best to give him a look of total devotion while she felt nothing but revulsion at the suggestion of what he wanted to do. At the same time, she knew she had to play her cards right or lose out on his money, lots of money, before it was a done deal.

"Knowing that will help me have lovely dreams in anticipation of tomorrow," she told him with another pout. "Also, I hate to bring this up, but I will need $50,000 dollars in cash to pay the extras we need to hire for tomorrow's movie shoot."

Josh reached for the brown leather pouch tucked away in the inside pocket of his lightweight, camel-colored, cashmere jacket.

"Are you sure that will be enough?" he asked, excited at the news the shooting of his movie would start tomorrow. "I came prepared," he assured her.

Elaina blushed demurely. "Well, I didn't want to ask, but if you could spare another extra $50,000, that would help cover the cost of hiring the extras and purchasing their wardrobe and make-up without me having to hit you up for any more money until it is needed to pay the stars and production crew."

"Not a problem," he said as he discretely counted out $1,000 bills as though they were ones and hand them to Elaina. She immediately stuffed the wad of bills down the front of her blouse into her bra before she stood to carefully lean over and give Josh another deep lingering French kiss.

"See you tomorrow at noon. My room or yours?" she whispered in his ear as she pressed the weight of her breasts and money firmly against his shoulder after coming up for air.

"Your room, since I don't know for sure when the whale will head to the beach," he said, anticipation and lust shining in his rheumy, contact-covered eyes. "I will tell her I'm headed for the boat show in case she gets a later than usual start."

"Be sure to bring a couple of condoms and those little blue pills," she whispered in mock passion before she headed for the curved, wrought iron stairway leading down into the main bar.

Elaina made a beeline straight for the ladies room as soon as she made it down the stairs into the main bar. She remained seated in the mirrored make-up lounge area for half an hour to make sure nobody else was in any of the stalls before removing the money stashed in her bra. She hastily stuffed the bills in her oversized beaded purse then zipped it closed and headed out to the bank of elevators located directly across the lobby. Pushing the call button, she stood back and waited for the one car exclusively programmed to take her to rooms located on the penthouse floor. Thinking herself alone in the elevator, she started to giggle. "Another sucker down and maybe another one waiting to be fleeced," she murmured. "I love Miami Beach!"

She was totally unaware the car had been fitted with a tiny camera and voice-activated tape recorder stuck to the wall in such a way as to look like part of the mural featuring exotic birds, flowers, and coconuts in one of the palm trees scenes attached to the back wall.

It didn't take her long to stash the money, her clothing, and her cosmetics into several suitcases once she unlocked her door and entered her plush oceanfront suite. After the first hurried call, she placed another call for a bellman to help her down to the waiting stretch limo in the next ten minutes. That call was followed by still another call to the front desk to let the clerk know she was checking out. "Just mail the bill to my home address," she curtly instructed. When the clerk told her she couldn't do that without a signature, Elaina instructed her to bill it to the credit card on file. She gave a fleeting thought about leaving without paying for the room but changed her mind. Such an action would bring the police into the picture, and she didn't want that to happen, at least not until she had time to make her getaway. The credit card she planned to use was one given to her earlier that morning by another mark to cover any costs associated with the making of his movie. She felt sure he wouldn't know she would be using his credit card until it was too late.

CHAPTER 17

Rick sprinted up the back stairs and waited in the exit stairwell, listening for the elevator Elaina was in to stop on the penthouse floor. He didn't have to wait long. With the stairwell door open a tiny crack, he watched Elaina exit the elevator car, but he lost her once she walked down the hall into another hallway, out of his line of sight. This made it impossible for him to see which room she had entered. It took Rick only a moment to extract the tiny camera and recording device from the penthouse elevator and shove it into his pocket before making his way down to the front desk.

"Damn!" he muttered. "Guess I'll have to hurry to the front desk and start asking questions before she has the chance to leave her room again. I can't go knocking on doors. Somebody is sure to get spooked and call security." He left the stairway quickly and walked across the hall to push the button for the elevator to take him down to the lobby, hoping against hope Elaina would not come out of her room and see him.

It took a good nine minutes to charm the young lady behind the check-in desk to provide him with Elaina's room number. This happened only after a $100 bill mysteriously ended up on the counter between them. But by the time Rick was able to summon the elevator and make it back up to the penthouse, nobody answered the knock on Elaina's door. While Rick was negotiating with the desk clerk, Elaina, shielded by a cart filled with luggage, made her getaway through the lobby and stepped into the waiting limo.

Janice was sitting on the sofa in the living room situated between the bedrooms. She was having a nightcap and a snack from the mini bar when Rick returned to their suite. She could tell he was upset, but so was she. She waited wordlessly for Rick to tell her what had taken place. Rick, who was equally as stubborn as Janice, poured himself a stiff scotch on the rocks from the mini-bar and wandered over to the large window overlooking the ocean. He still did not speak. Janice held her ground and remained silent while tapping her left foot on the marble floor. Except for the sound of ice cubes swirling around in her glass of a splash of dark rum, cola, and lime twist, the hostile silence between them continued. Unable to tolerate it any longer, Rick finally spoke.

"I know you are upset with me," he began. "But I was able to get Elaina's undivided attention from the moment of the phone call you made to me. You should have seen her eyes light up when I mentioned the ten million to "Harry" when I was talking to you. I feel sorry for that poor bastard she was with. She did agree to meet me in the bar tomorrow night at six so we can work out a deal to make my book into a movie, but I have the feeling she might have split. I'm hoping the thought of fleecing me out of some big bucks may make her change her mind."

"If what you are telling me is true, why the long face? It seems to me that it won't take much to arrange for the police to become a part of that meeting when she shows up. You did manage to get something on tape and the camera for backup evidence in the elevator, correct?" she questioned.

"I did," replied Rick. "But by the time I learned the location of her room she had apparently taken off for parts unknown," he said glumly. "She didn't answer when I knocked on her door saying I was the maid to turn down her bed. By the way, that little caper to get information has cost you another hundred bucks."

"How do you know she took off?" Janice asked without referring to the money used to bribe the hotel desk clerk.

"I checked back with the desk clerk when nobody answered my knock on her door. She told me Elaina had just checked out via phone shortly after I talked her into giving me the room number. Come to think of it, I do remember seeing someone walking on the other side of a luggage cart stacked with suitcases, but I never dreamed it was Elaina."

Janice took another sip of her drink before she answered him caustically. "And what about Percy telling me you are one of the best investigators in the business? Well, Mr. Crack Investigator, where does this leave us, me in particular? I presume holding the bag and writing more checks for your so-called expertise?"

"Look, Janice! I'm doing my best. We both know Elaina is as slippery as an eel. The next week of the investigation is on me. Take it out of my pay."

"How kind of you," she replied sarcastically. "The problem is we don't have any idea where she is going, so we're back to square one."

"I checked with the bellman. He was able to provide the name and phone number of the limo service who picked her up. I told him I had found the wallet she left at the bar and wanted to return it. I was able to make contact with the taxi driver and told him the same story. He didn't hesitate to tell me he took her to the terminal at Miami International Airport. That means I'll have to call in a favor and find out where she was headed from there."

"So what is keeping you from doing that?"

"My cell phone needs charging."

"Here. Use mine," replied Janice as she thrust her cell phone at him. "Or you could use the phone here in the room, but then you would have to pay through the nose. And this time, the charge would be on your dime."

"Watch it!" challenged Rick as he reached out and took her cell phone. "You're snipping at me again. I thought we had a truce."

Tightlipped, Janice didn't answer him, instead concentrating on what remained of her drink as he dialed, walked away into his bedroom, and closed the door behind him. He came out of the room a few minutes later smiling. "Hurry up and get packed. We are going to take a little road trip up the coast." When Janice started to speak he shook his head. "Not now. I'll fill you in during the drive. We need to get moving or we could lose track of her!"

CHAPTER 18

Rick helped a slightly inebriated Janice get seated as the bellman loaded their bags in the trunk of the rental car. Few words passed between them during the checkout and departure process. When they pulled onto the northbound, I-95 freeway entrance ramp, Janice could not hold her tongue any longer.

"So when do you plan to fill me in on where we are headed?"

"Melbourne," he commented without adding any more information.

"Melbourne?" questioned Janice. "That's not just a little road trip! That's in Australia! Shouldn't we be headed for the airport?"

"There's a Melbourne, Florida," stated Rick. "They have an airport, and that's where Elaina is headed, according to my source."

"I'm aware there's a Melbourne in Florida, but I can't imagine Elaina would be headed there," said Janice with a touch of sarcasm. "I find it odd she would go there when she could go almost anywhere she wanted."

"Not odd at all. It's a small town close to the beach where she can get lost in relative comfort in the tourist scene until she decides it's time to return to South Beach where the pickings are better."

"Shouldn't we just wait here until she comes back instead of racing up the coast like a couple of deranged people?" challenged Janice.

"I thought about that, but Melbourne is only an hour and a half drive from Orlando. If she gets bored and thinks it's still not safe to return here to Miami Beach, she may head there where the pickings are good, though not as good as here at this convention." replied Rick. "Besides, it should be easier to spot her in Melbourne or Coco Beach, since there aren't as many large major hotels or tourists. I'm sure she thinks nobody would give a second thought about her going there. Why don't you sit back and enjoy the scenery? We've got about a 180-mile drive ahead of us."

Janice said little except to express hunger as they rolled past exits leading to the towns of Fort Lauderdale, West Palm Beach, Hobe Sound, Stuart, and Vero Beach on I-95. "When are we going to stop for something to eat?" she asked. "I'm starving!"

"We're almost there, so hang in there," said Rick, as though he was speaking to a petulant child. "I know of a good Italian Restaurant called Rosa's on the way to Melbourne. Trust me. It will be worth the wait. We should be there in time for a late dinner."

"I certainly hope so, since all I've had are a couple of drinks, a few peanuts, and no real solid food since yesterday's lunch. And don't you dare count the candy bar from the mini bar! With this traffic, I have my doubts we will get there in time for dinner."

There was no mistaking the fact Janice was cranky. "Since you seem so familiar with the area, where do you suggest we spend the night?" she continued.

"I thought you knew the area since Percy told me you once lived in this part of Florida. I was counting on you to make that decision," answered Rick. "As for dinner, it's Friday evening. Many restaurants stay open until eleven, some even midnight. Since we are well past the city limits of West Palm Beach, Fort Pierce, and Vero Beach, it will be relatively open country from here to Melbourne. I can exceed the speed limit by at least ten miles an hour without being pulled over by highway patrol." He looked at his watch. "With luck and a heavy foot, I figure we'll be in downtown Melbourne around 10:30 p.m. at the latest."

"If you are counting on accommodations like The Fontainebleau, I'm afraid you're out of luck," snapped Janice. "Melbourne proper is not on the ocean, but I'm sure you already know that. I suggest we find one of the motels out on Coco Beach or Cape Canaveral. If Elaina plans to stay in the area, my guess is she will probably head out to the beach, but what do I know? You're the big time, bad ass investigator with all the answers!"

"Come on Janice. I know you're tired and disappointed that we didn't nail Elaina in South Beach, but so am I. Give me a break," pleaded Rick. "At least we can enjoy the ocean until I can figure out where she has gone."

"Sure we can enjoy the ocean!" retorted Janice. "I can see us now, hand in hand, strolling on the beach like a couple of lovesick teenagers. By the way, what is this *we* stuff? You made it clear you are the investigator, and I'm just a pain in the ass along for the ride."

"Would it be so bad if we walked on the beach hand in hand?" asked Rick, ignoring the last part of her remark.

"I can't think of anything I would rather be doing, except eating a nice big salad and a plate of spaghetti with marinara sauce and wild mushrooms." scowled Janice.

"My, we are cranky, aren't we?" said Rick quietly.

"Yes, I am tired, hungry, and madder than hell that you let Elaina slip through your fingers at my expense! But since you are paying for this week, I want to check into the resort on the beach. You can forget about parking lot view rooms. I want rooms, too, as in PLURAL, two, king-bed, non-smoking rooms, directly on the ocean!"

"Let's eat first since we're already practically to Rosa's. Then you will get your wish. Resort it is," replied Rick. Janice frowned, but agreed they needed to eat first. She knew Rosa's had good food since she and Clayton had eaten there many times in the past.

"With our luck, Elaina be scarfing down a big plate of spaghetti and meatballs when we get inside. I would not be surprised if she makes her escape out the back door as soon as she spots us," Janice replied dismally.

"Why don't you try to think positively for a change?" Rick muttered. "I don't see her car parked anywhere near the restaurant."

Good for you, thought Janice. Elaina could have parked anywhere.

CHAPTER 19

"Looks like I'm home free, at least for now," uttered Elaina to the person on the other end of her mobile phone line. "Nobody will guess I have gone for a little jaunt up the coast until things cool down on South Beach . . . No, I don't think you guys need to follow me here. That will look even more suspicious. I am reasonably sure there won't be any easy marks up here that require your help. If I get bored I can check out the scene in Orlando . . . I just told you guys to just continue playing tourist on South Beach! . . . Josh never met you, so he won't have a clue we are connected. And as for that guy, Rick, I don't think he's a writer. . . . Don't you dare argue with me, you sorry ass! I said stay put and I'll be in touch just as soon as I think the coast is clear for me to return . . . Don't you dare threaten me! If it weren't for me, you would still be collecting a few dollars per copy on the sale of anthologies instead of making thousands of dollars in a matter of days with every sucker I manage to talk into making a movie!"

Elaina was so angry she ended the call abruptly. "Who do those guys think they are?" she fumed as she paced back and forth in front of the picture window of her motel room located directly on the ocean. "I do all the hard work, and they rake in their share of the dough! That is going to change just as soon as I make it back to South Beach. I don't need them anymore!"

Elaina was unaware Rick and Janice had already checked into the resort and decided to have dessert in the oceanfront dining room adjacent to the Oak Tree Lounge. They chose to sit there because they knew Elaina might end up in the restaurant or lounge. At Rick's request, they were seated in a secluded corner of the large dining room. Anyone looking for them would have to go out of his or her way to find them.

Night fell as they watched couples through the restaurant's windows walk arm-in-arm along the well-lit beachfront. The serene ocean looked like glass. Several preteen children wandered ahead of their vacationing parents and chattered with glee when they found shells washed ashore. While Janice or Rick would never admit it, the scene made them miss something, a meaningful relationship with someone special. They both sat, quietly sipping their coffee, and pretended to eat apple pie. They explained to the waiter they had already eaten dinner at Rosa's.

"Just let me know when you need more coffee," the waiter, a young man wearing a white dress shirt and black slacks, had told them. "There is entertainment in the lounge tonight. The last set starts at midnight and ends at two. If you want, I can reserve a table for you. The third set starts in about fifteen minutes, give or take."

"That would be nice, as long as it isn't heavy metal," said Rick. The midnight hour was approaching, and it had been a long day, but his gut felt there was a distinct possibility Elaina might end up there.

The waiter laughed. "Not a chance of heavy metal happening around here. I think it's a duo featuring a female, guitar-strumming torch singer and her husband on the keyboard. They throw in a few jokes and like to talk to members of the audience."

Rick gave Janice a questioning look. "Are you game for a little entertainment? You never know, we might run into someone we know."

"Sure, why not? It will be like old times," answered Janice, picking up what Rick meant.

"It sounds like you have been a guest here before," said the waiter. Rick had never been a guest at this particular hotel complex before, but he confirmed his guess anyway.

"It sounds like fun," Janice responded, even though she really would have preferred turning in after such a long day. She wasn't even hungry after the meal at Rosa's Italian Café, and was exhausted after the long car ride.

"Good, I'll take care of reserving a table in the bar area with the bartender," said the waiter.

When the waiter left, Janice gave Rick a look of disgust. "How is it possible that you can lie with such ease? I think you would sell your grandmother if it got you what you wanted! We both know you have never been a guest here before."

Rick took a sip of his coffee and gave her a sly grin. "Lying comes with the territory. How do you think I've been able to become one of the top investigators in the state of California? I tell people what they want to hear and they often tell me more than I really need or want to know. I think of lying as a tool of the trade."

"No wonder you are still single," quipped Janice. "Any woman in her right mind would avoid having a relationship with you at all costs."

"I keep my work separate from my personal life," replied Rick, defensively.

"And I'm supposed to believe that?"

"You are going to believe what you want, so I won't make excuses for what I do to take care of business," stated Rick. "You hired me to do a job, and that is what I intend to do. Feel free to fire me if I don't meet your standards. But be aware if you do, you are on your own. Percy told me that if I mess up on this case I'm toast as far as working for him again. I'll make sure he won't be so eager to give you a helping hand when I fill him in on how you came to the decision to fire me."

"Don't be so touchy," said Janice. "Where I come from people don't feel the need to lie in order to get what they want."

Rick raised his eyebrows and gave her a questioning look. "Oh, really, is that a fact? I tend to disagree. What about what happened between you and Jack a few years ago? If I'm not mistaken, he lied to you about his relationship with Elaina, and that's why we find ourselves here in Florida, clear across the country from where we both now live in California."

Janice took a big sip of her water and her face turned red. "All right, I concede. Jack lied. What do you want me to do? Beat my fists on my chest and tear out my hair and say I was wrong to leave Tennessee, only to eventually rescue then marry him?"

"No, that's not what I want at all. I want you to understand that sometimes I have to stretch the truth in my line of work to get to the meat of the problem and help put the bad guys away so they can't hurt anyone else. As I stated before, I'm not a liar when it comes to personal relationships. I've been lied to, and I know what it feels like when someone you love lies to you. You, of all people, should understand."

"I'm sorry if I upset you," said Janice. "I think we need to forego the entertainment and go back to our respective rooms. We can meet for breakfast in the morning in order to start the search again. We are both tired and bickering like this isn't helping us find Elaina."

Rick drained his coffee cup. "There you go again. When things don't go the way you think they should, you're ready to cut and run. I must have misjudged you. I thought you were someone who would fight for justice. We're here to do a job, and by God, that's what we are going to do—or at least that's what I'm going to do! If you want to run away and hide in your room go ahead. If you don't like the way I work, you can fire me right now. I'll be on the first plane out of here back to California before you can say monkey's uncle! It's your call."

There was no mistaking Rick was angry, and rightfully so. He slapped his credit card on the table. "Here, take care of the bill. I'm going to the lounge. You do what you want."

Janice knew he had called her bluff. "Do you mind if I join you for the entertainment?" she asked contritely.

"Only if that is something you want to do," he curtly replied. At the same time, he was hoping she would go to the lounge with him. Before she could confirm her intention, the waiter presented the bill.

"Are you two still interested in going to the lounge?" he asked. Rick looked at Janice, who nodded.

"Sure thing," he replied. "We need a little entertainment to help us relax."

"Nothing like a little music and a nightcap to top off a long day," said the waiter.

"You got that right," said Rick. "Thanks for the suggestion."

"Of course, you could go for a stroll on the beach, but I don't recommend going beyond the lighted area. I'll make sure the bartender tells the waitress to hold your seats."

Janice spoke up before Rick could respond. "We won't be taking a stroll tonight. The music and nightcap will do the trick."

"Will it be a table for one?" inquired the waitress as soon as Elaina entered the bar and surveyed the crowd.

"That's right, unless you know some tall dark, handsome and loaded man who would like some company," she replied as she stood at the entrance to the Oak Tree Lounge.

"If I had someone like that in my life, do you think I would be working here?" the waitress replied with a bitter laugh. "Right this way. I have a table right down in front. Maybe if you sit there you'll get lucky when one of the cowboys wanders in off the ranchland looking for female company. When they get themselves cleaned up they don't look or smell too bad. Most of them aren't that poor and won't hesitate to buy you a drink."

"Don't you have anything a little farther back in the room?" asked Elaina. "I'm not actually looking for companionship tonight."

"Sorry, but those tables are reserved for hotel guests."

"Oh, all right," groused Elaina. Her demeanor immediately changed after being seated when she was approached by a good looking 40-something-year-old, well-dressed man who introduced himself as Ed Granger.

"May I join you?" Ed asked, assuming she was alone. "I'm here on a buying trip to purchase some oranges direct from the groves over at Indiantown. I own a chain of fruit and vegetable outlets up and down the east coast."

Elaina checked his left hand ring finger. There was no sign of a wedding ring, so she sized him up for the possibility of free drinks and a roll between the sheets.

"It's a free country, and I'm not meeting anyone, so feel free to use the empty chair," she said with a grin. The two of them were soon engaged in conversation and enjoying the drinks he ordered and paid for. Elaina was thus engrossed and did not see Rick and Janice enter the lounge through a back entrance and take their reserved seats near the back of the dimly lit room, several occupied tables away. With her back to them, they did not spot her until Elaina and Ed got up to dance on the small dance floor located in front of the equally small stage.

"I don't believe what I'm seeing," whispered Janice.

"Neither do I," replied Rick. "I'm glad it's dark enough in here. She seems to be taken with her partner, and he's obviously into her. I think we would be pushing our luck if I asked you to dance," he said with a wry smile. "Keep your head down if she happens to look this way, even though I don't think she can see us," he urged. As if on cue, Elaina stared directly in their direction longer than necessary. Rick leaned over and kissed Janice on the lips in an awkward attempt to hide her face. Neither one of them were prepared for the sensation that resulted.

"Don't read anything into the kiss," said Rick thickly. "Elaina was looking this way. I was just doing my job to keep her from focusing on us, make that you, in particular.

"Of course you were," replied Janice, weakly. "You were just doing your job, but don't you think it's time for us to leave before she takes another look?"

"No, I don't think we should leave. I need to know which room she's in," replied Rick. "I'm going out that door over there. It leads back into the dining room. It will eventually lead to the men's room, where I can slick back my hair and add a fake moustache and some dark rimmed glasses. I keep them handy in my pocket. She won't recognize me. You sit tight and don't take up with anyone else while I'm gone," he added with a smile in an attempt at levity.

Janice glared at him with indignation before replying, "You don't need to worry. I don't make it a habit of taking up with strange men. Do you mind telling me what you plan to do next, or am I supposed to sit here wondering?"

Exasperation filled Rick's voice. "Like I just said, I'm going to find out what room she's in. That means I will need to use my charms on the desk clerk. And while I'm doing it I run the risk of Elaina seeing me if she and Romeo decide to leave and walk across the lobby to her room. Any more questions, or may I do my job without you challenging my every move?"

Rick barely made it back from the men's room when Elaina and her newfound man got up and headed for the lobby door. "Looks like we might have struck out again," Rick announced when he returned to stand beside their table. "Be prepared to leave in a hurry when you see me at the lounge's front entrance door. I assume Elaina and that guy will get into a car and take off up the beach after a couple more heavy duty kisses. The desk clerk said Elaina didn't check in here, but the guy did, and he never takes dates to his room. That means they are headed for wherever she is staying." He didn't add that the simpering desk clerk charged twenty dollars for this information. "Janice, you need to go to your room. I'm going to scout the parking lots of area motels and try to find her car."

"Not on your life! I'm going with you," insisted Janice.

"You will do as I say! Go back to your room and get some sleep. I don't need to be concerned about you while I'm working," replied Rick.

"Aren't you forgetting something? You are working for me." said Janice, indignantly.

"Aren't you forgetting this week is on me?" he replied with equal indignation. "I do not intend to stand here arguing with you while Elaina is somewhere close by. Now be a good girl, go to your room, and stay there until I come to get you."

"How dare you treat me like a child," she began. This was before he grabbed her by the shoulders, pulled her firmly against his chest, and passionately kissed her.

"I don't do things like this with children," he heavily breathed before he let her go and quickly walked away. Stunned by his behavior, Janice meekly walked to her room with her heart pounding in her ears.

The time was approaching 3:00 a.m. when Rick spotted Elaina's car in the lot of a small motel located several miles up the beach. It was the sixth lot he'd checked. Unfortunately, the parking area made it impossible to determine which room she had rented. *Looks like I'll need to give Janice a call to let her know I'll be staying put in our car until Elaina decides to get around to making her next move,* Rick thought. He pulled his cell phone from his pocket and pressed the button for Janice's cell phone number.

It rang six times before her sleep-filled voice answered. "Where are you?" she asked, irate.

"I'm sitting in the car in the lot where Elaina's car is parked," he replied.

"What do you hope to gain by sitting there?" asked Janice.

"If you must know, I am planning to stay here until daylight, with the hope that I can make contact when she comes out of her room."

"When did you plan to include me in this little detail?" asked Janice.

"I didn't plan to include you," Rick shot back. "My next call will be to the Coco Beach Police Department to have them help me get a warrant for her arrest."

"And you think I'm going to sit here and wait for that to happen? I want the name of the motel and location where you are right now!" Tired and sleepy, Rick gave her the motel's name without thinking.

"I am going to pack and call a cab. I'll be there in less than an hour. I can't imagine Elaina getting her lazy fat ass out of bed at 4:00 a.m. for any reason." She hung up before Rick could protest. Exactly 42 minutes later, a cab pulled into the designated motel parking lot. Rick got out of his car and flagged it down. Janice got out of the cab and paid the cabbie. He helped her unload not one but two suitcases, one of which was Rick's.

"How did you manage to get my things?" he questioned. She gave him a sly smile and a determined look before giving him an answer.

"You aren't the only one who is able to fib a way into a room," she replied. "I told the desk clerk we had a fight and you locked me out . . . and wanted to make peace with my husband. And to add a little to the drama, I told him I lost my key while walking on the beach. He didn't hesitate to make me a new key for your room. You should be proud of me. I learned from arguably the best investigator in the state of California."

"There is nothing arguable about me being the best. I am the best," replied Rick. "Now hurry up. Help me get those bags in the trunk and get your fanny in the car!"

It turned out to be a long wait. Elaina did not step outside her door until right before ten in the morning, her travel bag in hand and her new gentleman friend right behind her. They parted after a brief hug and kiss. The man flagged down the retreating cab whose driver immediately came to a screeching halt just before exiting the motel parking lot. He backed up five feet, picked up the man, and went on his way.

Janice was hungry and needed a cup of coffee but knew this wasn't the time. Elaina got into her rental car, pulled under the motel portico, and went inside to presumably check out and pay her bill. Despite also needing coffee, Rick was ready to tail her wherever she decided to go.

It didn't take long after exiting onto the highway before Elaina pulled into a local Denny's restaurant, parked, and went inside.

This is when Rick reapplied the fake moustache and dark rimmed glasses. "Have you got a comb? Mine's packed," he asked. Janice pulled one from her purse, and he slicked back his still greasy looking hair. "I'm going inside to order some breakfast to go. What do you take in your coffee, and what do you want to eat?" he asked.

Tossing her healthy diet aside, an exhausted Janice said, "A bacon and fried egg sandwich with cheddar cheese and coffee, black," she replied.

"Too bad there isn't a fast food place next door. That would make things a whole lot easier," commented Rick.

"I thought I was making it easy by ordering a sandwich and black coffee," retorted Janice. "I could order eggs Benedict and a latté if that would make you happy." Rick had no response beyond rolling his eyes to make his feelings known as he made an exit from the car and walked into the restaurant.

They ate their food, drank their coffee, and sat in the car for what felt like a long while before Elaina returned to her car with a satisfied look on her face. It didn't take long before she headed up I-95 and exited the westbound ramp onto State Route 50.

"I knew it!" stated Rick. "She's headed for Orlando. Want to take bets on where she decides to hole up? I say the Grand Cypress Hotel. Loser buys dinner."

"You're on. I'm betting it will be the Peabody," said Janice with a straight face. "She strikes me as someone who would be fascinated by the duck parade since they, and she, waddle when they walk."

Rick tried, unsuccessfully, to stifle a laugh. "Do I detect a note of cattiness in that statement?"

"Whatever do you mean?" asked Janice in a fake southern accent. "Me catty? Surely you don't think little ole me could be catty." They both burst into laughter. Rick turned on the radio and they began to sing to the pop songs at the top of their lungs as they trailed behind Elaina far enough away to not arouse any suspicion she was being followed.

Janice won the bet. Elaina checked into the Peabody Hotel. "You owe me dinner," she announced.

"I don't recall making a deal that whoever won would buy dinner," replied Rick. "But that sounds like a nice thing for me to do."

"Nice has nothing to do with it." insisted Janice. "I won fair and square. You are the one who decided the loser would buy dinner, so don't try to get out of it by claiming amnesia."

"Don't gloat. It doesn't become you," replied a smiling Rick. "Since I am still incognito with the moustache and glasses, I'll check us in and hope Elaina has already checked in. Any thoughts as to how I can get her room number?"

"Oh, I'm sure you will figure out a way to get the number once you turn on the charm," she answered.

Elaina was walking across the lobby toward the bank of elevators when Rick approached the check in desk. "Be right with you, sir," said the harried clerk. "I just need to finish up the information on our last guest. My assistant called off sick today." Familiar with the computer keyboard in use, Rick was able to determine Elaina's room number by the location of the computer keys the clerk punched into the system.

"You don't have any rooms on the third floor, do you?" asked Rick. "Friends who have visited here told me that's where the duck parade to the fountain ends. My wife and I don't want to miss it." He wanted to slap his forehead when he realized he had called Janice his wife. *There goes my request for two rooms,* he chided himself. "Can you make that a queen room with two beds? She claims my tossing and turning keeps her awake. I never sleep well on the first night or two of a vacation," he quickly offered.

"I'm sorry, sir. We don't have any more queen rooms in the entire hotel. I do have a king room in 312 with a pull out sofa on the third floor though. It's close to the fountain where the ducks end up."

"I'll take it," said Rick without hesitation, even though he knew he would have some explaining to do even if it was next door to Elaina's room. He decided not to let Janice know about the accommodations until after they had dinner. That way, the news couldn't ruin the entire afternoon and evening. He hoped she would agree to stay and not send him to spend the night in the car.

"What took you so long?" asked Janice. "I'm starving."

"I figured you would be. Why don't we just head for Epcot at Disneyland? I have been there before and I know the French restaurant is great, unless you prefer Canadian, German, Scandinavian, or Mexican restaurant instead.

Oops, I almost forgot. You might be interested in dining in the American restaurant where the vegetables are grown hydroponically underneath the building. That one is quite interesting. It features a rotating panorama of what farm life is like—lightening, thunder, and rain included."

"What about Elaina? Won't we lose track of her if we go to Epcot?

"She's already checked into room 310. I'll be close by in 312," he said without revealing the type of accommodations they would be sharing. "That means we will have ringside seats for the duck parade in the morning. I'm sure she will stay long enough to see the ducks perform, or she wouldn't have checked in here."

Janice felt she had no choice but to agree with him. "I like the French restaurant idea. I dined there many times when Clayton and I lived in Florida and visited the park. The food and service are excellent," she told him.

"Good. I'll make a reservation for a late lunch just as soon as we enter the grounds. How about we do the Under the Sea experience for dinner and spend some time seeing the exhibits and riding the rides, since we're going to be there. I don't think Elaina is going anywhere today that I can't find her. She may even end up at Epcot, too." Rick sighed with relief when Janice agreed they should spend the entire afternoon and evening at the theme park. *At least I'm off the hook explaining the accommodations for a few more hours,* he thought.

"This is a marvelous idea, our going to Disney World, especially since you are going to be paying for it," added Janice with an angelic smile. Rick swallowed hard but managed to return a smile.

Both meals were fantastic. They laughed like a couple of kids as they waited in long lines to enjoy the rides. Janice could not recall a time she had felt this carefree since Jack's death. The theme park was large and crowded enough that they did not see any sign of Elaina. Rick began to sweat as the hour approached for the park to close. Janice wanted to stay after the fireworks display while the crowd dispersed. "I like to be here after the fireworks finale on the lake when the giant silver sphere is still lit. It makes me feel like I'm the only person left in the world."

I'm going to feel like I should be the only person in the world when you find out we're sharing a room again, Rick thought to himself. And he was right on the money.

"Why didn't you tell me it was one room up front?" demanded Janice when she learned they would be sharing a room with one king bed.

"I didn't want to spoil the day. I tried to get two rooms and when that didn't pan out, I tried getting a room with two queen size beds," explained Rick. "This was the only room they had close to Elaina's room. You take the bed and I'll take the pull out sofa. You can use the bathroom first," he said in an effort to placate her.

"How thoughtful of you," Janice hissed between clinched teeth.

"Come on, Janice. You have to admit we did have a nice day," said Rick. "In case you are wondering, I don't snore or pass gas when I sleep, so I've been told. How about you? Can you say the same?"

Janice ignored the remark, grabbed her makeup kit and nightwear, and headed for the bathroom to slam and lock the door behind her.

"Now what do I do?" she mumbled. "My frilly nightwear isn't exactly geared for sharing a room with someone I barely know, especially a man."

Rick was sprawled out on the pull out sofa when Janice exited the bathroom. He pretended not to notice what she was wearing but couldn't pull it off.

"You look beautiful," he said hoarsely.

"Don't get any funny ideas," Janice shot back.

"How do you expect me not get any ideas when you look like that?" he asked.

"Go take a cold shower," she replied. "You are the one who got us in the same room, so make the best of it!" She slipped under the covers. "Good night. Don't forget I get first dibs on the bathroom in the morning."

Janice snapped off her bedside lamp, which left the room illuminated by the pale blue light on the TV screen. Rick was obviously aroused and had no way to help the situation except hope the feeling would go away. True to his word, Janice had to admit Rick didn't snore or pass gas and hoped the same for herself. Clayton or Jack had never mentioned this was a problem, but she felt neither of them would have said anything, even if it had happened.

Rick was still sleeping soundly when she quietly slipped out of bed the next morning. She had to admit he looked peaceful and harmless, almost like a young boy who was dreaming about things young boys dream about as his eyelids twitched and a slight smile played around his mouth. She was tempted to reach out and push back a lock of his hair that had fallen across his forehead, but she told herself to stop. *Go get your shower and get dressed before he wakes up*, she admonished herself. *Now is no time to get sentimental!*

Rick was still asleep when she returned from her shower, dressed. She checked her watch. The duck parade was scheduled to begin at nine and it was already a quarter after eight. "Rick, you need to wake up," she said as she shook his shoulder. "The parade starts in 45 minutes and you need to shower, dress, and have some coffee. Otherwise, we could miss the chance to see if Elaina shows up."

Rick groaned, opened his eyes, and closed them again.

"Give me a couple of minutes," he mumbled.

"Only a couple of minutes," she answered. "I'll make some coffee to help you wake up."

The hotel room's kitchen consisted of a small refrigerator, microwave, and coffee pot tucked in a small alcove located under one of the two windows facing the street. While the coffee percolated, which took only about four minutes, Janice turned on the TV to a local news station, taking her attention away from Rick. She became annoyed when she turned around to note he had gone back to sleep.

"Hey! Sleeping Beauty, wake up, or I'm going to make sure you wake up to a glass of ice water in a place you won't like!"

This time Rick sat up and tossed the bedsheet aside. This is when Janice saw he was naked, except for a pair of bright yellow briefs barely covering the morning erection a lot of men experience. She quickly turned away in embarrassment at the sight and the sound of his laughter.

"What's the matter? Haven't you ever seen a man in his shorts early in the morning?" he said. "Of course, I could lie back down and let you take care of my problem with some ice water, but then I would have to take further measurers in retaliation. I don't think you would mind all that much if that happened, if you were to be honest with yourself."

"Just get up and get dressed," said Janice icily. Unable to look at him, she focused her attention on the newscast.

"You're no fun in the morning," was Rick's reply. But he did as she asked.

The silence between them was deafening when Rick returned from his bathroom ministrations and dressing. Without looking in his direction Janice announced he had only ten minutes to have some coffee, and then they needed to go out into the hallway to observe not only the duck parade but also Elaina if she graced them with her presence. Yet, she knew beyond a doubt she had to share what she had seen on the newscast.

Elaina had awoken that morning with her mouth feeling like the inside of a garbage can. "I need coffee and some breakfast," she mumbled before she noted there would not be time for more than a cup of in-room coffee, or she would miss the reason she had checked into the Peabody Hotel. She continued to grumble while she was forced to make coffee in the room because room service would take too long. While she waited for the coffee to perc, she turned on the TV.

"Oh shit!" was first thing out of her mouth once she realized what the newscaster was reporting. The newscaster said a man had filed a complained with the Miami Beach Police Department, revealing news of someone being scammed out of a large sum of money in exchange for a movie being made from one of his books.

"A Mr. Josh Riggins has filed a complaint with Miami's South Beach Police Department," reported the television news caster. "It seems Mr. Riggins paid in excess of $50,000 dollars to one Elaina Albright. He alleges she told him shooting of his movie was to begin yesterday. It appears the Albright woman left the area with the money, and the movie deal was not a viable option. No pictures of the alleged scammer have been released by the police at this time. We will show them on a future newscast as soon as they are made available. The two unnamed men mentioned as producers as part of the scam have not been found, and Mr. Riggins could not provide a description. It is assumed they, too, have left the area for parts unknown."

Elaina felt certain she was not the only one to see the newscast. "Damn! Damn! Damn!" she exclaimed as she continued to watch the newscast. "Looks like I'll miss the duck parade and a day at Disney. It's time to move on." She quickly repacked. Without waiting for a bellman's assistance, she made her way through the crowd gathering in the hallway for the parade to slip unnoticed down the exit stairway. Entering her rental car, she sat contemplating her next move. "If I leave now without paying, maybe the clerk won't remember me, but then again, if I leave without paying that will only bring the police into it. I can't afford that happening since nobody knows where I've gone." Several more minutes passed before Elaina decided to pay her bill in cash and take her chances on not being recognized.

"Are you sure of what you saw?" asked Rick when Janice told him what she had seen on TV.

"I may be blonde, but I'm not stupid! Of course I'm sure of what I saw!" she insisted.

"Then it looks like we're going to miss the duck parade. You can bet Elaina won't stick around, either. Hurry up and get your things together before she leaves."

There was no answer on Elaina's door when Rick knocked on it, pretending to be room service with a complimentary breakfast. Pushing his way through the gathering crowd, he managed to get a good look out one of the hall windows into the parking lot. Elaina was walking toward her car.

"We have got to hurry or we'll lose her," he mused as he shoved his way back to the room where Janice stood waiting. "Come on. We can't be nice about making our way down to the lobby. You check us out. While you take care of that, I will block Elaina's car so she can't leave."

Racing to their rental car, Rick was surprised to see Elaina exit her car and return to the hotel lobby. "What the hell is that crazy bitch doing now?" he mumbled. "I've got to beat her inside and get Janice out of the way before she recognizes her." As a second thought, Rick turned the key and stepped on the gas, deliberately bumping into Elaina's car, all the while hoping she would not recognize him.

"Hey, lady," he called as he scrambled out of his car. "Sorry. My foot slipped off the brake. I don't think there's any serious damage, but you need to take a look. I'll call the police if you want to involve them."

Thinking she had met this man before, but uncertain where, Elaina suspiciously approached the two cars to inspect the damage.

"I don't think there is any need to involve the police," she said. "It's only a slight scratch to the paint. Besides, I was on my way to check out, and I don't want to wait for an officer."

"If you are sure that's what you want to do," replied Rick.

"Haven't we met before?" asked Elaina.

"Not unless you've visited Deadwood, South Dakota. That where me and the misses live. It's our first vacation since we opened a restaurant there."

Out of the corner of his eye he could see Janice approaching. He knew he had to do something fast before the two women met. He patted his jeans pocket. "Oh my gosh!" he exclaimed. "I must have left my cell phone in our room! If you're sure you don't want the police called I need to go get it before housekeeping cleans the room." That said, he sprinted toward Janice and twirled her around to head back into the hotel lobby before Elaina could get a good look at her.

"Honey, we have to go back to the room. I left my cell phone lying on the nightstand."

"Have you lost your mind?" replied Janice. "I saw you put it in your jacket pocket just before we left."

"Shut up and go back into the lobby right now!" hissed Rick. "I just hit Elaina's car."

"You hit her car? What in the world were you thinking?"

"I didn't have a choice or you would have come face to face with her, so don't question what I did!"

"But didn't she recognize you?"

"I don't think so, since I told her the Misses and I owned a restaurant in Deadwood, South Dakota, and this was our first vacation in years. She was ready to head back inside to pay her bill just as soon as I stopped you. Thank heaven she didn't want the police called! Now stop talking and get moving to our car before we lose sight of her. Just pull that scarf from around your neck and cover your head. I don't think she will recognize you in her haste to make a clean getaway."

Fate was, for the moment, on Rick and Janice's side. After checking out, Elaina had to wait for the traffic light to change before entering Colonial Drive from the hotel parking lot. From where they were parked Rick could see her car, so he waited until the light changed before heading toward the same exit. This allowed enough time between their cars that Elaina would remain unaware she was being followed. At one point Rick was forced to run a yellow light, but he kept her in sight until they had cleared the congested area.

"It looks like there is a directional app she's checking on her cell phone. It's a good bet she will take a back road south toward the town of Windermere," he announced. "We need to be careful not tail her too closely, since that is a two-lane, less congested road out of town. We don't want her getting the idea she is being followed."

"That will change to a four-lane the closer we get to Windermere, if my memory serves me correctly," said Janice. "That area was becoming a popular tourist destination before Clayton and I moved, but I am thinking it is still a heck of a lot smaller than Orlando. There are less expensive, family-style restaurants and more locally-owned motels available that won't wreck a family budget in that area. What time is it? I'm hungry! We didn't have any breakfast."

"For as slim as you are, you sure like to eat," remarked Rick.

"Only when I miss meals," she replied. "And we seem to have a knack for missing meals, especially at times when normal people eat."

"That's part of the job," he replied. "Do you have any suggestions where we can catch an early lunch since it's only eleven o'clock? Of course, we will have to figure out where Elaina will stop to eat, since she probably hasn't eaten lunch either. I don't think she misses too many meals."

"My guess is she'll stop at the barbeque restaurant located in the hotel on the edge of town since we've already passed through main part of Windermere. The barbecue place used to be the only restaurant out here outside of a couple of hash houses in the downtown area. After that, we'll see open grazing and vegetable farmland until we're back in the Orlando suburbs, or at least that was the case fifteen years ago," offered Janice. Just as Janice thought she would, Elaina pulled into the barbecue joint parking lot, got out, and went inside the restaurant.

"Do we take a chance and go inside, or do we wait out here in the car until she comes back out?" asked Rick.

"They have high dividers between booths," offered Janice. "And I'm starving!"

"I take it that means we go inside."

"You got it," smiled Janice. "Just don't order the salad bar where we could easily be spotted from most of the other seats, especially the tables down the middle. Be sure to ask for a booth on the wall that doesn't have windows. That way it will be a little darker and harder for her to see us."

"Don't take offense, but I think we should sit side by side and act like we're a couple of lovestruck honeymooners," suggested Rick in an attempt to get a reaction.

"I think that kind of behavior will only call attention to us, so it's a big, fat *no* to us making out! I am beginning to suspect you had something to do with us not getting separate rooms. Quite frankly, I'm getting tired of you trying to put the moves on me. I think I made it clear that ours is purely a business relationship."

Instead of denying making the moves on her, Rick tried to make light of her comments. "Me? Make the moves on you? Surely you jest. Just because I am trying to keep us close to Elaina, and at the same time out of her line of sight, you think I am trying to make moves on you?"

Janice turned her face away from him toward the dark, wood-paneled wall to silence him with a slight wave of her hand. He took the hint to shut up. This allowed her to turn sideways and look past him across the room.

"Don't look now, but Elaina must have been in the ladies' room. She's taking a seat in a booth directly across the room. Thank God there's a table full of ranch hands sitting between us and her."

Rick casually glanced in that direction to find two tables pushed together, creating enough room to seat eight men wearing well-worn jeans, dusty boots, and pearl snap buttoned, western-style shirts. Each of them ordered a beer and large barbeque sandwich with a side of slaw and fries. It didn't take any time at all before they started laughing, joking, and talking loudly as the beers kept coming. As luck would have it, their antics soon caught the attention of Elaina, who began to outrageously flirt with them between bites of her food.

There was no doubt her racy comments encouraged the men. It didn't take any time at all before they began to exchange raunchy comments, gaining her undivided attention. This allowed Rick and Janice to quickly eat their sandwiches and fries without detection until it was time for Elaina to pay her check and leave. This caused Janice to hold her breath. It seemed as though Elaina paused to take a good look in their direction. She apparently decided they were the tourists she had made contact with at the Peabody and were no threat to her. Rick was slow in paying their check in order to give Elaina time to pay hers before he and Janice made their way to the cash register and out to their car.

"What makes you think you don't need to speed things up and ask for our check faster?" Janice irritably questioned. "We will lose her if you keep waiting for the waitress to come by again. Forget about using your credit card. Just leave the cash on the table and let's go!"

Rick gave her an exasperated sigh and a dirty look before he started to chastise her. "Why don't you go running out to the parking lot and introduce yourself? Obviously, you don't know timing can be everything when tailing a suspect. In this case we need to allow her time to head out ahead of us. It isn't like she has that many options of where to go, since this is a two-lane road through an almost barren wasteland for the next 100 miles until we get to the Florida Turnpike. Do I need to remind you I am the investigator, not you?"

It broke Rick's heart when Janice's lower lip began to quiver and she looked like she was going to cry. But he stood his ground, knowing it was necessary to keep her at bay if he was going to crack this case.

Just as Rick thought would happen, Elaina continued to drive south on the two-lane road, but following her became a little more difficult once they entered the busy

Florida Turnpike approaching Orlando. To his surprise she didn't make the exit he expected toward Miami's South Beach. She continued on to take the famous Alligator Alley exit across the Everglades, resulting in a turn toward Everglades City deep within the confines of Everglades National Park via a skinny, two-lane road going through alligator-infested water on each side of the road.

"I think she knows she's being tailed," groaned Rick. "I don't see any other option except to follow her. I swear she isn't going to get away from me this time! There aren't too many places she can stay or hide around here, plus she has to deal with the fact police are onto her in the Art Deco District." After what happened at the restaurant earlier, Janice kept her comments to a bare minimum. "I suppose you are right," she murmured.

As it turned out, Elaina was unaware she was being followed. She checked into the Everglades Motel, a sprawling, one-story building constructed of weathered wood with a large restaurant attached out back under an overhanging roof on the edge of a deep waterway. Built to accommodate boaters, the back door of rooms opened out onto a wood plank deck overlooking the pleasure watercraft and airboats anchored there. The setup offered easy access while occupants enjoyed a meal or stayed overnight in the motel.

"Let me check us in," said Janice. "You wait in the car. That way I can be sure we have separate rooms." Rick didn't miss the sarcasm in her voice, but he chose to ignore it after what transpired between them at the restaurant earlier in the day. "I'm not being a smart aleck, but just as a reminder, if you check us in you will be paying the tab.

My credit card is set up so it can't be used by anyone but me. I took that measure after Lola and I split. She kept using it, leaving me no choice but to cancel that one and get another card."

"It will be worth it to me," snapped Janice. "I can always deduct the room charges from your final bill. But that doesn't mean you can't pick up any other charges, including dinner, for the remainder of the week should we have the misfortune to remain here that long."

"By all means, anything to make you happy. You are my client. That means I am at your beck and call as long as you understand I'm the investigator and you don't do anything stupid." The words came out more sharply than he intended.

"I think you've got that backwards. I am the one writing the final check. That makes you my employee, but there is no need to quibble. And just in case you have forgotten, you are picking up the tab for this week because you blew it back in South Beach."

"Ouch! How can I forget this week is on me with your constant reminding?" Janice merely smiled and got out of the car to head for the motel lobby.

Ten minutes later she returned to hand Rick the key to room number ten. She kept the key to room number eleven across the hall.

"I hope you don't mind the rooms only have a double bed and no in-room coffee," she explained to him. "They don't have king beds here. They do have coffee service on a cart near the check-in desk. I have to warn you it smelled like it had been sitting there since early this morning. As you can see from the exterior this place is a bit rustic, but if my memory serves me, it's a whole lot better than the few other motels in the area. I remember the restaurant has good food, especially if you like fresh fish and chips with a side of cold slaw. But, sorry, no alcoholic beverages are sold since the restaurant is on State Park land. You can always check out the Quick Mart we passed coming in and see what they offer along that line when you gas up the car. While you take care of that, I'm going to my room and take a short nap before dinner. Come to think of it, there is a bar next to the restaurant if you feel the need for alcohol, but you still need to gas up."

A frown crossed Rick's face at the thought of what awaited him in the motel room. "Thanks for all that information. What time do you want dinner? I presume this place is the best place in the area?" he questioned.

"Trust me. The food is good, even if the accommodations are not luxurious," she responded over her shoulder as she took her suitcase from the trunk.

CHAPTER 20

The sunset was spectacular when Janice and Rick entered the restaurant later that evening. They asked to be seated out on the open deck. Janice sighed then exclaimed, "What a view! I'm sorry I've been so out of sorts today. You don't deserve the way I've been acting."

"I'm sorry, too. I know this change of plans has been hard for you." Rick reached out to cover one of her hands with his. Janice made no move to remove it for several minutes, focusing her attention on his face to see if he was sincere in the apology. The intense look he gave her caused her to drop her gaze. There was no doubt he was sincere, but there was something more, something that caused her to take a deep breath while remembering his angry kiss and the effect his hand had on her back at Melbourne Beach. This memory prompted her to quickly remove her hand from under his and let it fall into her lap.

"I'm not a snake that is going to bite you," said Rick softly.

She nodded and began to focus on the crab salad she ordered that the waitress had placed in front of her.

"I didn't say you were," she said defensively.

"Actions speak louder than words," he replied.

"I think we need to concentrate on the scenery and these tasty salads."

She avoided looking at him for fear he would be able to read her mind. That was the last thing she needed right now. Rick was deciding whether to respond further when he saw Elaina enter the restaurant.

"Don't look now but guess who is waiting to be seated."

"I'll bet it's not the Queen of England or the Pope," Janice responded with a frown.

"Let's hope she isn't seated close enough to recognize us. I don't have the right paperwork I need to arrest her yet." Their hopes were dashed. Elaina was seated only two tables away. Unfortunately, she was facing Janice.

At first Elaina concentrated on the menu then the sunset and ordered a drink before she saw a woman who looked vaguely familiar. There was also something familiar about the size of the broad-shouldered man seated across from the woman. "I know I've seen those two before," mused Elaina. The time that had passed in five years, along with the change in the color and cut of Janice's hair, left her wondering, "But where?" The waiter interrupted her thoughts.

"Are you waiting for someone or are you ready to order, Miss?"

"I'm not waiting for anyone, but I would like to order a double scotch. What do you suggest food-wise?" she asked while taking in the build of the good-looking, young college kid who was apparently working as a waiter for the summer. She batted her eyes and left no doubt she liked what she saw standing beside her table.

Used to being hit on by female tourists, he maintained a professional attitude. "I'm sorry, but we can't serve alcohol. We do have soft drinks, root beer, and iced tea. I recommend the seafood plate".

"You can't be serious! What do you mean you can't serve alcohol?"

"The motel and restaurant are on State Park land. That means no alcohol can be served. What else would you like to drink? Would you like to hear the specials?"

"Only if you are on the menu," said Elaina, a wicked gleam in her eyes. "Otherwise it's the seafood plate and a diet cola."

"One seafood plate and diet cola coming right up," he responded. "Would you like coleslaw or a salad with that?"

"Since what I would like is not on the menu, I guess I'll have the salad." This comment sent the young man scurrying toward the kitchen.

Elaina was not happy when her meal was served by a waitress. "I must be losing my touch," she mumbled before resuming her interest in the couple seated two tables away from her. "No, that couldn't be Janice. She can't have aged that well, and from what I've heard she lives in California," she muttered under her breath. She couldn't help thinking, *What would Janice Crenshaw be doing in Florida Everglades National Park, especially with that hunk of a man? I still laugh when I remember Jack telling me she said she would never trust a man again after he chose me over her. I know that isn't Jack with her. He's probably still crying in his beer over me taking his money and leaving. Stop it! You are letting your imagination run wild!* But the nagging thought that she had seen this woman before made it difficult to enjoy the seafood plate, so much so that she didn't order dessert as she typically would.

Instead, she paid her bill, again in cash, and wandered into the adjacent bar on Seminole land to take a seat beside an older man dressed in worn Levi cutoffs, a white tank top, and skanky, once-white tennis shoes. Unable to resist the urge to see if she could still get a man's attention, she struck up a conversation. "Do you live around here or are you on vacation?" she asked.

"Born and bred hereabouts. Own an airboat concession up the road about half a mile. No, I ain't married and no, I ain't interested in lookin' for female companionship!"

Being shot down didn't stop Elaina. She looked at his rejection as a challenge. "What makes you think I am looking for companionship?" she purred.

"Lots of empty seats at the bar, but you had to take one beside me."

"Could it be I just wanted to talk?"

"Maybe, but that's not what most women want."

"And what do most women want?"

"First a free drink, then dinner, then some action."

"I just bought my own drink, and I've already eaten dinner, and I'm not looking for action."

"Well since you put it that way, maybe we can talk. What brings you to this neck of the woods alone?"

"What makes you think I'm alone?"

"I don't see any wedding ring or any man wandering in to take a seat beside you. You didn't answer my question. What brings you to this remote place? Don't see too many unattached females around here."

"I wanted to see the Everglades I've heard so much about."

"Then you need to come out to my place and take a ride in an airboat. No better way to see the Glades and the gators."

"Do I need to make a reservation?"

"Yep. I need to know how many people will show up for the last run of the day just before sunset. What's your name? I'll also need a phone number." She scribbled her name and cell phone number she was all too willing to provide on a cocktail napkin.

"Why do you need my phone number?" she questioned.

"I've been having some problems with the motor on the air boat. If I can't get it repaired before the last run I'll give you a call so you don't drive out there for nothing. I need to get going. The name of my place is Greg's Marina and Air Boat Rides. It really ain't much of a marina anymore, but I don't want to buy a new sign. Way too expensive." With a sigh, Elaina watched him slide a twenty dollar bill toward the bartender and tell him to keep the change before sliding off the barstool to walk away. She finished her drink and paid her tab but decided to sit a little while longer to take in the sight of colors reflecting off the bay. Rick and Janice were making their way between restaurant tables toward the back restaurant exit. To reach their rooms they had to walk past the window of the bar.

"Damn! That has to be Janice, and the man with her is that guy who approached me and Josh at the Fontainebleau Hotel!" exclaimed Elaina. "I had the feeling he was some sort of law enforcement, probably a private detective by the way he's dressed. I need to get the hell out of here!"

At the same time Rick looked in the open window and realized she was about to bolt. "Stop right where you are, Elaina! The jig is up!" he yelled. "I have you on tape and I know what you did to Jack Fairchild, Josh Riggins, and the others you have scammed. "Don't even think about trying to run!"

"You!" hissed Elaina in Janice's direction. "This is all you're doing!"

"In the flesh, you piece of trash! It's time to pay the piper, Elaina! You scammed Jack out of everything, including his life. I know what you did, and I have proof! You lied and told him you could get one of his books made into a movie, that I was controlling, and our love wouldn't last when you only wanted to use him to further your writing career and steal his money! I'm here because I want you to know you didn't win. Jack and I got together again after you scammed him. In fact, we got married, but it happened only after you stole what would have been the best years of our lives together. For that, I will never forgive you!"

"That had to be the romance of the century, being married to that impotent old man who didn't have all that much money," Elaina replied, venom dripping from her lips. "Jack got what he thought he wanted and deserved. He tried to use me, just like he used you, only I got him first!"

Elaina picked up and threw a chair at Rick after he entered the bar through a side door, but he ducked and missed it. This gave her enough time to race from the restaurant and jump into her car. Gravel flew as she took off east on Alligator Alley at high speed. The description of the air boat concession was the only thought in her mind. *Maybe I can steal that boat and make a getaway*, she schemed.

Stunned by the chair that grazed the top of his head, Rick took several seconds before could gather his wits and follow her. He had no knowledge of her conversation with Greg in the bar, so he was unaware where she was headed. He knew only the direction she was headed. "You wait here," he told Janice.

"Not on your life!" she replied, opening the passenger side door of their car. "I haven't followed that bitch all the way out here to Florida to miss taking her down!"

Rick didn't argue. Elaina already had a good head start. He knew there were several unpaved side sand roads leading to Seminole Indian encampments where she could hide.

Rick took the first road to the left, a narrow path rather than a road, where he knew the Seminole Chief, Billy Bowlegs, had once called home by the sign marking the location. Several young Seminole men ran toward the car as it approached. Rick stopped amid a cloud of dust. "Have you guys seen a woman driving a dark blue SUV in the past few minutes?"

"Ain't seen no woman, 'cept my woman," replied one man. "What do you want with her?"

"She's a fugitive."

"You a cop? We don't live by white man's law. You need to leave."

"Sorry to have bothered you. We will leave," answered Rick.

In a panic, Elaina whipped her car into Greg's Marina and Air Boat Rides and drove it behind the metal building covering the air boat. "I've got to get out of here!" she said. Jumping out of the car she ran to the pier built beside the wide, open, metal structure where the large vessel was berthed. Unfamiliar with how an airboat was supposed to look, she didn't notice the wire metal cage encircling the large fan-like propeller blade was not in place. Greg had removed it when he left for the evening in order to make repairs to the high performance engine the following day. He left the boat key stuck in the ignition because he planned to resume work early the following morning just like he had always done without any problems. He never got around to calling Elaina.

Elaina didn't hesitate when she saw the key in the ignition. "This is my ticket out of this God forsaken place," she muttered. When she first turned the key, the engine sputtered. It took a third try before it roared to life. Unfamiliar with the engine's powerful thrust, she pushed the throttle to full speed forward. The powerful craft, facing open water, literally shot out of the covered canal into the deep waterway just as Rick and Janice were pulling into the parking lot to begin exiting their car.

"Elaina! Stop the boat! There's no way you can escape!" yelled Rick. "Janice, you need to get on the cell phone and call 911! We need the sheriff out here on the double!"

He could have saved his breath. The air boat engine died, sending the boat dipping crazily forward and backward in the deep muddy channel throwing Elaina backward into the still rapidly spinning propeller blades! She didn't even have time to scream.

When the sheriff arrived with a patrol boat on a trailer behind his vehicle, all anyone could see were blood spatters on the airboat's blades and several large alligators surrounding what appeared to be Elaina's remains in the bloody water.

Janice felt sick to her stomach. "I wanted revenge, but this is not what I had in mind," she told Rick. "I wanted her to go to jail for the rest of her life, but not this . . ."

She would have collapsed if Rick hadn't caught her and pulled her to his chest before lowering her to the sandy ground. She lay there without moving for more than five minutes. She came to with Rick hovering over her.

"I know you didn't want it to end like this, but you need to remember Elaina, not you or I, caused things to happen this way. She was pure evil. She was a woman without any thought of the hurt her actions caused others. Her only goal was to get what she wanted, and it didn't matter who she hurt in the process."

He wiped the sweat and tears from Janice's face and helped her to her feet. They walked to stand on the pier where they gave statements to the sheriff. The sheriff shook his head and told them he had heard on a television newscast earlier in the day about what Elaina was suspected of doing.

"Never expected that woman to show up here," he muttered as he reattached the unused patrol boat trailer to his vehicle.

Back at the motel parking lot, Rick pulled Janice to his chest without hesitation and kissed her soundly. The local sheriff looked on. This time Janice responded to what her heart wanted, without any thought of never trusting a man again.

POSTLOGUE

One year after Elaina's terrible death, Percy was smiling and seated at his desk. In his hand he held a courier-delivered wedding invitation from Janice and Rick. Rick called shortly after the delivery and asked Percy to be his best man.

"I told you Percy usually has a reason for the things he does, even if you don't understand them at the time. Do you want to make a bet on who gets married next?" Rick whispered to Janice when they stood before the justice of the peace to take their wedding vows the next morning, the day before Christmas at City Hall in Palm Springs, California. Janice's housekeeper Bernice and Percy looked on as witnesses as the couple repeated their vows. "Just take a look at the two of them," Rick said.

"I don't think Bernice is interested in getting married again," whispered Janice. "She has been my housekeeper as long as I've lived here and has never shown any interest in a man."

"I think you need to start interviewing ladies for your new housekeeper," replied Rick.

"How about putting your money where your mouth is?" asked Janice. "Say a hundred bucks?"

"You, lady, are on!"

"You got that right," replied Percy, who did not hear the comment Rick had made to Janice about Bernice and him being next to tie the knot.

"I knew you two were meant for each other the first day I met you, Janice," Percy said. "It didn't take me long to know you could ask Rick to sit up straight, and he would do it without any hesitation." Both Rick and Janice had to smile at Percy's comments before they said their *I do*s in order to start another, much happier, chapter in both of their lives.

Three months later, Janice and Rick served as witnesses for Bernice and Percy when they were married by the same justice of the peace in Palm Springs City Hall. Janice had lost the bet but happily gave Rick the money he was owed. Janice couldn't help but think that, despite what the brain might think the right course of action is, it pays to listen to what the heart wants.

Linda Ellen (Petty) Lynch was born on a farm in rural Franklin County, Ohio. She is a retired registered nurse, business owner, and writer. She now lives in Southern California.

Also by Linda Ellen Lynch

Secrets on Sand Beach revolves around two sisters born nine years apart to a wealthy family on an island off the South Florida coast. The elder sister is spoiled rotten by a doting nanny but ignored by emotionally distant parents. Resentment toward her younger sister escalates from adolescence into adulthood. This dysfunctional family carries readers through misunderstandings, romance, marriage, and murder.

Blood, a sequel to Secrets on Sand Beach is a story of due revenge, mental breakdown, and prison time. It turns out that in one family, blood is not thicker than water.

Emerald Valley takes place in the remote mountains of West Virginia, where characters and events are as dramatic as the rugged and breathtaking landscape. A sheriff in love turns criminal for good reason. Setting his heart toward revenge, he experiences shifts in emotion and experience that will engage readers from the first page to the last sentence.

Available on Amazon and Kindle.

www.ingramcontent.com/pod-product-compliance
Lightning Source LLC
Chambersburg PA
CBHW070628180626
46817CB00006B/2077